SHAUN BAINES

Juniper Falls

Copyright © 2021 by Shaun Baines

All rights reserved. No part of this publication may be reproduced, stored or transmitted in any form or by any means, electronic, mechanical, photocopying, recording, scanning, or otherwise without written permission from the publisher. It is illegal to copy this book, post it to a website, or distribute it by any other means without permission.

First edition

This book was professionally typeset on Reedsy.
Find out more at reedsy.com

Contents

Chapter One	1
Chapter Two	8
Chapter Three	12
Chapter Four	18
Chapter Five	22
Chapter Six	26
Chapter Seven	29
Chapter Eight	32
Chapter Nine	36
Chapter Ten	40
Chapter Eleven	45
Chapter Twelve	50
Chapter Thirteen	56
Chapter Fourteen	61
Chapter Fifteen	66
Chapter Sixteen	71
Chapter Seventeen	75
Chapter Eighteen	79
Chapter Nineteen	83
Chapter Twenty	87
Chapter Twenty-One	92
Chapter Twenty-Two	96
Chapter Twenty-Three	104
Chapter Twenty-Four	110
Chapter Twenty-Five	116

Chapter Twenty-Six	121
Chapter Twenty-Seven	125
Chapter Twenty-Eight	135
Chapter Twenty-Nine	140
Chapter Thirty	149
Chapter Thirty-One	155
Chapter Thirty-Two	161
Chapter Thirty-Three	167
Chapter Thirty-Four	174
Chapter Thirty-Five	179
Chapter Thirty-Six	187
Chapter Thirty-Seven	192
Chapter Thirty-Eight	198
Chapter Thirty-Nine	202
Chapter Forty	209
Chapter Forty-One	215
Chapter Forty-Two	221
Chapter Forty-Three	226
Chapter Forty-Four	231
Chapter Forty-Five	234
Chapter Forty-Six	237
Chapter Forty-Seven	243
Chapter Forty-Eight	247
Chapter Forty-Nine	251
Chapter Fifty	257
Chapter Fifty-One	265

Chapter One

Holly Fleet stretched her arms as her weary body groaned. She tried to shake some life into her limbs, jostling on her office chair and making her double chin wobble. It was no good. Her computer's gentle hum was like a lullaby. The glowing screen made her eyes tired. Her day of writing at the Little Belton Herald newspaper had been a long one, but it was over now. Finally, it was time to go home.

Holly was a journalist in her forties with a fringe she'd cut herself. She wore a grey suit stretched over a growing midriff. There was never enough money for a decent haircut, but she didn't like to skimp on her daily snacks.

Checking her watch, Holly sighed. "It's not even lunchtime yet."

She rubbed her eyes and turned back to the article on her computer. Her home village of Little Belton was a sleepy one, set amongst the rugged beauty of Northumberland and composing of a village green and the will to persevere. It wasn't a hotbed of scandal, which the residents would have loved, surviving as they did on gossip and innuendo. It was a collection of quiet homes, twitching curtains and folklore.

With Little Belton on a standstill, Holly had been forced to write an editorial about Crockfoot, a neighbouring village and their bitterest rivals. Crockfoot was restoring its town hall spire and it was the most interesting thing to appear in her newspaper for months.

Holly flicked off the computer screen, yearning for actual news to print.

Following a recent phone call she'd received, she knew it would be a brief wait.

The Little Belton Herald office was situated under a railway line and Holly pictured countless passengers on their journeys to work. Or travelling to meet their friends. Or going anywhere that wasn't Little Belton. They were all moving. They all had a direction. Holly was in a windowless office with no one to talk to and nothing to do.

Thunder rumbled above her, causing the computer to shake. The ironing board where she kept the office kettle skittered across the floor. The wastepaper bin toppled. Empty biscuit packets spilled out, reminding Holly of her skyrocketing calorie intake.

Stifling a yawn, she held the computer in place until the 11.17 train to Newcastle had passed above her.

Determined to be on her own journey, Holly grabbed her coat and left early for an appointment.

Outside it was raining, a soft and constant drizzle colouring the air grey. With her head bowed, she marched along the Little Belton high street, counting the growing number of Closed signs in the shop windows. Mr Magus the key cutter was gone, having retired to the coast. Mrs Jaffrey had remained in Little Belton, but had given up on her wool shop when she'd realised she was her only customer. Meanwhile, a pair of enterprising teenagers had opened a shop selling refurbished smartphones. Holly wished them well and hoped the village's intermittent phone and Wi-Fi coverage didn't damage their chances of success.

The shops were built from rocks hewn from the hills that surrounded them. Dotted around the hills were farmhouses and cottages with sloping roofs. Beyond the farms was the estate, a vast tract of moors, fields, and rivers. It belonged to the owner of Black Rock Manor, who

CHAPTER ONE

had made a promise to Little Belton.

So far that promise had proven to be as empty as the high street.

The village green was home to a conspiracy of ravens. They guarded the picnic tables with their sharp beaks and fought for space whenever the local council held a fete. The green had been a gathering place for all of Little Belton, but a recent deluge of rain had turned it into a quagmire, capable of sucking the shoes off anyone who dared to linger too long.

The Winnows' Convenience store sat snugly in the middle of the empty shops. Mr and Mrs Winnow were the first to greet Holly on her return to Little Belton from London. They were also the local poachers who were always hatching their next get-rich-quick scheme. The couple never rested.

Holly shook the rain from her coat as she entered their store.

Mr Winnow sat behind the counter, his feet up, reading a newspaper. His stomach rested on his thighs and he wore an oversized jumper sporting more holes than wool.

"Back for more biscuits?" he asked.

The Winnows sold anything they could. Fruit, vegetables, and free-range eggs from the allotments at Akin Lodge. Pheasants, chickens, and mutton from more nefarious sources. Holly wavered in front of a rack of various biscuits.

"Terrible weather at the minute," she said. "The rain just won't stop."

Mr Winnow whistled. "That's Long Robert for you."

Holly raised an eyebrow, and Mr Winnow continued.

"Long Robert lives on the estate near Thrashill. He's a nasty piece of work."

"Is he another of your local legends?" Holly asked, studying the biscuit display.

"I know you don't believe in this stuff, but Long Robert is a weather sprite," Mr Winnow said. "My father saw him once."

"Was your father coming home from the pub?" Holly glanced at Mr Winnow in time to see his Adam's apple bob as he gulped.

"That's not the point," Mr Winnow answered.

Holly returned to her biscuits. "It's a little difficult to swallow, that's all."

"Unlike all those biscuits you've been eating recently," Mr Winnow said into his chest.

"Pardon?"

"I didn't say anything," Mr Winnow said, "but you should believe in these things. All this rain. The roads are treacherous."

"Are you saying Long Robert controls the weather?" Holly asked, eyeing a packet of praline whirls.

"Of course he does," Mr Winnow said. "Mark my words, something has upset the old bugger."

The sound of creaking stairs above the shop told Holly a voice of reason was about to appear. Mrs Winnow, her make-up thickly applied, descended the stairs from their flat and perched at her husband's shoulder.

"Holly, dear," she said, a worried look on her face. "Back for more biscuits?"

"Mr Winnow was explaining how Long Robert is responsible for all this rain," Holly said with a smirk.

"Terrible, isn't it?" Mrs Winnow said. "They say he's roused to temper if he senses another's presence on the estate."

"Presence?"

"Something that harbours dark magic," Mrs Winnow said, "but never mind that now. What will you be having today? Mint choc or coconut surprise?"

Little Belton was an old village with records dating back to the Doomsday Book, a survey carried out on the orders of William the

CHAPTER ONE

Conqueror in 1086. It had been noted as *"a spirited place of things unnatural"* and its superstitions had never faded. In an era of satellites and predictive weather systems, the Winnows chose to believe in an ancient sprite with the power to make it drizzle.

True, Holly had seen things in the forests. Not seen, exactly, but felt. There was definitely something lurking in the bleak landscapes of the estate, but nothing that couldn't be explained away by science.

Or a good therapist.

Holly selected hazelnut cookies, reading their ingredients in full. "I'm actually here to do that article I promised. You know, the one about how Little Belton businesses are surviving the recent slump?"

Mr Winnow waved the Herald newspaper in front of her. "I'm looking forward to being involved. Got last week's copy here."

He opened it up and began quoting headlines with a sarcastic tone. *"Church Fete Cancelled due to Rain. New Lamppost Switched On.* And my personal favourite - *Dog Missing and Then Found Again."*

"What's your point?" Holly asked.

"Six months ago, Little Belton was about to be bulldozed to make way for a theme park by Mr and Mrs Masterly."

Holly ran a finger around her collar.

"We're business people," Mr Winnow continued. "That development would have brought tourists in from around the world. It would have put Little Belton on the map."

Mr Winnow took the biscuits from Holly's hands. "All we're saying is, we were expecting more from Mrs Masterly. She moved into Black Rock Manor and promised to rejuvenate the village. She claimed to have a new way of bringing in tourists. What about her promise?"

Holly lowered her head. "I trusted her, too."

Little Belton was failing. With shops closing and families starting anew elsewhere, it was becoming a ghost town. Mrs Masterly had promised to inject some life back into the village. Holly felt sure there was a plan, but so far, she had kept it to herself.

Mr Winnow moved to Holly's side and gave her a gentle nudge. "Hey, don't worry about us. We'll get by. We've got some great ideas. We've invented a game everyone will want to take part in. It's just we keep checking the Herald for news of what's happening, but there's nothing in there."

"Mrs Masterly has been really quiet," Holly said. "I couldn't get through to her."

Mr Winnow crushed the newspaper in his hands. "Well, that's typical, isn't it? She gets her big house and her big estate, and then she turns her back on the people who helped her get them."

Holly held up her hands and smiled. "I won't worry about you if you don't worry about Mrs Masterly."

"I think all that sugar has gone to your head," Mr Winnow said. "What are you talking about?"

"You're not my only appointment today. Out of the blue, she called. Mrs Masterly wants to see me and she's going to tell me how to save the village."

Mr Winnow did a little jig. "That's fantastic. I knew she wouldn't let us down. I said that from the start."

Holly caught his wife's eye and they shook their heads.

"So as I'm the bearer of good news," Holly said, "does that mean I can have those biscuits for free?"

Mr Winnow looked at her as if she'd sprouted a second head.

"Well, you can't blame a girl for trying. Why don't we get started on your article instead?"

They settled around the shop counter and Mr and Mrs Winnow described their next get-rich-quick scheme. As the couple talked, Holly's mind drifted to Black Rock Manor and her appointment with Mrs Masterly. There had been months of silence, visits where the front door had never been opened. No doubt the new owner of the manor

CHAPTER ONE

had been busy, but in Holly's experience, an unexpected phone call was never a good thing. It spoke of someone without a plan, the opposite of what Little Belton needed.

And why had Mrs Masterly asked Holly to come alone?

Chapter Two

Leaving the village, Holly drove through the estate in her ancient car. The vehicle was held together by rust and a prayer, and was too temperamental to navigate the rain-washed mud tracks. She took the roads slowly, circumnavigating the potholes and avoiding the soft grass verges hungry for her tyres.

Journeys like this were usually taken in Callum's Defender, a steadfast, all-terrain animal, like the owner himself. Holly glanced at the empty passenger seat beside her before refocusing on the road. She was on her own, and it wouldn't do to have an accident while Callum was not around to save her.

The road brought her through a forest where the trees blocked out the sun. Without light, branches grew like twisted ribbons, their foliage heavy with rain. Water bubbled over the cracked tarmac, and Holly thought of Mr Winnow's warning - the roads were treacherous.

Back at the shop, surrounded by people, the notion of Long Robert the weather sprite seemed preposterous, but the rain had been constant for weeks. It was abnormal and unsettling.

A gap in the trees grew before her. Grateful for an escape route, Holly pressed down on the accelerator. She bumped along the driveway to Black Rock Manor, her car juddering with exhaustion.

The manor cast a long shadow. Since Holly's last visit, the grounds had been mown. An overgrown nest of rhododendrons had been pruned to a manageable size, exposing stone statues she hadn't known were there. They were of topless men and now she could see them, she struggled to adjust her gaze.

The building itself remained the same. It was a square fortress of a home. Thick chimneys, blackened by soot, stood on the roof like sentinels. Ivy curled around the brickwork, its green fingers searching for a path through the rectangular windows. Battered by years of unseasonable weather, it remained as resolute as the craggy hills surrounding it.

Holly hesitated on the front step of the manor. Callum had always made her wait until she'd been invited inside. No one was more protective of the manor than he was, not even the new incumbent Mrs Masterly. The Acres family's history and the manor went together like the mortar running through its bricks, and impropriety was not allowed.

Holly tugged on her fringe and puffed out her chest. Whatever Mrs Masterly wanted from her, she was ready for it.

Trying the handle, the door was wrestled out of her grasp, swinging open to reveal Mrs Masterly on the other side.

She towered over Holly. Her face was pale and beautiful, with cheekbones sharp enough to cut through leather. She wore an animal print dress clinging to a slender frame.

"What a lovely surprise," Mrs Masterly said, retreating into the manor.

Holly followed her into a reception room with a polished slate floor. Originally, it had been used as a greeting area for the good and the wealthy. Its opulence was designed to intimidate. These days, it was empty, save for the marble busts of important people. Holly didn't recognise them, but their blank eyes seemed fixated on her.

"It's not a surprise," Holly said. "You invited me and I've been trying to contact you for ages. Where have you been?"

Mrs Masterly wove in and out of the statues like a ghost at a mausoleum. "I've been here, where I always am, but I've been rather preoccupied."

"The last time I saw you it was in the middle of a promise to rejuvenate the village," Holly said. "The residents of Little Belton are getting restless. They want to know what's going on. You don't want them turning up with their torches and pitchforks, do you?"

Mrs Masterly peered down her nose. "Why would they do that?"

"No one has seen you for months," Holly said. "When you took over Black Rock Manor, it was with certain expectations."

She stood in front of a bust of the previous owner. Mr Wentworth had built the village using money from his coal mines. He'd been lauded as a hero. Even after he was bankrupted and he had fled Little Belton, he remained on a pedestal.

"Callum taught me there is a line between the landed gentry and the rest of us," Holly said. "I'd hoped we were all on the same side."

"Perhaps I've been guilty of hiding in my ivory tower, but it's not without reason," Mrs Masterly said, coming to Holly's side. She studied the marble bust and placed a hand on Mr Wentworth's cold shoulder. "Do you like this statue?"

In the course of a prior investigation, Holly had learned some unsavoury facts about Mr Wentworth. Although he had appeared respectable on the outside, he had proven himself to be otherwise.

"It's okay, I suppose," Holly said. "Depends on what you think. It's your statue, after all."

Mrs Masterly smiled and pushed it over. Mr Wentworth fell backwards. As his cold head hit the floor, a crack appeared between his eyes and he rolled to a stop at Holly's feet.

"I don't like it either," Mrs Masterly said. "It's time for a fresh start."

Shaking marble fragments from her shoes, Holly stared at her host, wondering if her time in isolation had broken her.

"What have you been doing on your own all this time?" Holly asked.

Mrs Masterly's smile widened.

"I've been making good on my promise," she said, taking Holly's arm. "I know how to save the village. Come with me to the ballroom. You're going to like this."

Chapter Three

Holly was greeted by a circus. A paint-spattered radio played music Holly could only recognise as being too young for her. The room was vast with an open fireplace and polished oak floorboards protected by plastic sheeting. Large windows invited the Northumbrian landscape inside or would have done if they hadn't been covered in protective grills.

Scaffolding bridged the room from one side to the other. It passed under a ceiling rose being secured by two young men.

Holly couldn't help but notice they were topless. Like the statues outside.

"I'm turning the ballroom into a gift shop," Mrs Masterly said. "Drink?"

Holly's legs followed Mrs Masterly to a set of table and chairs. Her eyes remained fixed on the decorators, causing her to stumble.

There was a plate of cheese cubes on the table and Mrs Masterly produced a bottle of champagne, filling a glass for Holly.

"Take a seat," Mrs Masterly said, offering her one of the two wing-backed chairs.

Holly did as she was told and settled down. She sipped her drink and noted how the chairs faced into the room so the young men were always on view.

CHAPTER THREE

"Do you spend a lot of time here?" Holly asked.

Mrs Masterly charged a second glass and spoke over the rim. "It's for supervising."

It must have been hot nearer the ceiling because the two decorators were sweating. Glistening beads clung to their muscled chests. Their skin was tanned and glowing. Their backs were broad, like the sails of a ship caught by the wind.

Holly rolled the champagne glass over her forehead, hoping to bring down a sudden temperature. "Their faces," was all she could say.

"They have the types of jaws you could strike a match on," Mrs Masterly said. "It's why I wanted you to come alone. I thought we could have a girly afternoon watching the show."

"Who are they?" Holly managed to ask.

"They're brothers. Twins, actually. The one on the right is called Paul. You can tell them apart because he has a faint scar on his bicep. You must stare very hard, but it's there. The other one is called Saul. Otherwise, they are identical."

Holly worked a mouthful of champagne around her gums and swallowed. "Paul and Saul?"

"Evidently, their parents had little imagination," Mrs Masterly whispered. "Something that has been passed down, genetically speaking. As beautiful as they are, let's just say, neither of them will complete a crossword anytime soon."

"They remind me of those old Pepsi adverts," Holly said.

Paul placed a screwdriver between his teeth and grabbed a length of rope secured to the scaffolding. He leapt into the air and swung to the other end of the room, shaking his blond hair as he landed.

Saul applauded his brother.

"Total legend," he said between claps.

"This is what you've been doing?" Holly asked. "Supervising topless men work up a sweat?"

"Did you see my brother?" Saul shouted to Mrs Masterly from the ceiling.

"Yes, dear."

"Do you want to see me do that?"

Without waiting for an answer, Saul grabbed a rope and swung over Mrs Masterly's head, close enough to part her hair.

"I think they like you," Holly said.

Topping up her drink, Mrs Masterly smiled. "Oh, nonsense."

"It's hard to see why they wouldn't," Holly said, studying Mrs Masterly from the corner of her eye. She had high cheekbones and pouting lips. Her figure was trim with long, gazelle-like legs. Mrs Masterly was as beautiful as the trapeze brothers. Holly doubted if she'd even seen a packet of hazelnut cookies, much less eaten one, but Holly noted a tiredness in Mrs Masterly's eyes and lines around her mouth that had not been there previously.

Something at Black Rock Manor was getting to her.

"Well, this is it," Mrs Masterly said, opening her arms. "This is my plan. This is a regeneration."

It was clear significant changes had been made to the manor, but Holly didn't follow how that related to the village.

"Your plan is to decorate your new home?"

"Have you ever researched the manor?" Mrs Masterly asked. "It is steeped in history. It should be a heritage site, but it has been empty for so long. We need to bring it up to standard. I want to show them we are committed to its restoration."

"Who are 'they'?" Holly asked.

"A group called Historic England, but ultimately, it is the Secretary of State for Culture, and they don't just take anyone. We need to prove the manor is of special interest and highlight as many of the original features as possible."

Saul and Paul had finished showing off to Mrs Masterly and had

CHAPTER THREE

returned to reinstalling the ceiling rose. Craning her neck, Holly saw its intricate details, tracing the lines and curves of a sprawling pattern. It almost looked like the sun, shedding a warmth on the rest of the room.

"Once we're registered on their database," Mrs Masterly continued, "we'll become part of the National Heritage List for England."

Holly's eyes drifted to the brothers' buttocks and she realised she wasn't paying attention.

"And then what?" she asked.

"Tourists," Mrs Masterly said, tapping her champagne flute with a manicured nail. "Enough for the manor and the village."

Holly was dizzy with champagne and the room seemed to glow. "You did all this? With your own money?"

Mrs Masterly nodded. "I'm surprised your husband didn't tell you."

Holly's husband Derek worked for Mrs Masterly as an estate manager. He'd been unemployed for so long, he now worked with the dedication of a zealot. His role was sacrosanct, and he guarded the estate's secrets as unfailingly as he did his own.

Holly set her glass aside. "I can see the effort you've gone to. The manor looks amazing, or it will do once it's finished, but do you think being a Heritage site is enough? There are hundreds of them around the country. What makes this place so different?"

The paint-spattered radio changed its tune to something fast and electric. Its pace was matched by the excitement in Mrs Masterly's eyes.

"I've taken delivery of a very special item," she said. "Believe me, Holly, our fortunes have changed. No one has seen this item in a long time and they'll flock to see it now. We just need to get the manor restored."

The plastic sheeting at the end of the ballroom parted and a third man appeared.

It was obvious he was related to Paul and Saul. He had the same powerful features, the same tanned skin. His shoulders were broader and he was the only brother to wear a T-shirt. It stretched over his rounded muscles, threatening to split.

"This is the boss," Mrs Masterly whispered into Holly's ear.

He walked toward them with a phone in his hand.

"Mrs Masterly," he said. "Lovely to see you again."

Mrs Masterly played with her hair. "Thank you, Hector."

There was a lingering pause while Mrs Masterly batted her eyelids.

Holly cleared her throat, attempting to attract Mrs Masterly's diverted attention.

"Oh, and this is Holly Fleet, editor and journalist for the Little Belton Herald," Mrs Masterly said, suddenly awake.

Holly shook Hector's outstretched hand, feeling the roughness of his skin. "I thought your name might rhyme with Paul and Saul."

Hector glanced at his brothers by the ceiling rose and then down at his feet. "I'm nothing like them."

"It seems odd that your parents called them Paul and Saul, but named you Hector."

A frown darkened Hector's brow. "Why is that?"

Holly struggled to pursue her train of thought. "It just singles you out."

"I know what people think of my brothers," Hector said. "That they're silly. That their names are silly, but it doesn't give anyone the right to make fun of them."

The temperature dropped and Holly clamped her mouth shut, concerned she may have inadvertently insulted Hector.

Mrs Masterly cast her a glance, confirming Holly's suspicions.

"I'm sure she meant nothing by it," Mrs Masterly said.

"It's my fault," Hector said, blushing. "I'm being tetchy. There's a problem, I'm afraid."

He produced a crumpled sheet of paper from his pocket. "I was preparing your latest invoice and I received a phone call from my bank."

Mrs Masterly chewed a fingertip. "I made sure every invoice from Spectre Renovations went to the top of the pile."

Holly almost choked. "Your second name is Spectre? You're called Hector Spectre? Were your parents poets?"

The decorator turned to Mrs Masterly, his face falling. "Could I talk to you about this in private, please?"

"I've got nothing to hide from Holly," Mrs Masterly said.

Running a finger across his chin, Hector took a deep breath. "I've reached my overdraft limit."

Mrs Masterly linked her arm through Holly's. For a slender woman, her grip was uncomfortably strong.

"Well, you know how much we enjoy working here," Hector said. "The boys can't stop talking about you and we know how important this project is."

The grip on Holly's arm constricted further.

"How nice," Mrs Masterly said.

Hector forced a pained smile while Holly did the same.

"The bank says you haven't paid any of our invoices," Hector said.

Mrs Masterly loosened her hold and Holly flexed her hand, pumping blood back into her fingertips.

"I'm sorry," Hector said, "but we must down tools."

Running a hand through her hair, Mrs Masterly swallowed. "Yes, I was wondering when that would happen."

Chapter Four

By the time Holly had returned home, she had regained sensation in her arm where Mrs Masterly had held her like a boa constrictor.

Earlier, Holly had watched Hector ordering his brothers down from the scaffolding and they'd silently filed out of the room, their grim faces speaking volumes.

"We'll collect our tools later," Hector had said. "When it's more convenient."

Holly assumed he'd meant *less awkward*.

"You won't have to wait long," Mrs Masterly said, rushing around the ballroom, collecting her possessions. "You'll get your money. Meanwhile, please take something for your efforts."

She'd forced a half-empty bottle of champagne into Paul's arms. Saul was given a cheese platter and Hector was given a pleading look. Mrs Masterly followed them to the front door, waving stiffly as they climbed into their van.

Holly stepped over the shattered statue in time to see their taillights disappear into the estate.

"I don't believe it," she'd said, turning to Mrs Masterly. "What just happened? And what about this special item of yours?"

But Mrs Masterly had disappeared as quickly as the decorators had done. Sensing this wasn't the time to ask questions, Holly decided to go home.

The rain had continued throughout her drive. Holly lived in a cottage she'd inherited from her parents. It wasn't much, but after her husband declared his London estate agency bankrupt, they'd returned to Little Belton to start afresh.

The cottage overlooked Knock Lake, a deep expanse of water with a terrifying history.

Parking with her windscreen wipers batting left to right, Holly was surprised to see Derek on the roof of their home. He was wearing tattered jeans and a woollen jumper. His hair was slick to his scalp. He was on his knees, showing an eyeful of bum crack, sorting through a collection of tools, some of which still had the price tag on.

A rickety ladder leaned against the cottage wall.

If this was her Pepsi advert, Holly thought, she was switching to lemonade.

Sheltering under a tree, she watched him loosen a slate and pitch it to the ground. He stared at the hole he'd created and scratched his head.

"What are you doing up there?" Holly shouted. "Be careful. You might fall."

Derek jumped and skidded some way down the roof. "Bloody hell. Don't scare me like that."

"I said, what are you doing?"

"There was a cracked tile. I'm fixing the roof."

Holly sighed. "But you don't know how to fix a roof, Derek."

"Our cottage is on estate land. Residents must maintain their property at all times. To keep up appearances."

"Well, it appears to me that you've made a hole in the roof in the middle of a rainstorm."

Wiping wet hair from his eyes, Derek looked into the gap he'd created. "Water is getting in."

"Do you need a hand?" Holly asked.

Derek's eyes widened like a lost puppy. "I'd be grateful if you could."

"I might as well," Holly said, chuckling to herself. "Thanks to you, I'll be just as wet indoors as I will be on the roof."

An hour later, they were both inside, their teeth chattering with the cold. They'd done what they could to fix the hole. Only time would tell if they'd succeeded. They stripped off their dripping clothes and shoved them straight into the washing machine. Dressing quickly, they sat at the kitchen table with cups of hot tea.

"Sorry," Derek said.

Holly kissed his cheek. "I can't fault your enthusiasm, darling, but your common sense has been on holiday for years."

Her body ached. It had been an odd and draining day, and Holly longed for a bath. Maybe she'd use some of the expensive bubble bath she received as a birthday present last year. Maybe some of the skin cream, too. She didn't have Mrs Masterly's bone structure, but she could do more with what she had.

Plus, it would give her time to mull over what she'd discovered at the manor.

"Why didn't you tell me about the renovations?" she asked.

Derek stared at the clothes swirling around the washing machine. "I can't talk about that stuff. It's confidential. It's private estate business."

Holly knew he was right. It was a conflict of interest, but what was the point of having a man inside if she didn't exploit it every now and again?

"Of course you can talk about it," she said. "You don't work at the Secret Service. And I know that's why you're fixing the roof. You saw those three brothers swinging about with their shirts off and thought, I can do that."

"The tile needed fixing," Derek said, "and what do you mean, with their shirts off?"

CHAPTER FOUR

Holly sipped her tea, wishing it was wine. "There's something odd going on at the manor. I need to figure out what it is. The villagers are relying on Mrs Masterly to save them."

Derek held his hands up in surrender. "I never actually spoke to Mrs Masterly about her renovation plans, but I saw the accounts. I saw she was struggling financially, so I did some research."

"What kind of research?"

"Just some poking around," Derek said. "I saw she could apply for a grant, but it came with provisos. Mrs Masterly had to guarantee she had a way of attracting tourists."

"That must be her mysterious item," Holly said. "Did she apply?"

"I don't know. She became guarded, as if there was something she didn't want me to know."

There wasn't much more Holly could do at the moment and she decided to relax before bedtime. It was going to be another odd day tomorrow, she thought.

Upstairs in the bathroom, Holly sat on the edge of the bath as it filled with water, gazing at the new tiles Derek had installed. Each one was wonkier than the last. They looked like a chessboard that had been fed through a grinder. She comforted herself knowing that not all men were great at DIY. Derek's talents lay elsewhere. He was a whizz with numbers and as soon as Holly could persuade him to go undercover, she'd get the answers she required.

In the meantime, she might need to get her hands dirty, but Holly had someone else in mind for that.

Chapter Five

The wooden picnic table on the village green sagged in the middle where it had been battered by the brutal winter weather. The rain made it slippery and Holly tensed as she raised her arm above her head, waving her mobile phone in the air. If she positioned it just right, she'd get a single bar, enough to make a phone call.

"Be careful. You might fall," said a deep voice.

Holly's feet skated beneath her, threatening to slither in opposite directions. She steadied herself and looked down into Callum's upturned face.

Callum Acres was the estate's gamekeeper. He was in his early twenties with thick hair and a muscled body that strained through his clothing. He had helped Holly search for a missing pensioner and, in doing so, saved the village from a hostile corporation.

He was just the man Holly needed.

"What are you doing?" he asked.

"Trying to call you," Holly said, searching for a safe way to climb down from the picnic table.

Callum held out his hand.

"Don't worry, I can manage on my own," Holly said, stepping onto one of the seats. Her foot flew from under her, rising to head height. She toppled backwards, flapping her arms in a futile attempt to fly.

CHAPTER FIVE

Above her, the ravens cawed in an imitation of mocking laughter.

Callum raced forward.

Bracing for an awkward fall, Holly dropped into his open arms where he lowered her to the ground.

"Thank you," Holly said, adjusting her ruffled clothing.

They stood on the village green, facing each other, a sheet of grey rain falling in the space between them.

"How have you been?" Callum asked.

Holly shook her hair, spraying Callum with water as if she was a wet Labrador. "Damp, mainly. What are you doing in the village? I thought you'd be tracking deer or mending fences on the estate."

Callum jerked a thumb over his shoulder toward The Travelling Star. "Picking up a parcel. Since the post office closed down, Big Gregg runs a delivery service from behind his bar."

Everyone had been hit by the downturn in Little Belton's fortunes and the landlord of its only pub was no exception.

Holly linked her arm through Callum's. "I'll come with you. I want to talk to you about a problem at the manor."

Marching past his yellow Defender jeep parked outside of The Travelling Star, Holly and Callum bundled into the comfort of the pub.

The inside was empty, save for the one-legged landlord meticulously polishing the brass rail running the length of the bar. Big Gregg was a large man, more of a square than human-shaped. His ginger curls had a smattering of silver in them these days, but his ears still stuck out at right angles to his head. Despite his enormous frame, Big Gregg moved like a ballerina, dipping and extending at the rail, ensuring every inch gleamed.

The fireplace had been swept clean, but there was no fire. Above the mantle was an oil painting of a dark raven called Black Eye Bobby; one of Little Belton's folkloric myths. According to the villagers, Black Eye Bobby was a portent of disaster. Those who saw him were in for troubled times, but if they kept his image in their homes, he would never call at their door.

Big Gregg hopped from good leg to false leg as he cleaned.

"You missed a spot," Callum said.

Dropping his rag in surprise, Big Gregg hurried to the other side of the bar. "Please tell me you're here to get drunk."

"I'm driving," Callum said, "but I'll have a lemonade."

Big Gregg's face crumpled in disappointment until he saw Holly.

"There she is," he said, grinning. "I can always count on you to keep my cash register busy."

Holly ignored the obvious implications of Big Gregg's words. "How are things?"

"Slow, as always. Not a lot of money around to be spending on the finer things in life."

"Well, I'll take a gin and tonic," Holly said. "A small one."

"Great. I can finally retire." Big Gregg turned his back while he drained an optic.

Holly took out her purse and ran an exploratory finger through the lint inside.

Big Gregg placed her drink on the bar, reading the embarrassed expression on her face. "Don't tell me. It's on the house, yes?"

"I'll pay," Callum said, slapping down a five-pound note.

Holly sipped her gin, welcoming its alcoholic warmth. "Thank you."

"By the way, I've got that parcel for you, Callum," Big Gregg said, searching under the bar. I didn't want to see the post office close, but I have to admit, it's been good for me. It's the only reason people come in here."

"I don't understand why the postman didn't leave my parcel with a neighbour," Callum said, producing a red and white collection card.

Big Gregg cursed from under the bar. "You live in the middle of nowhere. You don't have any neighbours. Unless you count the sheep.

CHAPTER FIVE

Ah, there we are."

Callum swapped the card for the parcel. It was no more than a padded envelope addressed to *Callum Acres, Little Belton*.

"I've never received a parcel before," he said.

"What? Never?" Holly asked. "Given the lack of an address, I'm surprised you received this one."

Callum studied the envelope, turning it over in his hand.

"Aren't you going to open it?" Holly asked.

Callum stood away from the bar as Big Gregg returned to polishing the brass rail. Holly watched as Callum tore open the envelope, reaching inside for its contents.

"What on earth is this?" Callum asked, showing it to Holly.

In his hand was a straw doll. Its arms stuck out at right angles from its body so it took on the form of a cross. The doll had long hair and wore a tattered wax jacket. There was no face, but there were two eyes made from blades of grass tightened into a spiral. As Holly stared at the doll, the blades uncurled, hypnotising her, making her dizzy.

"Looks like you've got a secret admirer," she said.

Callum studied the ugly doll in his hand with a worried look. "With admirers like this, who needs enemies?"

Chapter Six

The blurred image of Callum appeared to Holly through the glass of her kitchen door. He sat at her wobbly table, his hands clasped in his lap.

"Everything okay?" Callum asked as she entered.

The kitchen needed an update, but Holly had banned Derek from attempting one considering the bathroom disaster. The room consisted of pale-coloured cupboards and a stone floor. A wooden counter ran around three-quarters of the walls. It was the same kitchen Holly had grown up in, except for one fresh addition. A wedding photo of Holly and Derek sat on the window ledge.

Holly stood over the straw doll propped against a butter dish in the middle of the table. Its lifeless eyes bore into her. She had wanted to speak to Callum about Mrs Masterly, but clearly there was something more pressing to discuss.

She dropped into the seat next to Callum and studied the doll.

"Have you seen anything like this before?" she asked.

Callum shook his head.

The kitchen door opened and Derek stepped inside. He sat on the counter, swinging his legs, but they stopped when he saw what was on the table.

"That looks like a voodoo doll," he said. "Why do you have one of those?"

CHAPTER SIX

The blood drained from Callum's face. "More importantly, why would someone send me one?"

Derek grinned. "It even looks like you."

Holly traced a finger through the doll's hair. "It feels real. Has someone stolen one of your locks recently?"

Callum put a protective hand over his head. "No one touches my hair."

"It's probably from an animal of some sort," Derek said.

"And you don't know who sent it?" Holly asked Callum. "There was no note?"

"Nothing, but it looks homemade," Callum said. "I think someone made it with me in mind."

Derek dropped from the counter in an awkward crumple. "Of course, they did. It's not like you can buy Callum-shaped dolls from the Winnows, is it?"

The sunlight through the window dimmed and Holly saw more rain clouds roll across the sky.

"Maybe it's a gift. Maybe someone is showing Callum that they care. It was sent to you for a reason," she said.

"What if it's got something to do with Mrs Masterly?" Derek asked the room.

Holly puffed a mouthful of air through her fringe. "I don't think so."

"It might," Derek said. "Two strange events have happened in as many days. They could be connected."

The expression on Derek's face told Holly he knew his claim was spurious, but that he was also looking for a way to be involved.

"You two are always off on adventures together," Derek added. "Maybe I can help this time."

Callum sat upright in his chair. "What was the other strange thing?"

Holly quickly told him about the renovations at Black Rock Manor, how Mrs Masterly was being oddly secretive about it and the fact that the richest person they knew in Little Belton now appeared to be as poor as the rest of them.

Callum listened quietly, steepling his fingers.

"And now we have an ugly doll," he said, his tone grave.

"Have you got something to tell us about Mrs Masterly?" Holly asked her husband.

Derek raised his chin, his face flushed with excitement. "I know you didn't ask me to, but I re-examined Mrs Masterly's accounts."

The only reason Holly hadn't asked was that she hadn't got round to it yet, but she let Derek continue.

"I'm afraid I've found some worrying anomalies," he said.

"Did you get Mrs Masterly's permission first?" Callum asked. "And why would a silly doll have anything to do with her?"

"I don't know, but you're not going to like this," Derek said. He rummaged in the back pocket of his trousers and laid out a crumpled piece of paper on the table. "Mrs Masterly is bankrupt and I've discovered why."

Chapter Seven

Derek's sense of triumph was palpable. He'd often complained about being left out in the cold. Now, here he was taking centre stage. Pressing out the creases of his spreadsheet, Derek preened like an overweight peacock. His manner reminded Holly of the businessman he'd once been. Proud and authoritative, taking to the spotlight with glee.

"What did you do, Derek?" Holly asked.

"You complained because I didn't tell you about the renovations at the manor," Derek said. "I wanted to show you I was listening."

As grim as it was to watch her husband gloat, Holly gave him a nudge, offering him a smile.

"What type of renovations?" Callum asked.

"Mrs Masterly has hired a team to rebuild the manor," Holly said, "but they haven't been paid. Lord knows how much she owes them."

"I can tell you that," Derek said, sweeping what was left of his hair from his forehead. "By my calculations, it's nearing the sixteen thousand pounds mark."

Holly whistled. "That much?"

"And that's not all. She owes Bimpton's Quarry for building materials. She's bought copper piping and electrical cables. There's an open tab at Roland's Hardware. Mrs Masterly has debts all over Northumberland. If she can't pay them back, she'll be banished from the county."

Callum raised a hand to his lips.

"The manor," he said. "We'll lose it all over again."

"Mrs Masterly won't lose the manor," Holly said, trying to instil calm into her voice. "It would become a shell again, and then Little Belton would be lost too. We can't afford to let that happen."

"That's why I went through her accounts," Derek said, waving his spreadsheet like a protest sign. "To find a way of helping her."

"And did you?" Callum asked.

"Not really, no."

Derek jabbed a podgy finger into the columns of numbers. "There was an initial cash deposit from when the manor was signed over to her by her husband, followed by further monthly deposits here and here."

"Housekeeping money," Holly said. "That's what my mam called the money dad gave her to run the house."

Callum scratched his bristled jaw. "In this case, it literally is housekeeping money. It's what's keeping the manor running and owning a stately home is pretty expensive. Never mind renovating it."

"It's a generous amount each month," Derek said, "but Mrs Masterly has continually spent over her budget."

Holly smiled at her husband. "I know you did this for me, but you're not telling us anything we don't already know. Mrs Masterly is broke. The question is why?"

"What you're not seeing is this," Derek said, indicating the last entry on his spreadsheet. "Two days ago, she had over forty thousand pounds in her account and now she doesn't."

"So where did it go?" Callum asked.

"Was it for a new car? Or a spa treatment?" Holly asked. "And let's not mention her wardrobe. Some of her clothes are pretty expensive."

Callum tugged at the frayed edges of his wax jacket. "Mrs Masterly wouldn't do that. It sounds like she is pouring her heart and soul into this renovation."

"He's right, hun," Derek said. "There's no sign she's spent any money on herself."

Avoiding their eyes, Holly felt that familiar sense of jealousy she always felt when picturing Mrs Masterly. She was rich, beautiful, and now appeared to be altruistic as well. How could Holly compete with that?

"Well, the forty thousand pounds went somewhere and it didn't go to the Spectre brothers," Holly said.

"That's where we hit the problem." Derek patted his round stomach, studying the spreadsheet. "Each outgoing is categorised. Here's money for a downstairs carpet. Here's money for steam cleaning the curtains. Here's money for "

Holly pressed into her chair. "Yes, we get the idea. What's the problem?"

Derek chewed the inside of his cheek. "Mrs Masterly's accounts go blank with no clue where the money disappeared to. It's there one minute and gone the next. If I had to make a guess, I'd say whatever she used the money for, Mrs Masterly wanted to keep it a secret."

Chapter Eight

The rain fell like silver bells, causing a ringing noise in Holly's ears.

"They say, it's Long Robert," she said, shaking water from her hair. "He's punishing someone, but you don't believe that, do you?"

Callum kicked at the step outside the front door of Black Rock Manor. "My boots are leaking. The only person who feels like they're being punished is me."

Holly knocked on the door again. "People around here talk like Long Robert is real."

"Oh, he's real, all right," Callum said. "Why do you think it's raining so much?"

There was no point in arguing with him, Holly thought. Unlike her, Callum had spent his entire life wallowing in the tales of Little Belton. *The Bell Tower Bog-Goblin. The Plains of Muckle. The Curse of the Horse Ghost.* It was nonsense, all of it, but to Callum and the rest of the village, they were a reality.

Holly was more concerned with getting wet.

"It's not like Mrs Masterly to leave us waiting like this," she said, opening the front door. "Come on. I'm soaked through."

They stepped into a small lobby and faced another door. It had a pane of glass etched with a coat of arms depicting a lion climbing a mountainside.

CHAPTER EIGHT

Callum placed a hand on Holly's shoulder, drawing her away.

She sighed. "I know we're not supposed to enter without permission, but we have to speak to Mrs Masterly."

"It's not about permission," Callum said, pointing at a lightning-strike crack in the glass. "The window is broken. You could have cut yourself."

"So can we go in or not?" Holly asked.

"I'm surprised you're even asking," Callum said, opening the door with a flourish. "You're right. This isn't like Mrs Masterly. She's paranoid about people breaking in. I'm surprised the manor was unlocked."

The reception room filled with their echoing footsteps.

"Perhaps she's ill," Holly said. "She might be convalescing in bed."

The sound of something breaking came from their right.

"Come on," Callum said, hurrying through the empty manor.

By the time Holly caught up with him, he was stepping through the kitchen door.

The room was bigger than Holly's whole cottage. It was lit by an oval-shaped stained-glass window. It cast a shower of reds and oranges over the white granite tops and a deep Belfast sink. The floor was ceramic tile. Copper pans hung from a rack. They gleamed and Holly wondered if they'd ever been used.

Their owner stood over a broken cup on the floor, black coffee seeping into the grouting. Mrs Masterly was still dressed in her silken dressing gown. Her hair wasn't combed and she wasn't wearing any make-up.

Holly blushed and hid her gaze, feeling as if she'd stumbled in on someone naked.

"Are you okay?" Callum asked Mrs Masterly, scooping the remnant of the cup into his hand.

"It fell," she said.

Guiding her to a stool, Holly smoothed down Mrs Masterly's hair.

"Don't worry," she said. "We'll tidy everything up."

Callum flicked on the kettle and searched the cupboards for more coffee.

"What's going on?" Holly asked.

"I didn't sleep very well last night," Mrs Masterly said. "In fact, I haven't slept well for a while. I feel like I've had a series of nightmares, but now I can't remember what they were. I'm a little groggy."

"It's the stress of renovating an entire manor on your own," Holly said.

"But now you're here," Mrs Masterly said, cupping Holly's face. "Actually, what are you doing here?"

Holly freed herself from Mrs Masterly's clammy hands. "It doesn't matter. We'll get you sorted and come back another time."

"Don't go," Mrs Masterly said, accepting fresh coffee from Callum. "I don't know what got into me. I'm starting to feel more human already. What can I do for you?"

"It's nothing," Holly said, desperate to ask some questions. "It's about the renovations."

"Go ahead," Mrs Masterly said. "I take it you have something to ask me. You always do. Ask me whatever you like. I have nothing to hide."

Holly hoped that was true and licked her lips in anticipation. "We know you're spending all your money on this place."

"That's correct," Mrs Masterly said.

"But we were wondering... are you, though? Have you used the money on anything else?"

Mrs Masterly's eyes narrowed. "That sounds like an accusation."

"And that sounds like you are keeping something from us," Holly said. "We know you've just spent forty thousand pounds on something and I'm guessing that's related to this mysterious item of yours. So what exactly is it?"

Mrs Masterly's jaw tightened. A brief flash of indignation rippled

CHAPTER EIGHT

across her face, but it didn't last long.

"It's impossible to keep a secret in this village," she said, wringing her hands. "I thought I was being so clever. Did you ask your husband to go through my financial records or was he working alone?"

Derek had used his initiative, but he'd acted on Holly's behalf.

"I asked him," she said, unwilling to let Derek take the blame.

"I'll remember that the next time I try to embezzle funds." Mrs Masterly sighed and slipped from her stool. "You better come with me."

They left the kitchen and climbed the staircase to the second floor.

"I knew I was going to run out of money before the manor was complete," Mrs Masterly said, "so I had to get creative."

She held onto the bannister while Callum kept her steady from the other side.

"I was put in touch with a young woman. I paid her to turn our fortunes around."

They reached the second floor and Mrs Masterly gathered herself.

"Your husband," she continued, "the man who rifles through my accounts as readily as he might my underwear drawer suggested I apply for a grant. It was a good idea, except they are incredibly scarce. In times of austerity, culture is the first to suffer."

They stopped by a closed door. Next to it was a small table with a delicate-looking vase in the same shape as Mrs Masterly's figure.

She unhooked a key from a chain hanging around her neck.

"I couldn't tell a soul about the item," she said, turning the lock, "because in this room is a bribe. Knowing about it implicates you both so you better hope this goes without a hitch."

Swinging open the door, Mrs Masterly screamed into an empty chamber.

"It's gone," she said.

Chapter Nine

Holly pushed past Mrs Masterly and stepped inside. The room was empty, except for a robin beating its wings and frantically trying to escape.

"It's gone. It's gone," Mrs Masterly said. "I've been robbed."

"What has?" Holly asked, ducking as the robin flew to freedom. "What's gone?"

"A cabinet designed by a man called Greyston," Mrs Masterly said. "It's irreplaceable."

Holly bought most of her furniture flat-packed. The idea that a cabinet was irreplaceable was so alien to her she had trouble picturing it.

"What's so special about it?" she asked. "And what has it got to do with your building work?"

Mrs Masterly held onto the doorway, her face marked with despair. "Alistair Greyston was a gifted craftsman in the 1800s. His work was much sought after by the middle classes. Greyston's reputation grew, so it came as a surprise when he disappeared for no apparent reason."

"Where did he go?" Callum asked.

"No one knows," Mrs Masterly said, "but when he returned, he'd changed and so had his work."

"And you have one of his cabinets?" Holly asked.

CHAPTER NINE

"His last one," Mrs Masterly said. "It was called *A Hallelujah to the Lord* and it was beautiful."

Callum approached the far wall where a hole had been drilled through the brickwork. It was about two feet wide and coloured orange from the sandstone. He inserted his hand through it, his sleeve gathering brick dust on its cuffs.

"The walls are thinner on this side of the manor," Callum said. "These were the old servants' quarters, but it's still quite a job to drill through this stonework."

He retrieved his hand and wiped it on his trousers. "Did you keep this door locked?"

Mrs Masterly nodded. "Always, and there's no way it could have been picked. It's ancient. It's hard enough to open with the key."

"And you kept the key around your neck?" Holly asked.

Mrs Masterly nodded again.

"Then they must have drilled into the room from the outside and forced the cabinet back through the hole," Callum said.

"It's too small," Mrs Masterly said, "and the cabinet was too big."

"At least, we know how the robin gained entry," Holly said. "Where exactly was the cabinet?"

Pointing to a bare section of the wall, Mrs Masterly choked back a sob. "It's all the money I had. I'm finished. We're all finished."

"We'll get it back," Holly said, "but what does a piece of furniture have to do with the manor?"

They listened to the robin beating against a window downstairs. As tiny as it was, it fought a fierce battle.

Mrs Masterly stood motionless in the centre of the room. "A few years ago, my husband and I applied for a heritage grant to restore a battlefield we wanted to use as part of a theme park. The man in charge of approving our application was Mr Xavier. We tried everything to reach an agreement, but we were eventually turned down."

37

"And he's the guy approving this grant?" Holly asked.

Mrs Masterly blinked repeatedly. "Getting to know him, we discovered he was obsessed with a furniture designer called Greyston. We attempted to procure a sample of his work as a— "

"Bribe?" Holly offered.

"My husband called it *oiling the wheels of progress*, but yes, it was a bribe. We found the cabinet, but not in time. When I discovered Mr Xavier would be handling this application, I made sure to buy it beforehand."

"You were going to give him a forty-thousand-pound cabinet?" Callum asked.

"In exchange for a grant worth hundreds of thousands," Mrs Masterly said, "but he doesn't want the cabinet. Just a chance to study it. That was the best part. I got to keep the cabinet, using it as an attraction for tourists whilst oiling the wheels of my application, but without it, Mr Xavier will turn me down."

A grey cloud settled over Little Belton and it was more than Long Robert's doing. It was rain, but this time it was hammering at the walls of Black Rock Manor.

"We better call the police," Holly said.

Mrs Masterly let out a desperate squeal. "No. Don't call them. I don't want the village to know I've been such an idiot."

"I have a friend on the force," Callum said. "He owes me a favour. He'll be discreet."

But Mrs Masterly shook her head and began pulling on her hair.

Holly rushed forward, pinning Mrs Masterly's hands to her sides. "Okay. Okay. We'll handle it. We'll find out who took the cabinet."

Mrs Masterly's lips trembled. "How? We don't even know how it got out of the room."

"If the door was locked," Callum said, "it could only have left via that hole."

CHAPTER NINE

"I told you, the cabinet was far too big."

Staring at her shoes, thoughts buffering like a bad internet connection, Holly saw her feet were coated in dust. An immaculate woman like Mrs Masterly kept a tidy household so what was it doing there?

Holly ran her finger along the sole of her shoe, feeling something gritty on her skin. She presented the evidence to the others.

"Sawdust. That's how they did it." Pinching some between her thumb and forefinger, Holly walked across the room. She placed her arm through the hole and released the tiny shavings to the wind. "They dismantled the cabinet first."

Chapter Ten

Mrs Masterly disappeared into her bedroom to dress while Holly and Callum chased the robin out of the manor. Leaving through the front door, they continued to the rear of the building, their boots squelching through the wet grass.

Set against the grey sky, Black Rock Manor loomed above them.

"Where are the servants' quarters?" Holly asked.

"Right wing," Callum answered, pointing toward them," but it's difficult to be exact."

Holly followed his finger but saw nothing. The walls were matted with climbing ivy. Heart-shaped leaves dripped with water. A wind blew across them, causing them to flutter, like the wings of a thousand butterflies. The weaker ones were dislodged and tumbled to the ground.

Holly watched them fall.

"What's that?" she asked.

She reached down and found the end of a rope. Tugging it, Holly yanked it free from the ivy. It was damp in her hands and she struggled to keep a firm grip, but as she pulled it from the wall, they saw it stretched to the hole in the servants' quarters.

"Whoever it was, carried the cabinet down with rope," Callum said, "and used the ivy as a climbing frame, but who?"

"The three Spectre brothers," Holly said under her breath.

CHAPTER TEN

Callum raised a questioning eyebrow.

"When they were working," Holly said, "they were like a circus act, swinging around on ropes, scrambling along the scaffolding."

"Maybe they saw the cabinet being delivered and hatched a plan to steal it."

The brothers seemed like obvious suspects, but Holly had her doubts. "It can't have been them. They were so... nice."

Callum examined the rope's end. "This is made of nylon. It's used by rock climbers. Does it look like the type of rope the decorators were using?"

Holly studied the rope. "No idea. All looks the same to me."

Callum tutted. "Someone carried the cabinet down the ivy, but where did they go next?"

"I have another question," Holly said. "Do you think Mrs Masterly is telling the truth?"

"She wouldn't lie."

Callum's face grew stern and Holly shrank under his gaze.

"I'm not questioning your loyalty to the manor," she said, "but we have no evidence the cabinet even existed."

"We have Mrs Masterly's word and that's enough for me."

And it should have been enough for Holly. Mrs Masterly was a lot of things, but she wasn't a liar, and if she had decided on a fabrication, surely she could have come up with something more plausible?

"I agree with you," Holly said, "but Mrs Masterly did keep this a secret. That seems suspicious in itself."

Callum paced the grounds, his boots leaving imprints in the grass. "She did that to protect us. Mrs Masterly has entered into a dubious contract with a dubious man. She didn't want us involved."

"Okay then, explain this to me. How did the brothers get into the room?"

Callum looked to the manor. "They scaled the walls using the ivy and

41

drilled a hole."

"How did they know where to drill? You grew up here and even you couldn't find the servants' quarters from the outside. You couldn't find it when the hole was already there."

"They were renovating the manor," Callum said. "They would have blueprints."

"Not necessarily. They were making cosmetic changes, not structural, and I met the brothers, Callum. They're lovely people, but they couldn't find their shoes until they looked at the end of their feet."

Holly remembered Hector's response to her stupid remark about his name. He wasn't like Paul and Saul. He was smarter, more clinical in his decisions. He'd seen how mortified Mrs Masterly had been when she couldn't pay. Another man, a man like Callum, might have continued working, trusting in Mrs Masterly's sincerity. Hector had ordered his brothers to leave, as if trusting someone wasn't his top priority.

"And there's another problem," Holly said. "How did Mrs Masterly sleep through a hole being drilled? I mean – "

Holly was silenced by Callum raising his hand. "Can you smell that?"

Sniffing the air, Holly detected nothing. She had spent most of her adult life living in London and was grateful her sense of smell had been dulled.

"It's coming from over there," Callum said. He grabbed her hand and they set off through the grass in leaps and bounds.

Holly lumbered after him, her heavy stomach bouncing in rhythm with her footsteps. Her breath came in quick gasps. No more biscuits, she repeated as a mantra. No more biscuits.

Jerking to a stop, Callum lifted his nose to the air, like a bloodhound seeking a scent. "The smell is getting stronger."

"What smell?" Holly asked at the space where Callum had once been. He was off again, trampling through a grove of withered trees.

Holly gritted her teeth, pin balling through the trunks, swallowing stray leaves and protecting her face from being scratched by branches. She found Callum in a clearing and pulled her coat tight to her frame. Despite all the running, she was cold. The clearing was a perfect circle with a proud poplar tree in the centre. The grass was grey and looked brittle.

"What's that chill?" Holly asked, rubbing warmth into her arms.

Callum glanced at her over his shoulder. "It's a witches' hall. That's why you're cold."

Her body shivered and Holly had lost sensation in her toes. "So it's witches who effect the weather now? I thought it was Long Robert."

"The coven would meet and practise dark magic," Callum said. "They say, their spells seeped into the ground. You can never stay warm on a sacrificial site like this."

"That's rubbish," Holly said with a snort.

Callum gave her a loaded stare. "Really? Well, are you hot or cold right now?"

If she hung around much longer, Holly thought her skin might turn blue. "That's not the point. Witches don't exist."

"Not anymore," Callum said, "but someone definitely made a sacrifice last night. Look at this."

Holly tip-toed into the circle, growing colder with every step. The grass snapped under her feet, emitting puffs of grey soot. A smouldering pile of ash sat at the base of the poplar tree, sending curls of smoke into its arms. Its bark wore wet bubbles where it had blistered and sap wept from its skin.

"There was a fire," Callum said, placing his hand on the darkened bark, "and even while it was being burned alive, the tree protected the flames from the rain."

Holly didn't know if the tree would survive its damage, but the bonfire was almost dead. Glowing embers turned white and floated away on the breeze. As the ash drifted, it exposed a charred skeleton of drawers and furniture fixings.

"It's the cabinet," Holly said, pressing fingers to her lips. "They burned it."

Callum joined her, his face flushed red. "Still think Mrs Masterly was lying?"

Chapter Eleven

Mrs Masterly leaned over the kitchen sink as if she was ill.

"I don't understand," she said. "Why burn it? It was worth more intact, surely?"

Holly and Callum stood shoulder to shoulder. Water dripped from their hair into hot mugs of coffee, which they nestled in their hands for warmth.

Holly shuffled on her feet. "Unless someone was jealous of it."

"It was going to be on show for everyone," Mrs Masterly said. "There was no need to be jealous."

There's never a need, Holly thought. It just kind of happens.

"What about Alistair Greyston?" she asked. "Perhaps there's an episode in his past someone objected to."

"But no one knew I even had the cabinet," Mrs Masterly said. "I did everything in secret. You only knew because you were snooping on me."

Holly watched the steam rising from her coffee, reminding her of the bonfire's smoke. It was clear the theft was not money orientated. The motivation to steal and then burn the cabinet lay elsewhere.

"Where do Hector and his brothers come from?" Holly asked.

The smooth skin of Mrs Masterly's forehead wrinkled. "Hartlepool."

"Outsiders," Callum whispered to Holly.

"They were staying at The Travelling Star, where everyone stays, but I don't know where they are now. Why do you want to know?" Mrs Masterly asked.

"It would be difficult for a resident of Little Belton to hide something like this," Holly said. "The place is too small to keep secrets."

"As I found out," Mrs Masterly said.

"Whoever did this needed the right tools to dismantle the cabinet and drill through a wall," Holly said. "They'd also need to be agile. I hate to say it, but I think it might have been the Spectre brothers."

"They're probably halfway home by now," Callum said. "We won't find them now."

"Are you finished?" Mrs Masterly asked.

Holly looked around the room before settling her gaze back on Mrs Masterly's questioning face.

"Listen, I'm sorry this has happened," Holly said," but I don't know what else we can do."

"No, I mean, are you finished with your coffee?" Mrs Masterly asked.

Before Holly could answer, the hostess whipped the mug from under her and poured its contents down the sink.

Holly listened to it gurgling.

"It wasn't the brothers," Mrs Masterly said. "They knew nothing about it."

"Are you sure?" Callum asked.

"They left when the money ran out," Mrs Masterly said. "I never mentioned the cabinet in front of them, and well, I always got the impression they liked me."

Holly wondered how Paul and Saul had performed their circus tricks so well with their tongues hanging out. However, their brother Hector had always remained professional. Between Mrs Masterly and money, Hector had sided with his bank account.

"Okay, then. Who else knew about the cabinet?" Holly asked.

CHAPTER ELEVEN

Mrs Masterly opened her arms. "Just us three," she said. "Oh, and the girl who arranged it. She's renting a bothy by Juniper Falls."

* * *

Callum's Defender slipped around the muddy roads. His forearms flexed as he struggled to keep the jeep from skidding into a watery ditch. He slowed to a stop, tapping his finger on the steering wheel.

Up ahead, a mass of dirty wool approached. Sheep wobbled shoulder to shoulder, tramping purposely along the road. Their heavy hooves fell in unison, as if they were a beleaguered troop of soldiers returning home from war. They marched in silence, their dark heads bowed under the rain.

"Sometimes they take to the roads when the fields get too marshy," Callum said.

"Can't we drive around them?"

"Too dangerous," Callum said. "The sides are unstable with the weather. It's not far now. We'll just have to wait."

The sheep appeared in no mood to hurry. For every inch they moved forward, they'd stop to chew grass or headbutt one another.

Holly closed her eyes. "This is a fool's errand. Why are we even searching for this cabinet thief?"

"Look at what Mrs Masterly is trying to do," Callum said. "Bring business back to Little Belton and she's been doing it with her own money, risking her own home."

Holly opened her eyes to see a sheep staring back at her. Standing in front of the Defender, a dribble of water cascaded down its long face.

"There is another reason someone might want to destroy the cabinet," she said.

"Like what?"

"What if it was burned because someone knew about Mrs Masterly's bribe? What if someone wanted to stop her from getting the grant? Someone who doesn't want to see her succeed?"

Holly could imagine Mrs Masterly having a string of enemies. People who were jealous of her marriage, her status or her beauty. It took little to tip people over the edge these days.

But it was thoughts of Mrs Masterly's husband that Holly couldn't shake. He was an influential man with a fragile ego. When Holly, Callum and Mrs Masterly had ruined his plans for a theme park, they were three strangers thrown together by fate. Now they felt more like targets.

"Do you remember how we first met?" Callum asked.

The sheep swarmed around the jeep, bumping into it, making it rock.

"No," Holly lied.

Callum placed a bracing arm over Holly's chest as the Defender swayed left and right.

"You were being chased by a herd of sheep," he said. "They wouldn't leave you alone."

"Some things never change," Holly said, staring at the animals through the windscreen.

The sheep buffeted past the Defender, appearing in the rear-view mirror as a river of wool. The road became clear and they drove onwards with Callum's eyes fixed on the treacherous road.

Trees gave way to a stony outcrop yellowed with lichen. Ravens hopped about the rocks, cawing and flashing their beady eyes. The waterfall known as Juniper Falls tumbled through the boulders, ending in a pool of frothy scum where no fish would ever swim. Tufts of grass sprouted like hairs from a witch's chin.

"Are you sure she lives around here?" Holly asked.

Callum nodded. "Behind those juniper bushes is a bothy. That's where Mrs Masterly said she would be."

He jumped from the jeep and turned his face to the sky. "Bloody hell. It's stopped raining."

CHAPTER ELEVEN

The clouds parted and a ray of sunshine hit the waterfall, catching water droplets and filling the air with rainbows. Startled, the ravens beat a hasty retreat, their dark forms disappearing over the horizon.

Holly scrambled over the rocks, pausing when she heard someone coming.

A woman appeared. She was young and muscular with hair tucked behind her ears. Her black skin glistened from the mist of the waterfall. She wore a silver charm bracelet on her wrist and nothing else.

Holly's mouth fell open. She was too stunned to even look away. The girl must be freezing, she thought. What had happened to her clothes?

She turned to Callum for an explanation to find him struggling to remove his coat. In his blundering hurry, he'd forgotten to undo the zip.

"Put this on," said his muffled voice to the woman. "You'll catch a cold."

The coat was trapped around his shoulders. He twisted in a circle as if he was wearing a straitjacket. Panicking, he took the collar and yanked the jacket over his head, securing it tightly over his face.

Smirking, Holly picked her way through the rocks to free him. Her eyes were glued to the ground to avoid an embarrassing fall. Finding safer footing, she looked up to see the naked woman at Callum's side, gently taking the coat from him and wrapping it around herself.

"Thank you," she said in a Northern burr.

Callum mumbled something Holly didn't catch, but she saw the woman demur at his words.

Holly stepped backward, but the ground behind her was wet. She slipped and collapsed onto the bank of the pool. Her momentum was too strong and the bank was too steep. Holly didn't even try to fight it.

The last thing Holly saw was Callum and the beautiful woman, their faces aghast as she slid under the pool's surface.

Chapter Twelve

A fire roared in the bothy, but underneath Simone's blanket, Holly's teeth chattered like castanets. Introductions had been made after Callum and Simone had dragged her from the pool.

Callum handed a spluttering Holly to Simone, who carried her over the threshold of the bothy. He waited outside as Simone dressed and Holly stripped, and settled into a chair. When Simone called him inside, Callum avoided meeting anyone's eyes for a while.

Traditionally, bothies were used by shepherds who were forced to stay with their flock to protect them from predators. When shepherding was modernised, the practice died and bothies were used by hillwalkers hoping to shelter from sudden storms. When weather forecasts grew in accuracy, there was little use for bothies and most fell into disrepair.

Simone's bothy was decorated in furs, reminding Holly of Callum's cottage. They were sprawled on the floor and draped over the walls. There was a small area for cooking and a hammock strung between beams in the roof for sleeping. It was a single room with a bathroom separated by a curtain patterned in faded sunflowers.

"Drink this," Simone said, handing Holly a steaming cup of liquid. "It's borage tea. It will invigorate your vapours. Keep you warm."

Simone had changed into a white, laced dress flowing to her ankles. As she leaned over the fire to throw on another log, Holly saw her body again, silhouetted through the material.

Shaking her head, Holly turned her attention to the murky tea in her cup. Unconvinced, she took a sip and was surprised by the warming flowery taste.

"Aren't you having any?" Holly asked. "You must be feeling a chill after your naked stroll."

Simone smiled. "Don't worry. I'm used to it. I enjoy being close to nature."

Holly wiggled her toes through the furs at her feet. "Close enough to hunt it?"

"They're all fake," Callum said. "You can tell."

"Can you? Not all of us are tree huggers," Holly said.

Callum stood tall, bumping his head on the low ceiling.

"Why are you being so snipey?" he whispered to her. "We're guests."

"Snipey?" Holly questioned. "You're not even speaking English now."

"It means *critical*," Simone said. "It's a Northumbrian word. I haven't heard someone use it in years."

"Are you from around here?" Callum asked.

"Little Belton. Born and bred, but I moved away when I was a child."

"That's the same as me," Holly said, setting her tea aside, "but I don't remember seeing you in the village."

Callum cleared his throat. "Well, there is a bit of an age gap. You would have left for London before Simone was born. She's more my age."

The fire spat an ember onto the stone hearth and Holly watched it blaze.

"I don't remember seeing you either," Simone said to Callum.

She sashayed across the room, her white dress trailing over the furs. As she stopped in front of Callum, she clasped her hands together.

All she needs now is a wedding bouquet, Holly thought.

"I didn't go into the village much when I was a kid," Callum said.

"What about school?"

"Too busy helping my dad around the estate, and then the school burned down, of course. Dad was the head gamekeeper. Like I am now."

Holly shrank beneath the blanket, listening to them gossip. Callum's face was red, though she doubted it was because of the heat from the fire. At least not the one in the fireplace.

Simone looked equally enamoured. Her large eyes glistened, framed by eyelashes batting frantically.

Holly glanced to the door, needing to escape the idea of being the fifth wheel. Her clothes were drying by the fire and she didn't have Simone's confidence, or body, to walk out naked. Even if she did, she'd end up sitting in the Defender, still naked, waiting for Callum to drive her home.

"Oh, you're so funny," Simone said to Callum.

Holly wanted to disappear, to pretend like she wasn't there. As she turned to the fireplace, her buttocks rubbed on the chair, making a noise.

Callum and Simone stopped talking and stared at her.

Holly gulped. "That wasn't me. It was the chair."

"Well, borage tea affects the digestive system," Simone said. "Perhaps I made it too strong."

"I'm not so old that I can't tell when I've farted, you know?"

Callum smirked. "Maybe you should move away from those flames."

It wasn't Callum's joke that annoyed her. It was the fact it appeared to be shared with Simone that crawled under Holly's skin. They were there to do a job, to help a friend, and Callum seemed to have forgotten that. Typical man, she thought, to be so easily swayed by a naked woman.

Holly jumped to her feet, grabbing at the blanket before it fell around her ankles. "Actually, Simone, we were hoping to ask you a few questions. If that's okay?"

CHAPTER TWELVE

"Anything I can do, I will."

"We want to know about your involvement with Greyston's cabinet," Holly said.

Simone's face grew grave. "I'm not supposed to talk about it."

"It's okay," Callum said. "We're helping Mrs Masterly. She told us how to find you."

Opening a kitchen drawer, Simone produced an incense stick. She lit it and left it smoking in a vase. "Do you mind if I burn this? It helps me concentrate. I want to give you my full attention."

"Not at all," Holly said. "While we're on the subject, that pool water has left me feeling grubby. Could I use your bathroom to clean up a bit?"

"No," Simone said, her face hardening. "I mean, sorry. The bathroom is my private spiritual place. I find it difficult to share."

Holly sank into her blanket. "Not a problem. I understand. Why don't you tell us how you first came across the cabinet?"

"Well, I worked for Charleston Collectables, an antiques dealer in Berwick Upon Tweed. It's a one-man-band. Run by Mr Charleston. He said, there was a sales lead in Little Belton. Someone was interested in a Greyston piece. He asked if I could handle it. I met with Mrs Masterly and the deal was struck in under ten minutes."

"You arranged for transportation to the manor?" Holly asked. "Couriers? A specialist delivery company?"

"I did it all myself," Simone said. "I'm quite strong."

Holly's eyes drifted to the woman's powerful arms. "So no one else saw the cabinet or knew about it?"

"Mrs Masterly stressed the importance of discretion. It was part of the deal."

Holly dragged the blanket tightly around her shoulders and looked at the bothy's furnishings. "You seem to have made yourself at home after the delivery. What made you stay?"

"I love my village," Simone said, "and I thought it might be exciting."

Recalling her job at the Herald, Holly cringed at the articles she'd written lately. While cities thrived on news, Little Belton was driven by gossip. The biggest splash Holly had ever made was collapsing into a waterfall. Excitement was in short supply.

"You seem very interested in the cabinet," Simone said. "Is there a problem with it?"

"It was stolen," Callum said.

"And burned to ashes," Holly added, watching the fire.

Simone raised her hand to her mouth. "Oh, no. Is Mrs Masterly okay? She wasn't hurt, was she?"

Callum ran a hand through his hair. "She'll be fine."

"She is very upset about the theft," Holly said, shooting a look at him.

"Of course, she would be." Simone rushed to the door. "I better go see her. Could you give me a ride?"

Holly stumbled over the blanket to reach her. "We're handling it. I just needed to find out how many people knew about the cabinet."

"I told you, it was me and Mrs Masterly," Simone said. "Wait, does that mean I'm a suspect?"

She certainly wasn't acting like one, Holly thought. Some criminals liked to return to the scene of the crime, but not to console the victim. As much as Holly hated to admit it, Simone seemed sincere. She appeared as devastated as Mrs Masterly.

Simone bit her thumbnail. "I swear, I didn't tell a soul. You can ask Mrs Masterly."

Maybe Holly would, but now wasn't the time.

She inspected her clothes. They were still damp and smelled of pond water, but they would have to do. Snatching them from the drier, she dressed under the blanket, squirming with every awkward movement. She shoved her feet into squelching boots and cast the blanket aside.

CHAPTER TWELVE

Holly marched to the door. If Simone was going to the manor, it left her and Callum free to pursue other suspects.

It was time to do what she did best – talk to topless men.

Chapter Thirteen

Away from the bothy, the rain began again.

"You could have said goodbye to Simone," Callum said, guiding the Defender around a slippery corner.

"I was in a rush. Do you want to find the Spectre brothers or not?"

Holly's tone was sharp, sharper than she intended. She'd fallen into a pond and for most people, that would be humiliation enough. For Holly, however, it had been just the beginning. She'd also had to endure the mating ritual of two people who ought to know better.

Not to mention Callum's off-hand comment about her age.

"They'll be halfway to Hartlepool by now," Callum said, "and Simone helped us. You could have spared her five minutes."

The streets of Little Belton were empty, save for the growing number of puddles crowding the pavements as the rain continued to descend.

Callum parked outside The Travelling Star, his windscreen wipers beating like a metronome.

"I think I should go back," he said, scratching his neck. "See if there is anything more Simone can tell us."

Holly scrunched her hair, drawing out a bead of pond water. Callum had more than talking on his mind, she thought.

"Whatever," she said and jumped from the Defender and barged open the door to the pub.

CHAPTER THIRTEEN

Big Gregg greeted her from behind the bar, waving his damp cloth. "On your own again?" he asked.

When Callum stumbled through the door, Big Gregg's face split into a wide grin. "Drinks all round?"

"Actually, we're here to ask you a few questions," Holly said.

"God forbid I should make any money," Big Gregg said, settling his bar rag over his shoulder. "So what can I do for you?"

"You had some guests staying. The Spectre brothers?" Holly asked.

Big Gregg poured himself a gin. He downed it in a single gulp and gave her a nod.

"Can you tell us anything about them?" Callum asked.

"Well, they're not too bright, but I'd say they were okay. For outsiders, like."

Holly tapped the bar counter with her finger. "Can you tell us when they left?"

"Nope."

Curling her lip, Holly reached for her purse. "Is this because we haven't bought a drink? Honestly, what happened to a sense of comradeship?"

Big Gregg smoothed down his ginger mop of hair. "I can't tell you because they're still here. They're over in that corner booth."

Despite it being daytime, the bar was dimly lit. On entering, Holly had failed to see two heads huddled in whispered conversation. They were hunched over a small table, their brows almost touching.

"Oh," Holly said.

Big Gregg watched her expectantly, his eyes drawn to her open purse.

"Two cokes, please," Holly said.

Holly and Callum carried their drinks to the corner booth.

The Spectre brothers looked up as they approached.

"The other manor lady," they exclaimed together, peeling apart.

"I'm surprised to see you again," Holly said. "Are you staying here?"

Paul nodded with a grin. "We like it."

"Hector says, we've paid for a full week so we might as well stay," Saul said. "Plus, when Mrs Masterly sorts out our wages, Hector wants her to know where we are."

"Where is Hector?" Holly asked.

The brothers glanced at each other. Their puppy-like enthusiasm darkened a little. Although they sat together, they looked alone.

"Do you need to speak to him?" Paul asked with caution in his voice.

Perhaps, Holly thought, but maybe Paul and Saul would be enough for now.

"I was just remembering how you swung around the ceiling and climbed the scaffolding," Holly said. "I thought you were very good."

"Did Mrs Masterly?" Paul asked.

Saul sat up in his seat. "Did Mrs Masterly think we were good?"

"I'm sure she did," Holly said, attempting to ignore how she'd been passed over for another woman again. "How did you learn to do that? Those circus skills, I mean?"

"We're rock climbers," Paul said. "Been doing it our whole lives."

"And that involves ropes?" Holly asked.

The Spectre brothers nodded.

"What about Hector?" Callum asked, folding his arms.

"He was the one who taught us when we were kids. There's no one better than our Hector," Paul said.

Holly leaned over the table, closing the gap between herself and the brothers. Their foreheads weren't touching, but it was near enough.

"Do you think Hector could climb up the side of a house using a rope?" she asked.

Paul frowned. "Why are you whispering?"

"I think he could. Easily." Saul's eyes sparkled and he offered Holly a shy smile. "Would you like a drink?"

He pointed to his beer as if to explain what he meant.

CHAPTER THIRTEEN

Holly's mouth was drier than her clothes and it was a kind offer. Saul's sudden interest would be the tonic she needed to accompany a decent-sized gin, but she knew it was her ego talking. It had been bruised in the past few hours and needed attention.

"Maybe another time," she said with a smile.

Saul took the rejection admirably, she thought. Too admirably, if anything.

"Where did you go after you finished working at the manor?" Callum asked.

"Nowhere," Paul said.

Callum folded his arms. "You didn't go back? Maybe at night?"

"Why would we?" Paul asked, giving his brother a quizzical look.

"Hector told us not to go back until we'd been paid," Saul said.

Sensing another dead end, Holly climbed out of the booth. "Do you know where we can find Hector?"

Paul swirled the dregs of his pint around his glass. "I wish we did."

There was something in his tone that made Holly feel sorry for them both. Shirts on or off, Paul and Saul were two young men cast adrift with no place to go. She opened her purse again and slapped a ten-pound note on the table.

"Have a drink on us," Holly said. "Big Gregg needs the business."

Holly led Callum out of the bar, pulling her collar up against the driving rain. "I don't think they stole the cabinet."

"Because one of them offered you a drink?" Callum asked.

"No, because if I had stolen and burned a cabinet worth forty thousand pounds, I wouldn't be waiting around to be caught."

Water rolled down Callum's handsome face. "So we're back to square one?"

"Not exactly," Holly said. "Hector isn't around. He's the smart brother and by the sounds of it, capable of climbing up the side of a manor."

Callum found his car keys and motioned toward the Defender. "Do you want to come back to the cottage? Try to figure out where this Hector is?"

It was a tempting prospect. Holly pictured the roaring fire and the whistling kettle on top of the stove. The rain would beat against the window, but the cottage would be warm and dry.

Holly checked her watch. It was late afternoon. Derek would still be at work. He kept long hours and Holly would often return home to find him asleep in his business suit on the sofa. It was a comforting sight, not least because it meant he wasn't practising his DIY skills.

She had plenty of time to spare.

"Okay, then," Holly said, "but you'll have to get me back home before I turn into a pumpkin."

Callum looked to the roundness of her stomach and Holly dragged him to his jeep before he could make a comparison.

Chapter Fourteen

The cottage was as Holly remembered it from her first visit. The ceiling was low and stained by decades of smoke from the open fire. Lanterns lit by candles swung from the beams. The floor was carpeted in furs and a picture of Black-Eye Bobby hung above the fireplace.

Callum was at his stove, stirring a rabbit stew.

Its curdled smell made Holly's eyes water.

"Must you cook that while I'm here?" she asked.

Callum dropped the spoon into his stew. Holly was alarmed to see it staying upright.

"I thought you might be hungry," Callum said.

"I was until I smelled that," Holly said.

She leaned back in the armchair she was sitting in, her fingers finding a loose thread in the upholstery. Without thinking, she began to pull.

Callum watched her over his shoulder until a hole appeared. "That's my father's chair. It outlived him. Doesn't look like it's going to outlive you, though."

"Sorry," Holly said, covering the bare patch with her hand. "It's also the chair you slept in on the night we first met."

"I remember. You wrapped me in a blanket when I got cold."

"Did I wake you?" Holly asked.

"I'd say, startled is a better description," Callum said, a growing smile on his lips. "I wasn't used to female visitors."

"But you're used to it now?"

Callum's smile turned into a grin. "Absolutely. This place is like the Playboy Mansion now."

Holly doubted that. Callum lived an isolated life, wandering the estate with the deer and the sheep. There were no neighbours to take in a parcel, and as far as she knew, Holly was the only woman to have been to his cottage, much less slept there.

Her thoughts were cut short by a knocking at the cottage door.

Callum answered, his face widening into a grin.

"Sorry for dropping by unannounced. Is this a bad time?" Simone asked from the doorstep.

Holly stumbled from the armchair, brushing down her clothes. It wasn't the voice she recognised, but the scent. It was of the incense stick Simone had burned at her home, wafting into the cottage, strong enough to mask the smell of Callum's unctuous stew. Simone smelled of rose petals mixed with fresh rain, which was odd, Holly thought.

Peering through the window, she saw it had stopped raining.

"Why don't you come in?" Callum asked.

Simone accepted, drifting inside with a shy smile. She wore a velvet green robe that hugged her figure. She stopped when she saw Holly.

"Nice to see you again," Holly said.

"You, too," Simone responded before kneeling in front of the empty fireplace to build a fire.

Holly ground her teeth. "I was just about to do that."

Simone's hands worked quickly, balling dried grass into a mound. She built a pyre from the kindling and struck a match off the heel of her shoe. The flames flickered and her eyes danced in an orange hue. "This will keep you both warm."

"I thought you didn't feel the cold," Callum said.

"I don't, but I thought you might." With the fire crackling and the earthy smoke twisting up the chimney, Simone got to her feet and looked to the stove. "Is that rabbit stew?"

Callum tugged on his collar. "Yeah. Sorry about the smell. I suppose I'm used to it."

"I grew up eating rabbit stew," Simone said. "It was one of the things I missed most when we moved away."

"Where did you go?" Holly asked. "When you left?"

Simone drew a line on her velvet dress with a fingernail and then rubbed it out. "Initially, I went to London."

"I'm sorry to hear that," Callum said.

Holly watched the fire build. The flames caught Simone's charm bracelet hanging from her wrist. Its sparkle drew Holly in, mesmerising her, freezing her to the floor.

"It must have been difficult," Callum said to Simone. "Leaving your friends and family. Little Belton might be small, but it has a powerful hold over people."

"Is that why you stayed?" Simone asked.

Callum coughed into his hand. "Well, my jeep is quite old. I doubt it would carry me further than the outskirts, to be honest."

Simone's dress flowed like liquid moss. It poured over her limbs as she took a tour of Callum's home, but no matter where she was, her eyes never left his face. They shone through the muted light like headlamps.

But Holly couldn't tear her eyes away from the bracelet. Lights leapt from Simone's wrist, as if her jewellery was shedding fairies. They swam through Holly's vision and she felt sleepy.

"I like the people of Little Belton," Simone said. "They're a genuine community. They watch out for each other."

Callum nodded in agreement. "We're a family here."

"Luckily for us," Simone said, "we're not all related by blood. Otherwise, we'd end up like the people of Crockfoot."

"Did you know some of them have two belly buttons?" Callum asked with a smirk.

Simone paused in front of him.

Holly blinked. While Simone had ceased moving, her flowing dress had not. It continued to wash over her body in waves.

Simone took Callum's left hand and drew a finger along his palm. "No wedding ring, I see."

He shivered. "Holly is married. Not me."

"Well, perhaps I can read your future then? See if I can predict if love is on the horizon?"

With no one to attend the fire, the flames withered and the glow of Simone's bracelet went with it.

Holly rolled a sluggish tongue around her mouth. "Is there something we can do for you?"

Simone's face hardened, transforming from a seductress to a statue, as if she was a victim of a cruel spell. "After you both came to my house, I went to see Mrs Masterly. She told me to find you. She said, you'd never refuse a request to help."

Callum took back his hand and returned to the stove to remove his stew from the heat.

Holly was grateful for that, at least. "How did you know I'd be here?"

"I didn't," Simone said. "I came for Callum."

Callum grabbed his cottage keys from the mantlepiece. "Come on. Let's go, but the roads aren't safe after all this rain. We'd be better off walking. Are you okay with that, Simone?"

"Perfectly," she answered, giving him a wink.

"Cool your jets, Rocketman," Holly said. "We don't even know why Mrs Masterly wants to see us."

Opening the door, Callum glanced at his feet.

"What on earth is that?" he asked.

Sitting on the doorstep was another straw doll.

"It wasn't there when I arrived," Simone said.

CHAPTER FOURTEEN

Holly rushed to Callum's side as he picked it up.

"It's the same as the last one," she said.

Callum rolled the doll around his hand, but unlike the last one, this doll's eyes had finished unwinding and lay as strips of grass. Holly guessed it had been sitting there for some time.

She looked to Simone, who was inspecting her fingernails.

"It's not exactly the same," Callum said, holding the doll for Holly to examine.

It was of a similar size and the tousled hair looked the same. The wax jacket was comparable to the last one, though it seemed less well fitted, as if it had been constructed in a rush.

But Callum was right. There was one striking difference and Holly gulped.

This doll wore a straw noose around its neck.

Chapter Fifteen

While it had stopped raining, the roads remained flooded. Callum and Holly trudged through a copse of trees whose branches were caught in the wind, swaying like a body at the end of a rope.

Holly's head rattled with thoughts of dolls and hangmen. The images scuttled in the shadows behind her eyes. When she tried to focus on them, they vanished, reappearing as faces in the gnarled bark of trees or as shimmers in a puddle.

"We should stop thinking about those dolls for a while," Holly said. "Concentrate on helping Mrs Masterly."

Callum kept his eyes trained to the boggy ground. "I agree."

"But who's sending them?" Simone asked. She cut a distinctive figure, clambering through the rough terrain in her velvet dress, but she was true to her word. The cold didn't seem to bother her and she pushed on through the melted mud. "I mean, they must mean something to someone."

"That last one seemed quite malevolent," Holly said.

"And clearly targeted toward Callum," Simone said. "I swear I didn't see it when I first arrived."

Callum waded through a marsh, disturbing a host of yellow flies from their slumber. "This is the quickest way to the manor. Come on."

The group continued on in silence, save for the squelch of mud.

"Oh no," Holly said, pointing at her walking boots. "These things are leaking again."

"I think someone is stalking me," Simone said, interrupting.

Why was it always about her, Holly thought?

Callum scanned the horizon, his ears keening for the slightest sound. "How do you know?"

"In the morning, there are footprints around the bothy and they don't belong to me."

"It could be animals," Callum said.

"Not unless they're wearing size ten boots."

Simone's face was impassive, but Holly saw the worry lines around her mouth.

"Have you seen anyone?" she asked. "Have they tried to get inside?"

"No, but I sense them sometimes. It's as if some creature is prowling around my front door." Simone wrapped her muscular arms around her waist in a hug. "I'm so alone out there. I don't know what I'd do if they got in."

At night, the estate was pitch black. There were no streetlamps, no nearby glow of a neighbouring town to cast a glimmer of light. It was as if their world was soaked in black ink. Holly wasn't surprised Simone was fearful. As a child, Holly had been reluctant to leave the family home after sunset, scared she might lose her way in the night and never be found again. Even as an adult, she rarely ventured out after dark.

Until Callum had bought her a torch.

Living on her own and surrounded by alien noises, Simone had a right to be nervous.

"I'm sure it's nothing," Holly said, "but maybe Callum can take a look after we speak with Mrs Masterly."

"I'd be happy too," he said, breaching the summit of a small hill and studying the oncoming clouds. "We're gonna get wet soon. Let's move it."

"This way," Simone said, turning south.

But Callum grabbed her hand. "It's too dangerous. There's a bog. We'll get stuck."

He stared into a valley below. "And that's Crosskeys down there. It's riddled with swallow holes and caves. One false step and we'll never be seen again."

Simone shuddered. "I don't want to run into Easter Mary."

"Who's that?" Holly asked.

"She's a ghost," Callum said.

The ground under Holly's feet was saturated from weeks of rain. Her feet were sinking and she trotted on the spot, fearful of being dragged under. "Please. Not another one of your mystical stories."

"Two hundred years ago," Callum said, "Mary Malstead of Gosport was hiding duck eggs for an Easter Day egg hunt. Her twins - a boy and a girl - set off to find them in a merry rush, not realising their mother had made a fatal error. Mary had hidden the eggs in the caves during unpredictable weather. A furious storm erupted, causing a flash flood that ran into the caves and drowned her two children."

Whether it was the gruesome nature of the tale or the way Callum related it as fact, it caused Holly to shiver and she turned her back on the Crosskeys caves.

"Easter Mary was so bereft," Simone said, continuing with the story, "she never left the caves again. She spent the rest of her days searching for her children."

"Don't tell me you believe in this nonsense too?" Holly asked Simone.

"She lives there still," Simone said, "luring in travellers, petrifying them into statues so they can never leave."

"My dad told me that story," Callum said.

Simone smiled. "Mine, too."

"Well, your dads obviously had a broad definition of what an education means," Holly said, wrenching her feet from the mud and almost losing her leaking boots. "Couldn't they have taught you algebra instead?"

Callum and Simone gazed at the crumbling walls of Crosskeys valley, silent, lost in their own thoughts.

"We should get moving," Simone said, suddenly. "I say, we risk the bog."

"It's safer to use the road circling the manor," Callum said. "If we get stuck, Mrs Masterly will be coming to help us. Not the other way around."

Simone laughed, as if Callum had said something funny. "Catch me if you can, then."

She took off at a lurch with Callum in quick procession. Holly followed from behind as she struggled through the wood. Her legs grew leaden, unable to match their blistering pace. Eventually, Callum noticed and waited for her to catch up.

"I can manage," Holly said, but Callum braced an arm around her waist, carrying her wayward form until they broke free of the wood's clutches. They staggered onto a cobbled road to where Simone was waiting with her hands on her hips.

The road was winding and slippery. There were snaking ditches on either side, filled with running water, gurgling and spitting as it bounced over debris under the surface.

Holly massaged her aching limbs while Callum approached the last tree in the wood.

"What's going on?" she asked.

The tree had fallen, obscuring their path. Its roots were exposed where it had been yanked from the earth. They looked like muddy fingers stretching to the sky. Water pooled around the trunk, swirling in circles, gathering dead leaves into its hold.

The fallen tree was surrounded by its neighbours, all standing steadfast against the elements.

"Why has this one fallen and none of the others?" Callum asked.

"It's probably weak and diseased," Simone said, casting an eye over a sweaty Holly.

Holly drew herself to her full height, her muscles shaking with the effort. "I'm sure it's fine. It just doesn't get the chance to exercise as much as it should."

Callum leaned over the tree, as if he was mourning its destruction. He rubbed his fingers over the rough bark, shaking his head.

"What's the matter?" Holly asked, going to his side.

Callum pointed downward, his mouth dropping open.

On the bark were two handprints in white, as if the tree had been pushed over by a gigantic ghost.

Chapter Sixteen

The handprints vanished in front of them, leaving Holly biting her lip.

"Where did they come from?" she asked. "Did someone shove this tree over?"

Callum looked uncertain. "No one is that strong."

As the flood grew, water filtered through the snapped branches, pouring over Holly's shoes.

"The rain must have loosened the ground around its roots," Holly said, stepping back. "It toppled over."

"I don't think so." Callum traced a finger along the knotted bark where the handprint had been. "This isn't possible."

"Why?" Holly asked. "Why are you saying that?"

Callum sucked air over his teeth. "Because this tree is older than I am. It wouldn't just fall down."

"Then we're back to the original idea. It was pushed over."

"That's not possible, either," Callum said. "What would push over a tree and leave behind white handprints?"

"Don't you dare say, it's a ghost," Holly said. "We need to be serious. What else could it have been?"

"A really big clown?"

Holly forced down a string of expletives. Ignoring her wet feet, she examined the tree where the handprints had been. "There has to be an explanation. What are those?"

Nearing the top of the trunk were two gouge marks running parallel to each other.

"I don't know," Callum said. "They weren't made by an animal and they look fresh. The marks have cut through the bark layers into the sapwood. This tree is still bleeding."

Holly swallowed down her unease. "Trees bleed?"

"They bleed sap. Not blood and these wounds haven't had time to heal over."

Appalled and fascinated, Holly clambered closer to get a better look. As she did, she felt something wrap itself around her ankle. When she looked down, a green face stared up at her.

She screamed.

Callum vaulted the tree trunk, splashing down at her side, his teeth bared. "What is it?"

Holly's shoulders dropped and her heart returned to its normal rhythm as she wondered how often a woman could make a fool of herself before it became a habit.

"It's a plastic bag," she said, pointing at her feet.

Entwined around her ankles was the tattered face of a man. His skin was wrinkled, and his beard was pointed. Callum wrestled it free and splayed it out on the trunk.

Holly hid her embarrassment behind a snort. "What's it doing here?"

"It must have been carried here by the floods. It's from Roland's Hardware," Callum said.

"The shop in Woolscroft?" Holly asked, searching around her feet. "That's miles away. How could it get all the way out here? And there's no other litter anywhere else."

"Well, that's definitely Old Man Roland's face on the bag," Callum said, rummaging inside it. "There's nothing in there, though."

"Wait a minute," Holly said. "Didn't Derek say Mrs Masterly owes

Roland money?"

"He did," Callum said, scratching his head. "Could this have something to do with her?"

"More likely it has something to do with the renovations the Spectre brothers were completing. It is a hardware shop, after all." Holly leapt onto the tree trunk, using it as a balance beam. "We should look around. See if there is anything else here."

She paused as she scanned the estate. "And that includes Simone. Where is she gone to?"

They both turned at the sound of Simone's giggling as she stumbled out of the tree line, holding two mushrooms over her head.

"I've been foraging. How lucky are we?" Simone said. "Angel's parasols."

The mushrooms had a brown cap pitted with white dots.

Simone bit down on their flesh and her eyes lit up.

Callum scrambled from the tree, hurdling over puddles to get to her. He tugged his jacket sleeve over his hands and batted the mushrooms out of Simone's grasp.

"Put them down," he shouted.

"What's the matter? I've eaten these before," Simone said. "I had them in a risotto in London."

"Gathered by someone who knew what they were doing," Callum said. "For every edible mushroom, there is another that looks just like it. This one could be riddled with poisons."

"I've been a forager all my life," Simone said. "Don't worry. I know what I'm doing. I'm one with nature."

"Even experts get this wrong," Callum said. "Please. Be careful."

Holly lifted her face to a pewter sky, feeling the first cold splash of rain on her skin. "How far away is Black Rock Manor?"

The rain was gathering pace, falling in glittering sheets, but Callum and Simone didn't appear to notice. Their clothes took on a darker tone as the damp in them spread.

Simone walked in circles. "I was trying to do something nice for you."

"It's best to do as he says out here," Holly said. "You could have died."

"That's very kind, but I didn't ask for your help," Simone said. "That was Mrs Masterly. I've been on my own long enough to know I don't need a knight in shining armour."

Lightning split the sky. When it vanished, the sky was awash with angry clouds.

"The manor is about a mile away," Callum said. "If we cut through the brush, we'll be there in a quarter of an hour."

"What if we follow the road? It might be quicker," Simone said.

The exhaustion in Holly's limbs was forgotten as she stamped her foot. "Whatever you both decide to do, make up your mind before we're washed away."

A puddle swelled around them, growing by the second. Under the opaque sky, it looked like oil, reflecting the clouds above it.

"Wait," Simone said, pointing into a ditch overflowing with water. Her finger trembled and her lips moved as if she was trying to speak.

Inwardly cursing, Holly followed the direction of Simone's finger.

"What is it?" she asked.

"I can't see," Simone said and her eyes rolled into her head. She wavered, her feet attempting to find purchase on solid ground. Blood drained from her lips and she scratched at her throat.

"The mushrooms," Holly said.

Simone's body twitched, as if she'd been compelled to dance to a deadly tune, but the music was brief and Simone swooned, unable to dance any longer.

Chapter Seventeen

The grounds of Black Rock Manor were fringed with rhododendrons. Their oval leaves dripped water as the new purple flowers were battered by the rain. Birds cowered in the recesses of their canopy, waiting for a brief window of light weather before they sprung forth and foraged.

Callum burst through the bushes in a starburst of petals. He lurched forward, his arms heavy with a recumbent Simone.

Holly staggered after him, swatting away startled sparrows.

"Get inside," she shouted.

They cut through the grounds, heading to the front door.

"It'll be locked," Callum shouted over his shoulder.

Powered by panic, Holly's legs worked like pistons. She ran past Callum and threw herself at the door. Surprisingly, it was open. Her momentum carried her through the porch, where she skidded on her knees through the inner door and rolled like a damp heap into the reception room.

"Help me," came Callum's voice from behind.

Her joints ached and her lungs felt as if they were filled with sand, but Holly clambered upwards and helped Callum lower Simone to the floor.

"What on earth is going on?" Mrs Masterly asked, emerging from the kitchen. Her willowy figure was ramrod straight, but there were dark smudges under her eyes. She moved as if dragging a heavy chain behind her.

Holly did a double-take at Mrs Masterly's appearance but said nothing.

"She picked up a panther cap. They're everywhere at this time of year," Callum said, loosening the neckline of Simone's dress. "She thought it was an Angel's parasol."

Mrs Masterly looked on with an open mouth.

Dropping to her knees, Holly pressed two fingers to Simone's throat. "Her pulse is weak. What should we do?"

"I'm calling an ambulance," Mrs Masterly said, a phone against her ear.

Callum shook his head. "That'll take too long. Go to the bonfire outside."

Holly pelted to the front door and then stopped "What? Why?"

"Where the cabinet was burned," Callum said. "Get some charcoal."

It didn't answer her question, but Holly didn't have time to query further. Bouldering out of the manor, she raced around its circumference and cut through the tall grass to the forest. When the temperature dropped, she knew she was in the right place. She'd found the Witches' Hall.

The blackened poplar dripped water on her as she scooped wet charcoal into her pockets.

Holly's stomach flipped at the thought of Simone losing her life. She was too young, too healthy, too everything to die because of a stupid mistake.

With her pockets full, she prepared to run back to Callum, but found her legs useless. She stared into the forest. On the outskirts of the Witches' Hall, a man stood with his hands clasped over his heart. He was young with golden locks pinned behind pointed ears. He was talking, calling out, but Holly couldn't hear what he was saying.

The man's mouth moved to the drum of rainfall hitting the ground.

"What do you want?" Holly asked.

But the man evaporated, as if he was a dissolving pillar of salt. Holly tore her eyes from the last of the apparition and hurtled back to the manor, hoping she wasn't too late.

Holly was greeted by Mrs Masterly holding out a glass of water. "Put the charcoal in there."

Turning out her pockets, Holly dribbled the runny charcoal into the water, turning it milky grey. Something slipped through her fingers, landing in the glass with a clunk.

"What's that?" Mrs Masterly said.

Holly pulled a twisted lump of metal out of the glass. It was a small brass handle.

"It's what's left of the Greyston cabinet," she said, jamming it back into her pocket.

"She couldn't have ingested much of the mushroom," Callum said, "but I can't be sure. I don't know if this is going to work."

He took the glass and pressed it to Simone's lips. She stirred, her eyelids flickering open.

"Drink," Callum said.

Simone sipped, her face twisting at the taste and she turned away.

Callum lifted her head back to the glass. "You have to drink this."

The breath was caught in Holly's hammering chest. Simone was conscious. That had to be a good thing and Callum appeared to know what he was doing.

"The ambulance will be here soon," Mrs Masterly said.

Holly's shoulders sank in relief, knowing help was on its way. As the panic subsided, her mind turned to what she'd seen at the Witches' Hall as she searched for a rational explanation. Nothing was forthcoming. Instead, she remembered the stories of strange goings-on around the estate; the tales of Little Belton not being quite right.

"I have to tell you something," Mrs Masterly said, dragging Holly back to reality.

"Is it good news?" she asked.

But Holly could tell by Mrs Masterly's face it was not.

"Someone is going to pay us a visit," Mrs Masterly whispered.

"Pardon?"

Mrs Masterly's frown was highlighted by the blue flashing lights of the approaching ambulance. "Mr Xavier, the assessor in charge of our grant application, has arranged to come to the manor."

"But we don't have the cabinet," Holly said.

"Which I couldn't really tell him." Mrs Masterly chewed at the side of her thumb. "But when he finds out, I'll be saying goodbye to Black Rock."

Chapter Eighteen

On the following day, Holly and Callum trooped over a road awash with rain.

"The paramedic said you did the right thing," Holly said, hopping over a grey puddle.

Callum marched through it. "She'll be fine. It was a mild case."

The rain fell in a repetitive drum beat as it hit the trees, the ground, the hills, and everything it could reach within its bitter touch. Long Robert struck with an indiscriminate hand.

"Mrs Masterly will look after Simone in the hospital," Callum said. "She'll be out later today."

Rainwater squished inside Holly's boots as she walked. "Did you notice anything about Mrs Masterly? She wasn't quite her immaculate self."

"I was a bit preoccupied with Simone."

"Saving damsels in distress seems to be your thing," Holly said. "And just how preoccupied are you with Simone?"

"She wasn't in distress until I met her."

Holly placed a hand on his arm, stopping him on the slippery cobblestones. "You can't blame yourself for Simone trying to eat a mushroom."

"I still placed her in danger," Callum said, his face twisting. "There's something off about Little Belton right now. Long Robert doesn't normally stay this long. It's causing havoc. I'm afraid Mrs Masterly might have brought it here."

"Why would you say that?" Holly asked.

"Nothing happens in Little Belton. It's why I like it, but there have been two new arrivals of late. The cabinet and Long Robert."

"They aren't related," Holly said.

"What if they are?" Callum asked. "Long Robert is a jealous sprite. He protects his territory. He won't tolerate interlopers. If Mrs Masterly has unleashed something in Little Belton, Long Robert won't rest until it's washed away."

Holly opened her mouth to speak, but Callum silenced her with a hand.

"I know what you're going to say," he said. "It's all nonsense. It's not feasible, but I've lived here long enough not to dismiss it so readily."

Holly dried her face on the sleeve of her coat.

"What is it?" Callum asked. "Something's wrong. I can tell."

Pairing the cabinet and Long Robert together was ridiculous, thought Holly. It was faulty logic, like making a link between wearing certain underwear and avoiding a car crash. But Holly couldn't deny everything Callum was saying. There was definitely something strange going on in Little Belton and Holly had been there to witness it.

"I saw a figure," she said. "When I was getting the charcoal for Simone."

"At the Witches' Hall?"

"It was a man," Holly said. "He was trying to tell me something, but it was like he was under water. Like his volume had been turned down."

"What do you think he wanted?"

"I don't know," Holly said, "but he scared me."

Callum blinked rain from his eyes. "If we trust in the stories, then the Witches' Hall is a powerful place, drawing in warmth and energy from the whole of the estate. I think Long Robert is drawn there."

"That's who was speaking to me?"

"Either that or you were in a heightened state of anxiety causing you to see things that weren't there." Callum gave her a weary smile. "Depends on what you believe, doesn't it?"

Holly wasn't sure what she believed anymore, but the figure at the hall seemed as real to her as Callum was now.

"Well, Long Robert needs to be clearer if it wants its message to get through," she said.

A low rumble of thunder rolled over the estate, causing the trees to shed the water clinging to their leaves.

"We'd better get going," Callum said, wincing at the sky. "The rain is getting heavier. The Defender is over the ridge. Let's pay a visit to Roland. Maybe he can tell us why his plastic bags are littering my estate."

"Better still," Holly said. "Maybe he can tell us what was inside it."

The ground was loose as Holly summited the ridge. Her feet faltered as her breath came in short gasps. Her mind concentrated on staying upright, dismissing all other thoughts. She kept her eyes on the ground until she saw something in the Crosskeys valley below.

On a grey landscape of rocks and swirling streams, a red cowl drifted through the rain. Whoever was beneath it picked through the peaks and troughs with a hand pressing the hood deep over their face.

Fearful she was suffering from another hallucination, Holly looked to Callum, who was watching the same figure with a frown.

"They'll meet Easter Mary if they're not careful," he said. "We better warn them."

Before Holly could protest, Callum was slipping down the hill, his heels ploughing tracks through the mud, making his way to the valley floor.

She could wait for him to return, she supposed. On top of a hill. In the driving rain. Maybe go looking for the Defender herself. Possibly get lost. In the driving rain.

The figure in the red cowl disappeared among the jagged rocks. Soon Callum would do the same.

Cursing, Holly followed as quickly as she could.

Chapter Nineteen

The rain bounced off the valley walls and the sound of gushing water made Holly's bones tremble. The stones vibrated under her feet, moved by an unknown force.

"This place is made from limestone and it's riddled with holes and caverns," Callum said, shouting above the noise.

The floor was worn smooth. There was no moss or ferns clinging to their surfaces. They had long since been washed aside. If Holly ever visited the moon, she imagined it would remind her of Crosskeys. Apart from all the noise.

"Where is this guy?" Holly shouted. "We haven't got time for this."

"He was heading over there," Callum said, taking her hand.

Holly stared at their interlocking fingers and the wedding band she wore.

Callum must have registered the look on her face.

"Don't get any ideas, madam," he said, tapping his foot to the ground. "Beneath us are hundreds of caves and tunnels and rivers. We're currently standing on a roof that's thick in some places, but as thin as an eggshell in others."

Holly wished she'd started her diet earlier.

"If you fall through," Callum continued, "I want to have a tight hold on you."

Water coursed down the valley walls, bursting into a mist as it struck the ground. Gathering itself into streams, it rushed ahead of Holly and Callum, racing through the gargling mouth of a cave.

Holly and Callum paused in its shadow, listening to the distant rumble.

"Let's go," Callum said.

"You want me to go inside?" Holly asked.

Callum wiped wet hair from his brow. A stubborn curl clung to his forehead.

"I've got you," he said.

"You've got me," Holly said, "but who's got you?"

He cocked an eyebrow and nudged her inside.

Holly clung onto Callum so he was almost carrying her. If they dropped through a hole, she was likely to drag him down with her, but Holly was reassured by his presence. They proceeded carefully, moving away from the light of the entrance. Soon, they were engulfed in darkness, surrounded by the roar of unseen rivers.

"I can't see a thing," Holly said.

She heard rustling and a beam of light cut through the cave.

"Where did you get a torch from?" Holly asked.

"Who doesn't bring a torch to a cave?" Callum swept it over the jagged stalactites and stalagmites. They hung from the ceiling and grew from the ground. If the cave was a mouth, Holly thought, those were the teeth, except for their shape. They weren't conical. They took on various forms, looking like teddy bears or children's dolls. Others were garden gnomes or wind chimes. There was even something resembling a bicycle.

It was as if Medusa had turned the contents of a home into stone.

The roof dropped by a few inches, forcing them to stoop.

"Is he in here?" Holly whispered.

Callum swung the torch around, chasing away the shadows. The cave

CHAPTER NINETEEN

was pockmarked, its walls pitted with brittle spikes. The water gushed along, coating every surface with damp. It tipped into a velvet black drop where it continued under the estate to the North Sea.

"They aren't here," Callum said.

"Did they get swept away?"

"If they did, there's no helping them now." Callum searched the walls, the floor and the twisted rocks caught in mid-metamorphosis between children's toys and limestone. "They could have slipped by us. It's dark and with the sound of the river, we wouldn't have noticed."

Holly preferred that idea to the notion they were currently hurtling underground toward the sea.

"What were they doing here?" Holly asked. "They weren't running away from us. They didn't know we were following them."

Callum focused his beam on a section of the floor, narrowing it down to a pinpoint. "Plus, we were only trying to help."

"Where are they then?" As Holly searched the cave, her eyes roamed to Callum's face and the smile upon it.

"I used to play in here as a kid," he said. "Lots of us did."

Holly stared about the bleak and dangerous environment, listing all the ways wayward children could perish, from disappearing down a hole to drowning in the dark. "Unsupervised? And what about Easter Mary?"

Callum squatted to the ground. "We'd leave our toys here or a trinket of some kind. The waters are rich in minerals. They drip over the toys and cover them in stone." He pointed to the ground. "This is one of my Matchbox cars. It's a jeep, like the one I drive now."

"I came here, too, but it was on a school trip," Holly said, pointing to a shape next to Callum's toy car. "That's my doll. I wanted to leave something of myself here. Even at that age, I must have known I would move on."

A thought came unexpectantly. Holly looked to the car and the doll encased in stone.

"Just think," she said. "We've been sitting together in this cave for all those years."

Callum grinned. "And we're still sitting here now. In the dark and getting wet. We never came here when the weather was this bad. Why would someone risk their lives coming to this cave now?"

"Give me your light," she asked.

Callum shook his head in despair. "So I bought you that torch for nothing?"

"Look who's being snipey now," Holly said, holding out her hand. "Maybe the person in the cowl left something behind, too."

Callum gave her the torch with a sniff and Holly pointed it into every corner, searching the craggy rock faces and the baubles left behind by generations of Little Belton residents.

"There," she said. "By the stalagmite shaped like an Action Man."

They scurried over the ground to a pile of objects glinting under the torch's light. Holly picked one up and examined it. "In a few months, these would have been unrecognisable."

"They're unrecognisable now," Callum said. "What are they?"

Holly rummaged in her pocket and produced the charred cabinet handle she'd accidentally fished from the bonfire's ashes.

"They're handles," she said. "Like this one."

Chapter Twenty

After their aborted attempt yesterday and with Callum busy on the estate, Holly decided to visit Old Man Roland herself. It was a short drive, but long enough to take her away from Little Belton. As she did so, the rain lessened and the sun emerged. Its sudden brightness forced her to rummage in the glove compartment among the sticky toffees and lint for her sunglasses.

Woolscroft was a stone-built market town on the north-east coast. It was renowned for its smoked kipper sandwiches and the beauty of the surrounding countryside. Its car park, however, was a nightmare, and Holly circled it three times before she swooped down on an empty bay like a vulture.

Roland's Hardware was on Venison Street. As she approached, Holly saw the outside pavement was filled with brooms, metal buckets, wheelbarrows, and bags of compost and coal. The glass door entrance was hidden behind a mass of garden hoses.

Holly stumbled inside and Old Man Roland peered at her over half-moon glasses. He was so old, it was impossible to guess his exact age. Maybe seventy, maybe ninety. He was dressed in a velour tracksuit and wore gold sovereign rings on his fingers.

"Can I help you?" he asked.

The shop wasn't cluttered, suggesting most of his sales were conducted on the pavement outside. The shelves had boxes and packages bleached by years of sunlight. There was an air of must and Holly was unsure if the smell came from the shop or the man himself.

Holly handed him the plastic bag she'd found at the fallen tree. "Is this yours?"

"It's an excellent likeness, don't you think?" Roland asked, blinking rapidly. "Really captures my eyes. My grandson did it on one of them computers. Bright kid. Always coming up with new things. Probably blow himself up one day."

"I found the bag on the Black Rock Manor Estate," Holly said.

Roland stared at her, as if he didn't comprehend the gravity of her words.

"That's nice," he said. "Can I help you with anything else?"

"I was hoping you could tell me why it was there."

Roland flattened the bag on the ground and cupped his chin with his hand while he studied it. His brow knotted in a frown. He walked around it, viewing it from every angle.

"My guess," he said slowly, "is that someone dropped it. And then you found it. And then you brought it here. Am I right?"

Holly wasn't stupid, though Old Man Roland was doing a good job of making her feel that way. She understood the folly of asking these questions, but the bag didn't belong in Little Belton. It belonged in Woolscroft. That made it either important or a coincidence, and Holly didn't believe in coincidences.

"Do you get many customers from Little Belton?" she asked.

"I get a few," Roland said. "Couldn't tell you their names. I go mainly by faces. Yes, sir. Round up all of my customers and stand them in a line, and I could tell you who bought what and when."

Could Holly persuade the residents of Little Belton to join a line-up? It seemed like a tall order. Could she photograph the chief suspects and present them to Roland? Possibly, she thought, but she wasn't one

CHAPTER TWENTY

hundred percent sure who she suspected and who she didn't.

"Is there a reason you're asking me about a plastic bag?" Roland asked.

"I think one of your customers may have been involved in a crime," Holly said.

Roland's glasses slipped off the end of his nose. "Pardon?"

Holly strolled around the shop, gathering her thoughts. She stopped at a display of brass fittings and fished out the handles they'd found in the caves from her handbag, together with charred remains of the handle she'd found at the Witches' Hall. All three of them matched.

"Do you recognise these?" she asked Roland.

Fixing his glasses back onto his nose, Roland studied them as thoroughly as he did the plastic bag. "Yes. We sell them. They're part of a Regency collection."

"Do you remember selling any recently?" Holly asked.

"We sell them all the time," Roland said. "People use them to jazz up their furniture. Make their chest of drawers look more like antiques."

Holly's heart rate quickened. "Could you give me the names of anyone who bought them in the past month or so?"

"I told you," Roland said. "I don't do names. Only faces."

"Do you take credit cards?"

Old Man Roland looked affronted. "There's no need to offer me a bribe, miss. I'm telling you the truth. I don't know any names."

Holly attempted to hide her frustration. "No, I mean, if you take cards, then you'd have their details in your till. If you take cards, that is."

She breathed in the musty aroma of the shop. It was like being in a museum for nineteen fifties retail. The shelves were lined in dust and Holly suspected the products on them hadn't been moved in years.

"Of course we take cards," Roland said. "We went cashless years ago. Grandson's idea. He said most people don't carry money anymore. Did it all through his computer. He'll go far one day. If he doesn't turn to crime first."

At that moment, Holly could have kissed Roland. In fact, there was a danger she still might.

"So could you tell me who bought those handles?" Holly asked.

"I don't know how it all works," Roland said. "The till and the computer thing. That's the grandson's department."

"Could you ask him to do it for you?"

Old Man Roland's face clouded over. "He doesn't like to be disturbed when he's busy."

As he finished speaking, the shop was filled with the sound of a drill.

"That's him," Roland said, jerking his thumb to a door behind him. "Building something again. Honestly, I don't know where he gets his ideas from. Last week he made a robotic cat. Lost a fingertip in the process, mind you. The idiot."

The high pitch of the drill made it feel like it was being pressed directly into Holly's head, compelling her to raise her voice.

"Could you talk to him about it, please?" Holly asked, handing over her phone number. "It's really important."

Roland nodded, but something told Holly he hadn't heard her. She turned to leave, the din from the drill driving her from the shop. She'd return with Callum. Perhaps he could speak to Roland; persuade him more forcibly than Holly could.

And then a thought occurred to her.

"Roland?" she asked above the noise. "Is there such a thing as a quiet drill?"

"Pardon?"

"Can you buy a quiet drill?" she shouted.

Roland smiled in a way that reminded Holly she was acting stupid again.

"All drills are the same," he said. "It's what they're drilling into that makes the noise."

"What if they were drilling into stone?"

Roland's face contorted. "That would make a helluva racket. Worse than the one he's making now."

Holly thought back to Black Rock Manor and the night the cabinet was stolen. She pictured Mrs Masterly fast asleep in bed while the thief drilled holes in her walls.

"There's no way you could sleep through something like that, could you?" Holly asked.

Roland clapped his hands over his ears.

"Lord, no," he said. "It would be enough to wake the dead."

Chapter Twenty-One

Holly waited at Black Rock Manor for Callum. There was no one else around, but she didn't mind. It gave her more time to think. It was also an opportunity to poke around Mrs Masterly's belongings while she wasn't there.

Holly had returned from Woolscroft with the unshakeable notion the lady of the manor hadn't been telling the truth about her night-time habits.

On the second floor, Holly stood next to the vase on the table while she inspected the door to the servants' quarters. It was an inch thick and the lock remained intact. Peering closer, she could see there were no scratch marks to indicate it had been picked. Not that she would have recognised those types of marks anyway, but she felt better for checking.

The quarters were as she remembered them - small and soulless. The sawdust had collected in drifts, forming the shape of a question mark. The hole in the wall had gone. Without the skills or money to have it repaired, it had been hidden behind a poster of Raquel Welch. The breeze behind it was strong, forcing Raquel's stomach to bulge. Holly patted her own stomach, noting its decreasing girth. No one enjoyed marching around the estate in the rain, but Holly would tolerate it if she dropped another dress size.

CHAPTER TWENTY-ONE

She left the servants' quarters and tiptoed toward Mrs Masterly's bedroom. There was no one else in the house and no need to tiptoe, but Holly remained on the balls of her feet until she reached the bedroom door. It creaked open and she dared herself to cross the threshold. The bed was king-sized and littered with silken pillows. They were embroidered with words like *Love* and *Home*. As Holly snooped through the room, she was grateful there wasn't one called *Trust* or *Friendship*.

Her guilt levels were high enough already.

Holly examined herself in a full-length mirror before her eyes were drawn to an oak wardrobe. She knew what she would find inside and that it would have nothing to do with the missing cabinet, but she opened it anyway.

The wardrobe was filled with designer dresses. There were short ones, long ones, some that left little to the imagination, but they were all as beautiful as their owner.

Holly took one from its hanger and turned to the mirror, pressing it against her body.

The dress was a backless halter neck in green, tapering to a narrow waist. The colour reflected Holly's jealous face. It was far too small. The dress belonged with Mrs Masterly and not with her.

It wasn't fair, Holly thought. They were both penniless and yet, Mrs Masterly lived in a manor with stunning clothes. Holly lived in a cottage with a leaking roof and a husband who did not know how to fix it.

With a huff, she replaced the dress and closed the wardrobe harder than she intended.

Holly inspected the rest of the room, idly picking up trinkets and casting them aside. On a table by the bed was a gel mask and a tub of moisturiser. Mrs Masterly's beauty regime; her secret to staying young. Next to the cosmetics was an orange vial with a white top.

It rattled when Holly picked it up.

"Q12 Vitamin Nourishment Pills," she whispered, reading the label.

Holly popped the lid, shaking a pill into her open hand. Things fell into place. Holly had assumed Mrs Masterly maintained her beautiful figure through diet, but no one that thin ate more than fresh air. Instead, it appeared Mrs Masterly relied on a little help.

Holly continued to read the label. "Scientifically proven to counter signs of ageing."

She recognised a spurious claim when she saw one. For all Mrs Masterly knew, her vitamins could contain lithium or asbestos.

How silly. How dangerous, Holly thought before swallowing a pill.

If it kept Mrs Masterly looking so young, maybe it would work for her.

Leaving the bedroom with a smile on her face, Holly went downstairs to examine the manor's lower levels, but nothing had changed. The cabinet hadn't magically reappeared and neither had Callum.

Holly checked her watch. He should have contacted her by now. He'd been vague regarding his "business" on the estate and Holly wondered if he'd used it as an excuse to visit Simone in hospital. Perhaps Mrs Masterly, Callum and Simone were there together, their collective youth and beauty making people feel ill.

There were more lines on Holly's face these days and a tyre around her waist, but she'd find something to solve this case if it killed her. The manor had no new answers, but perhaps they'd missed something at the Witches' Hall.

As she approached the front door, Holly noticed the crack in the windowpane had widened. She wasn't surprised. With the number of people coming and going, she'd be more surprised if it hadn't shattered entirely. Stepping into the rain, Holly carefully closed the door behind her, not wanting to be the one who committed that fateful act.

She was met with a deluge and turned up the collar of her coat. The ground was saturated and her feet sank into the dirt. As she waded through the mire, she thought back to the wonderful dresses in Mrs

Masterly's wardrobe.

"When would I even get a chance to wear one?" she asked herself, mud splashing up her shins.

The walk sucked the life out of Holly's already tired legs. Blinking against the rain, she came to the edge of the Witches' Hall. The familiar sense of cold greeted her. Holly checked the perimeter for apparitions, but she appeared to be on her own.

The charred poplar tree waved at her under a gentle breeze. Holly leaned against it, listening to the branches creaking. The bonfire ash had been washed away, leaving a scorched circle of grass. Sitting in the centre was a frog, its skin slick with rain.

"Shoo," Holly shouted, waving her hands. "Get out of here, you sticky thing."

As if understanding it had just been insulted, the frog turned its bulbous eyes upon her.

Holly ignored it and did a fingertip search of the circle, her head heavy and bowing. There were no more brass handles and with the ash gone, no sign of the cabinet at all. There was just herself, the poplar tree and the frog.

"Holly," she heard the frog say.

She was feeling sleepy and struggled to focus on the frog.

"Get out of here," she slurred.

"What are you doing?" it asked.

Its lips were moving. The frog was definitely speaking.

"Trying to find something," Holly replied, unsure if she'd spoken at all.

The frog made to move and Holly reached out to grab it. Her hand moved through its green body and she flayed wildly, attempting to correct her balance. Her legs buckled and Holly dropped into the scorched earth, swallowed by an impossible blackness.

Chapter Twenty-Two

"Holly?"

The sound of her name drew her back to reality.

"Are you okay? What are you doing?"

Holly shook her head and squinted into the sky. It was a swirling blanket of shifting grey cloud and she realised she was lying on her back. Struggling to her elbows, a shadow danced in front of her.

"Callum?" she asked.

"What are you doing out here?" His features settled and Callum's handsome face materialised through a fog. "You're soaking wet."

"It was a frog," Holly said, her mouth dry. "Sitting in the middle of the circle. It tricked me."

Using Callum's lapels as leverage, Holly hoisted herself to her feet. The world was unsteady and it took her a moment to gain some stability.

"Where have you been?" she asked.

"The hospital," Callum answered, confirming Holly's suspicions, "but Simone had already checked out. Mrs Masterly was by her bedside, dozing and she walked out without waking her. The doctors said, she might still be suffering from the poisons in her system."

Holly thought back to the frog. Had she somehow digested the same toxins as Simone? Had they induced a hallucination?

"The frog. It was talking," she said. "Asking all these questions."

CHAPTER TWENTY-TWO

Callum searched the ground with narrowed eyes. "Like, will you kiss me so I can turn into a prince?"

"I know what I saw," Holly said.

"You don't," Callum answered, "but I do."

In the blackened centre of the scorched earth was another straw doll. Unlike the others, it wasn't made of straw. It was made from grass, its pale green body sparkling with water. Its eyes were made from rose petals pinned to its head.

"They're everywhere," Callum said. "What exactly are they saying to us?"

Holly rubbed her face, trying to clear the fugue from her mind. What had happened? Was it the strange power of the Witches' Hall? Or a new illness spawning hallucinations? Holly felt the way Mrs Masterly had looked on the morning the cabinet was stolen.

Callum held up the straw doll like a false idol. "What are we going to do about these bloody things?"

"Forget about them," Holly said, waving him and the doll aside. "Is Mrs Masterly back at home?"

Callum nodded and Holly made a few faltering steps toward the manor, gazing at its dark face. "I know what happened to the cabinet."

Holly urged her sleepy legs to move. They staggered to the manor where Holly and Callum found the front door open. Despite her ill-timed nap at the Witches' Hall, Holly distinctly remembered closing it. There had already been one theft from the manor. Did Mrs Masterly want to make it two?

Holly and Callum closed the door again and found Mrs Masterly in the kitchen, swirling black coffee around a china cup. She looked up as they entered, her tired face creasing further.

"Are you okay?" Mrs Masterly asked Holly. "You look peaky."

Holly poured water into a glass and sipped gently.

"I know what happened to your cabinet," she said. "The thing that always bothered me about this was how you slept through the theft. Holes were being drilled through walls. That would cause a lot of noise."

"I'm a deep sleeper," Mrs Masterly said, fidgeting with her hair.

"Your bedroom is just down the hall," Holly said. "You'd need to be more than a deep sleeper, and there's still the question of how they got into the room. The lock was heavy and rusty. No one could pick something like that."

Mrs Masterly folded her arms over her chest. "I don't see how the two things are related."

"You have a vial of vitamins by your bed," Holly said. "My guess is you take them because you don't look after yourself as much as you should."

Mrs Masterly's high cheekbones shone red and she stared at the floor. "There isn't always the time to cook and with the stress of the renovations... well, I felt I needed more support."

Some women possessed the "slender" gene, Holly thought bitterly, knowing she wasn't one of them. They were born that way and nothing they ate made a difference to their size. Others took a different route, chasing an unrealistic expectation of themselves.

At least, Mrs Masterly had foresight enough to take vitamins, but the practice hadn't been born by recent stresses.

"Ever since I've known you," Holly said, "you've been thin enough to slip through a crack in the floorboards."

"Aren't we trying to find a cabinet?" Mrs Masterly asked, forcing a laugh.

"Not if it means losing you in the process," Holly answered.

Black Rock Manor moaned as a gust of wind whistled through its eaves. Mrs Masterly turned her ear to the sound and closed her eyes. "I'm not weak, if that's what you think? I use how I look to get people to listen to me. I force them to pay attention because you can be dismissed when you look a certain way."

CHAPTER TWENTY-TWO

Or don't look a certain way, Holly thought to herself.

"But it isn't easy," Mrs Masterly continued. "My appearance is a tool and I'll take whatever help I can get. I'm being perfectly safe."

When Mrs Masterly opened her eyes, they glittered with the passion of the righteous.

Unfortunately for her, she was wrong.

"Remember the morning when the cabinet was stolen?" she asked. "You imagined you were groggy because you'd had nightmares all night, but you'd been drugged. Someone replaced your vitamins with sleeping pills."

"That's impossible," Callum said.

Holly's head was clearing and she walked around the kitchen as the fog lifted. "Mrs Masterly was so out of it, she slept through major DIY and she slept through someone taking the key for the servant's quarters from around her neck."

Mrs Masterly grasped at her throat. "Someone was in my room? They poisoned me?"

"I'm sorry," Holly said, "but it explains how they got into that room."

The coffee cup shook in Mrs Masterly's hand and Holly rushed over, taking it from her.

"I've been an idiot," Mrs Masterly said, her eyes clouding with tears. "But my bedroom. They took the key from around my neck and they returned it so I wouldn't know they'd been in my room. They... touched me? Twice?"

Holly swallowed. It was an ugly revelation and she hoped Mrs Masterly was strong enough to bear its weight.

"Why go through all that trouble just to burn a cabinet?" Callum asked.

"The bonfire was meant as a distraction," Holly said. "I found a brass handle in the ashes and assumed it was part of the Greyston cabinet."

Callum rubbed his chin. "But then we found more in the caverns at

Crosskeys."

"They were brand new," Holly said. "Part of a replica or some cheap imitation. Old Man Roland said people bought those handles to pretend they own valuable furniture, but this time around, they were bought to make us think something valuable had been destroyed."

Mrs Masterly tapped her foot on the floor, sounding like the drips of Chinese water torture. She wrung her hands and her clear complexion grew mottled.

"I was supposed to be safe here," she said. "This was supposed to be my home... the idea of a stranger in my bedroom... it's my most private place."

"It will be your home again." Holly drew her into an embrace, whispering in Mrs Masterly's ear. "Don't you understand what this means? Your cabinet is out there somewhere. We can find it."

"The thieves, whoever they are," Callum said, "sent us in one direction while they disappeared in another."

Holly gave Mrs Masterly a squeeze. "The window in the front door is damaged. I bet they caused that when they bundled the cabinet outside into a waiting van. They carried it from the servants' quarters and down the stairs. If you slept through someone drilling a wall, you'd sleep through that."

"So you can find it? Return it?" Mrs Masterly asked.

"The one person we haven't spoken to yet is Hector Spectre," Holly said. "He's disappeared, which is suspicious enough. Maybe if we can find him, we can put the pieces together."

"There's still something I don't understand," Callum said. "How do you know Mrs Masterly was drugged?"

"Trust me," Holly said. "I know."

Mrs Masterly pulled herself out of Holly's arms. "And how do you know I have vitamins by the side of my bed? Have you been in my room too?"

CHAPTER TWENTY-TWO

All eyes were on her Holly. Mrs Masterly's were wide and questioning, rimmed in red, but Callum's eyes were worst of all. He held the manor and its owner in high esteem. They were almost sacred and any kind of trespass was unforgivable. And he'd warned her, hadn't he? He'd warned her about seeking permissions and treating the manor with deference.

As usual, Holly had dismissed his concerns in the same way she had dismissed his fear of the straw dolls.

When she looked into his eyes, she saw his disappointment.

"I was searching for answers," Holly said.

"In my bedroom?" Mrs Masterly asked.

Callum adjusted his jacket. "I asked Holly to look through your bedroom. For clues, like."

Holly made to dismiss Callum again, to confess it was entirely her doing, but when she saw the relief on Mrs Masterly's face, the words failed to materialise.

"I can always trust you, Callum," Mrs Masterly said, her smile returning. "I should have known it was part of the investigation."

"I took one of your vitamin pills and fell asleep in the woods," Holly said. "That's how I figured you'd been drugged."

"But why would you take my vitamins?" Mrs Masterly asked. "You're right. I don't look after myself the way I should. That ends now, but why would you take one?"

"I wasn't feeling well myself," Holly said, horrified at how easily the lies came to her. "I thought a vitamin pill might pep me up."

"And how are you feeling now?" Callum asked, an edge to his voice.

"To be honest," Holly said, avoiding his gaze. "I think I'd like to go home."

Callum buttoned up his coat. "Good idea."

"Perhaps we should all take a rest," Mrs Masterly said. "We're all feeling under the weather and there's lots to do if we're going to find

Greyston's cabinet."

They said their goodbyes and Holly warned Mrs Masterly to replace the broken glass in the front door as soon as she could.

Stepping outside, Holly welcomed the onslaught of rain. It slewed the heat and shame from her face. She'd broken Mrs Masterly's trust to assuage her own petty jealousies. Holly was a lot of things, but it had been a shock to realise she could stoop so low.

Callum gripped her arm, grabbing her attention. "You went in Mrs Masterly's bedroom? What for?"

"I told you— "

"And don't say you went looking for something to pep you up," Callum said. "Even I'm not that stupid."

There was the disappointment again. Holly formulated a million reasons why she could have been in Mrs Masterly's bedroom, but none of them came close to the truth. She was selfish and nosey and pathetic.

"You went in there because you couldn't resist your own curiosity," Callum said. "You never once considered how it might affect Mrs Masterly. Anyone can tell the theft has left her shaken. And how many times do I have to urge you to treat this place with respect?"

"I wasn't in there long," Holly said, cringing at the weakness of her words. "There was no need to cover for me."

Callum climbed into the Defender and slammed the door shut.

Holly watched him as he took a deep breath and wound the window down.

"I'm going to spend tomorrow searching the estate for Hector," he said. "If he's as passionate about rock-climbing as his brothers make out, perhaps he's out there."

"Couldn't we do it together?" Holly asked.

"No. You need to find a way of making this up to Mrs Masterly. Find the cabinet, Holly."

Callum gunned the engine and guided the Defender through the curtains of rain falling from a dark sky. The tail lights faded and Holly was on her own.

Chapter Twenty-Three

Berwick upon Tweed was a coastal town sitting on the border of Scotland and England. The two nations had fought over its possession until it was finally captured by the English. It still retained a Celtic atmosphere, however, surrounded as it was by glens and rugged coastline. Holly had holidayed there with her parents when she was a child and remembered long walks along the River Tweed.

She parked her car overlooking the estuary and went in search of Bridge Street, breathing in the sea air as she walked. The buildings were stone-built, consisting of the sort of artisan shops Holly could happily spend her annual income in. There were bespoke curtain makers, potteries, art galleries, and a shop selling nothing but stained glass. Callum would hate it here, she thought.

She thought back to their last conversation and winced at its conclusion. Callum had given her an ultimatum, a way to redeem herself. It was a kindness, she supposed. If he ever betrayed her, Holly wondered if she'd be as considerate. It was time to make it up to him and Berwick was the place to do it.

She strolled up one side of the street and down the other, but couldn't find Charleston Collectables - the place where Mrs Masterly had bought Greyston's cabinet.

Gaining her bearings, Holly noticed a narrow opening between an

CHAPTER TWENTY-THREE

upholsterer and a wedding cake designer. Bridging the gap was an ironwork arch, orange with rust. Pinned to it was a handwritten sign. *50% Off All Wedgwood Tableware.*

Holly crossed the cobbled street. Although the gap was barely big enough for her to squeeze through, the alleyway beyond widened. She scraped between the two buildings and followed a broken pavement to the front door of Charleston Collectables. On either side of the door were two large bay windows made from several square pieces of glass.

A bell rang above her head as Holly entered. Charleston Collectables was a long single room with glass cabinets stacked against the walls. Locked behind the polished glass were china figurines, bowls, and jewellery. To her right was a small collection of blue Wedgwood plates. Even at their discounted rate, Holly couldn't afford them.

The central gangway featured a mass of furniture with tables and wardrobes carved from dark wood. Balanced on top were rocking chairs teetering precariously, together with ottomans and leather-covered footstools.

A narrow path took Holly on a tour of the displays and she tucked her elbows to her sides, fearful of knocking over something expensive.

"Can I help you?" a voice asked.

Holly turned in its direction, but there was no one there. She heard the hum of a motor, the grinding of gears as the sound drew closer.

"Where are you?" she asked.

A head appeared over a writing desk. "Sorry. Not as tall as I used to be."

Carefully navigating his way around the furniture, a man appeared in a motorised wheelchair. He was around Holly's age with a thick thatch of blond hair and he was dressed in a pinstripe suit with an open-collar shirt. Using a rubber joystick, he guided his chair through the antiques.

He caught Holly staring at it.

"Had the old girl customised," the man said. "I can reach almost five miles an hour with a strong wind behind me."

"Mr Charleston?" Holly asked.

"The one and only. How can I help? Are you interested in my Wedgwood?"

Holly let the question hang. There was a twinkle in his eye she wasn't comfortable with, but Holly owed it to Mrs Masterly to find the cabinet. Not to mention Callum.

"Why don't I make you a cup of tea while you think?" Mr Charleston asked. "The kettle is in the back room, if you'd like to join me. It will be a snug fit, but I'm sure we'll find a way."

"You're very kind, but I'm from the Little Belton Herald." Holly waited for a look of recognition and when it didn't arrive, she pressed on regardless, pulling a notebook from her pocket. "I wonder if you could tell me more about the Greyston cabinet you sold recently."

"I'd be happy to, but I can't divulge any information on the purchaser. That wouldn't do."

"You don't need to," Holly said, consulting a blank page. "It was bought by Mrs Masterly from Black Rock Manor."

Mr Charleston's eyes sparkled and he answered with a grin. "I'm so glad there won't be any secrets between us. I'd hate for our relationship to begin that way."

"Where did you get the cabinet?"

"It was gifted to me. Previous to that, it belonged to a farmer's wife whose husband was long since dead."

"That's sad," Holly said.

"Oh, it gets a lot sadder. He bought it for her on their twentieth wedding anniversary. She was so pleased, she placed it in her front room, which was only ever used on special occasions. The husband, who was as equally pleased to have made his wife happy, then went out to feed his cows and was trampled to death."

Holly pressed her hands to her cheeks. "You're right. That's awful."

CHAPTER TWENTY-THREE

"The farmer's wife was a superstitious one and blamed the cabinet," Mr Charleston said, adjusting his suit. "Hard not to, I suppose. Personally, I would have blamed the cows."

"That's how it came into your possession?"

Mr Charleston's face darkened and he tapped the armrest of his chair. "And my life changed not long after I took delivery."

Somewhere in Berwick, an ambulance raced to the scene of an accident. Mr Charleston turned his head to the sound of the sirens and ran a finger around his collar.

"These things are sent to try us," he said.

"I'm sorry," Holly said. "What happened? The cows didn't come for you as well, did they?"

Mr Charleston used his joystick to drive himself closer to Holly. He misjudged the width of his wheelchair and bumped into a Welsh dresser. "I'd finished writing up my notes on Alistair Greyston and I was a little careless. I'd had to make room for my new cabinet and I didn't stack things the way I should have. There was a collapse. I was trapped under a beautiful Victorian bookcase for two days."

With the shop being tucked away, Holly could imagine how few people found it. What she couldn't imagine was lying in wait, desperate for help to arrive.

"When I was finally rescued, I'd lost the use of my legs," Mr Charleston said.

What was clear was how tragedy followed Greyston's cabinet around. First the farmer, then Mr Charleston, and finally Mrs Masterly. How far back did its influence stretch? Were there tragedies before the farmer? Had it marred the aspirations of Greyston himself? Whatever the history of the cabinet was, its title of *Hallelujah to the Lord* seemed like a mistake.

"You look troubled. Are you sure I can't tempt you into my office?" Mr Charleston asked. "I've had it decorated recently."

"You have a woman working for you called Simone," Holly said.

"Not working for, exactly," Mr Charleston said. "She was more of a sales rep working on commission. It was her job to find a buyer for the cabinet. When I heard there was interest in Little Belton, I sent her there to secure the purchase."

"Because she was an expert in antiques?"

Mr Charleston shook his head. "She was a wonderful girl. Heart of gold, but she wasn't an expert. I don't think she's an expert in anything. I got the impression she drifted around a lot, taking work where she could get it."

"So why hire her then?"

"Because of her connection to Little Belton," Mr Charleston said. "There's a lot to be said for the personal touch."

There certainly was, thought Holly, picturing Callum and Simone together.

"Is there anything else I can help you with?" Mr Charleston asked.

"No, you've been very kind."

"Well, let me show you to the door," Mr Charleston said. "I have a date in half an hour and I wouldn't like to keep her waiting."

He led Holly through the furniture maze toward the door. "Are you interested in Alistair Greyston as an artist? You never said."

"Not really, no."

"I'm pleased to hear it," Mr Charleston said, bouncing into his Wedgwood display and accidentally knocking over a plate.

Holly caught it before it hit the ground. "Why would you say that?"

"Greyston's furniture seems to bring out the worst in people. They get obsessed. I know of someone who speaks of nothing else. The cabinet took my legs, but he's the real reason I wanted it out of my shop. He'd call me every week with fresh new questions. Do I know anything about Greyston as a child? Have I seen the court records for his trial?"

CHAPTER TWENTY-THREE

"Greyston was on trial? What for?"

Mr Charleston opened the shop door, his eyes on the bell ringing above him. "I'm afraid I don't know. I learned enough about Alistair Greyston to help me sell his work. I didn't like to learn too much. He may have carved his spiritual devotion into his furniture, but there was always something about the man that didn't sit right."

"But he was a man of God, wasn't he?" Holly asked.

"He was," Mr Charleston answered, "but I'm not sure which one."

"And the man who calls you, he's of the same ilk?"

"He's an obsessive, that's what he is. I wouldn't let him anywhere near the shop. He's not of sound mind. I still don't know how he found out it was in my possession."

"What's he called?" Holly asked, wondering if this man had made his way to Little Belton and the manor.

Mr Charleston checked his watch, clearly anxious not to miss his date. "Mr Xavier of Historic England."

"The grant assessor?"

"The very same," Mr Charleston said. "Do you know him?"

Chapter Twenty-Four

Holly watched the grey water, still digesting everything Mr Charleston had told her.

"Are you okay?" Simone asked.

They sat by the edge of Knock Lake on a granite boulder that had rolled down from the Ableman Hills centuries ago. It had come to rest in a marsh as moisture silently gathered around it to form a lake. Decades later, it was a promontory where Holly and Simone could perch and dangle their feet into the water.

"I should be asking you that," Holly said, feeling the cold bite her toes.

"I'm good," Simone said, "for a girl who was recently rushed to the hospital."

"You left just as quickly," Holly said. "You didn't even tell anyone you were leaving."

Simone wriggled her toes through the water. "I can't stand those places. They kind of go against how I live, but I should have said something. Especially after how everyone looked out for me. Callum saved my life."

Holly reached for a pebble and dropped it into the lake. "He has a habit of doing that."

"You're lucky to have him in your life," Simone said. "I think he wanted us to spend some time together. To see if we could get along better."

"We get along fine," Holly said, worried Simone could read the secret jealousies of her mind. "Why would he do that?"

The thrum of wings beat above them as a swan descended from the sky, its white wings casting a dark shadow. It skated along the water, coming to rest by a reed bed. Stretching its graceful neck to the sky, it circled in the shallows and waited.

"That's a Bewick's swan. A male," Simone said. "You can tell because it's mating season and the protuberance above the bill swells in size."

Holly nodded, attempting to forget the information before she accidentally repeated it. "You know a lot about the natural world. It's fascinating, really."

"I got the impression you didn't like that about me."

Holly's feet were like blocks of ice. She'd only agreed to put them in the lake because Simone was doing it.

"Not at all," she said, clamping her chattering teeth together. "I know I can be abrupt. I just have a job to do, that's all, and finding the thief who broke into the manor is proving difficult."

The first part was a lie, of course. Holly hadn't warmed to Simone, but Holly also knew it wasn't Simone's fault.

Holly sighed and stretched backwards so her stomach wasn't sitting like a rounded turnip above her belt. As she did so, she caught the contours of Simone's body through her flimsy dress and cursed at her taut muscles.

"How is that going, by the way?" Simone asked. "I asked around the village. Apparently, you have a reputation for getting to the bottom of things."

"I'm a journalist. I'm nosey by nature," Holly said.

"Well, I think I can help you there." Simone withdrew her feet from the lake and dried them with the hem of her dress. "I'm also nosey so I consulted some of my books."

Thankful Simone's feet were back on dry land, Holly whipped hers out of the water and frantically rubbed at their numbness. "You have something for me?"

"Callum's straw dolls are actually love tokens," Simone said. "He said, they were voodoo dolls. I don't know where he got that idea from, but my books are never wrong. Apparently, the cottagers and farmhands around here would send poems for their betrothed carved into the jawbones of cattle. When they realised that was pretty gruesome, the ritual evolved into the gift of straw figurines."

Holly's socks hung from her walking boots like woollen tongues falling from an open mouth. She grabbed one and strangled it.

"Why are you so concerned about those dolls?" she asked. "Don't you know we're looking for a priceless cabinet?"

Frowning down the length of her nose, Simone pouted. "Because we're Callum's friends. I thought you'd be more concerned for him."

Holly's eyes travelled over the lake, over the swan patiently waiting. She stared up the valley wall to where her cottage sat silhouetted by the setting sun. A figure staggered along the roofline and Holly heard it swearing.

Oh God, it's Derek. He'll end up killing himself, Holly thought.

"I can prove it, you know," Simone said.

Holly kept her eyes on her husband, fearing this could be the last time she saw him alive.

"Prove what?" she asked.

"Look."

Reluctantly, Holly turned to Simone and saw she was holding one of Callum's dolls.

"What are you doing with that?" she asked.

"Callum gave it to me when he suggested we meet," Simone said.

"When did he do this?"

Simone beamed and held the doll to her chest. "Yesterday. While you were out of town."

Callum was supposed to be searching for Hector. He'd been emphatic on the subject, and now Holly had discovered he'd been doing nothing of the kind. He'd been sharing intimacies with Simone.

"Have you been spending a lot of time together?" she asked.

"Some," Simone answered with a sparkle in her eyes. "He came to my bothy. We've been out walking and chatting. You don't mind, do you?"

Holly shrugged. "Why would I mind? Although, I would have preferred it if the pair of you had been searching for the cabinet."

"We were," Simone said. "I promise."

"And what exactly are your intentions toward Callum?" Holly asked.

The question was out before she'd had the chance to stop it. Holly was transported back to when her father had grilled Derek the first time they had met. It had been an uncomfortable situation then and it was uncomfortable now.

"I'm sorry," Holly said. "It's none of my business."

"I just want him to like me. It's why I researched the dolls. To see if I could ease his mind in some way."

"You told Callum the doll was a love token, which is the first thing I don't agree with," Holly said, "and in knowing that, he gave you the doll?"

"As a token, yes," Simone said. "A love token or at least that's what I'd hoped it was."

Holly used her sock to mop a perplexed brow as the pieces eased into place.

The swan in the lake honked and beat its wings against the water. Above him, another swan sank through the last of the daylight. It was a female. The protuberance above the bill, called a blackberry, was smaller than the males'. Callum had taught her that.

The two swans swam out to the centre of the lake, where they met with a gentle kiss of necks.

"Callum is obviously more worried about this doll nonsense than he's letting on," Holly said. "I think he wanted you to share your findings with me so I could figure who was sending them."

Simone climbed to her feet, brushing out the creases of her dress.

"So this love token isn't for me," she said. "It's for you."

Holly yanked on her socks and plunged her cold feet into the comparative warmth of her boots. "Yes, it's for me, but it isn't a love token. Callum wanted you to share whatever information you had. You said you could prove what you said?"

Biting her lip, Simone placed two thumbs on either side of the doll and split it open with a crack. A yellowed note drifted to the ground.

Holly took a sharp intake of breath. "How did you know that was in there?"

"From my books." Simone stepped over the note, backing barefoot into the heather. "I'd like to help you find the cabinet. I was hoping to return to Little Belton permanently, but I'll need a job and who will hire the person who cost Mrs Masterly forty thousand pounds?"

"No one is blaming you," Holly said.

"You are. I can tell." Simone's oval eyes shimmered in the growing darkness. It reminded Holly of a forest creature capable of seeing in the dark.

"If I helped you," Simone continued, "you might be more forgiving. You might let me get closer to Callum. You are married, after all."

Holly's own eyes flashed and though she might not be capable of seeing in the dark, she saw an attitude in Simone she didn't like.

"Callum and I are friends," she shouted after her.

Simone climbed through the heather and onto the path toward her bothy.

"Wait a minute," Holly said. "Are you jealous of my relationship with

CHAPTER TWENTY-FOUR

Callum?"

Simone melted into her precious nature and was gone, leaving Holly with the dusk call of a thousand hidden birds.

The swans paddled to a nearby reed bed to settle down for the night.

"I think she is, you know," she said with a satisfied smile.

Pulling a torch from her pocket, Holly searched for the yellowed note. That was something else Callum had taught her. Night fell fast on the estate and smart people carried torches. Since the events at Crosskeys caves, she'd decided to listen for once.

She found it fluttering in the breeze by the foot of a rotted tree stump. She examined it under her beam of light. Holly read it twice to make sure she wasn't mistaken, and then a third time to be sure.

The words were handwritten and underlined.

Holly Loves Callum

She recognised the writing. With a gasp, Holly knew who was sending the dolls.

It was her.

Chapter Twenty-Five

Having arranged to meet Callum on the following morning, Holly paced the driveway, waiting to see his yellow Defender score up the road to her cottage. The doll's mysterious note was folded into the back pocket of her jeans. Holly couldn't risk leaving it in her home. If Derek stumbled upon it, there'd be more than a hole in the roof. His temper was likely to blow the entire roof off.

Holly heard whistling from behind the house. Her husband was up early, preparing for another day of home maintenance. She tried not to think about it, certain that one day she would return to find her home maintained into rubble.

She was equally determined not to divulge the note's contents to Callum. It wasn't fair because she didn't love him. Not that way. Yes, she loved seeing him. Being around him, but that didn't mean—

Holly stopped pacing, a shivery feeling creeping over her skin.

Holly Loves Callum

How could she have been so stupid? Mr Winnow had called it a game, part of an entrepreneurial effort to boost his floundering income, but Holly hadn't known it would involve straw dolls and hidden notes.

And now that she did know - how could she tell Callum she was his secret tormentor?

The sound of a car engine ricocheted off the valley walls. The road to

CHAPTER TWENTY-FIVE

Holly's cottage was fringed with ferns and the dried tangle of brambles. She peered through the waving vegetation to see Callum's Defender emerging from a low hanging mist.

He parked in front of the cottage, and Holly joined him at the driver's door.

"Did you bring them?" she asked.

Callum reached into the glove compartment and produced the other two dolls. He handed them over to Holly.

"You didn't open them," Holly said, silently grateful.

Who knew what the other two notes contained? She didn't want Callum reading something that might stir his waters. Or land her in trouble.

"I thought it would be better if we did it together," he said.

That might be worse, she thought. She took one of the dolls and placed it between her two thumbs.

"That was the critter I received in the post," Callum said.

Counting down in her head, Holly reached one and broke the doll open, snatching the note before it fell to the ground.

"What does it say?" Callum asked, leaning out of the Defender.

"Home is where the heart is," Holly said, frowning. "That doesn't mean much."

"Not much of a love token," Callum said, looking disappointed.

"That's what Simone said they were."

Holly wasn't ready to disappoint him further. She broke open the second doll with more confidence.

"To discover what is known by all, Find me at the Witches' Hall."

She rubbed the paper through her fingers while she considered the secretive message. "This is from the doll Simone found on your doorstep."

"What did that note say?" Callum asked, his keen eyes shining.

Holly looked to her muddy boots. "Pardon?"

"I gave the third doll to Simone so she could give it to you," Callum said. "What did the other note say?"

Holly Loves Callum

More like a sick joke, Holly thought.

"Oh, I left it in the house," she said, fumbling the other two dolls back into Callum's hands.

He raised his eyebrows, prompting her into action. "Well, do you want to get it?"

Derek appeared, whistling a tune that made him sound as if he was in pain. He carried an aluminium ladder on his shoulder and a bucket of tools in his hand.

Callum shifted in his seat and struck the jeep's horn to say hello.

Derek leapt at the noise, spinning in their direction. The ladder made a sweeping arc, crashing through the sitting room window.

"Oh no," Callum whispered.

The glass shattered, spraying the inside and outside of the house. Derek dropped to the ground as if a bomb had gone off, his tools clattering out of his grasp. When the last of the glass settled, he lifted his head and stared at the Defender.

Holly's stomach lurched.

"Are you okay, hun?" she shouted.

"Okay?" Derek asked, scrambling upright. "What do you think? He's just smashed my window."

Callum slid out of the Defender, like grease off a frying pan. "I'm really sorry. I'll find someone to fix it."

"What would Mrs Masterly say if she saw this mess?" Derek asked. "We're letting the whole estate down."

Holly coughed into her hand. "Erm, 'we're letting the estate down'? Callum peeped his horn and you smashed the window. It was like watching Laurel and Hardy. I had nothing to do with this."

Derek and Callum looked at each other like scolded children. It shouldn't have made Holly feel better, but it did. There were more pressing concerns to attend to and she didn't have time to waste parenting to grown men.

"The important thing is the window will be fixed soon," she said. "Just like the roof will be fixed soon, right?"

Callum craned his neck to the roof, shielding his eyes from the rain. "Was that hole there when I was here last?"

Holly rolled her eyes. "Yes."

"I'm fixing it," Derek said, protesting.

"You could fall through that roof," Callum said. "Why don't I fix while I'm fixing the window? My treat."

Holly was desperate to see her cottage returned to normality. The love note in her pocket seemed to burn and she wriggled against its touch.

It was time to leave.

"We have to go now," she said. "I called Mrs Masterly. She's expecting us."

Holly ushered Callum into the Defender and leapt into the passenger seat.

"Don't worry about the roof," Derek called after them. "I'm all over it."

Callum pointed the Defender down the driveway. "He'll be all through it if he's not careful. It's an easy fix. Let me do it."

Holly wanted to accept the offer, but her thoughts were with her husband. It seemed important that he fix the roof, though Holly didn't understand why. Maybe it was a man thing? Whatever it was, if she woke up to one more morning of water dripping through her ceiling, she'd shove Callum onto the roof herself.

If he was still speaking to her, that is.

Holly had discovered the source of the straw dolls. It was a puzzle Callum had been brooding over, but there was no way she could tell him, especially when the dolls contained notes like the one she'd found last night. After Holly had blundered into Mrs Masterly's bedroom, Callum's disappointment in her was palpable. Their friendship felt strained and she didn't want to jeopardise it further. She hoped by telling Mrs Masterly what she'd discovered at Charleston Collectibles, Callum might recognise it as contrition.

But she couldn't lie forever and Holly worried at her lip.

How was she going to tell Callum what she'd done?

Chapter Twenty-Six

"No way," Holly muttered under her breath. "How do you know he'll do a good job?"

Callum kept his eyes glued to the road, ploughing through brackish puddles. "Mr Winnow has been replacing windows for years. I'll call him. He'll be glad of the business."

"But he runs a convenience store," Holly said.

"And a delivery service. And boat trips," Callum said. "Not to mention he's the number one poacher on the estate. I've been trying to stop him since I was a kid."

Holly folded her arms. "Jack of all trades. Master of none."

"There are some things I can do and some things I can't," Callum said.

"I don't believe that's true."

The rain pounded off the Defender, drumming its fingers on the roof.

"Well, you don't believe in Long Robert and that hasn't got you very far," Callum said, doubling the speed of his windscreen wipers. "And I get the impression you don't believe the straw dolls are love tokens, either."

Holly twisted her seatbelt into a knot. Casting a sideways glance at the driver, she paused before speaking. "They are getting to you, aren't they? You're bent out of shape over them. Over Simone, too."

The Defender carved its way along a muddy side road. It bounced over a hidden rock and Holly banged her head on the roof.

"If they are love tokens, do you think Simone is sending them?" Callum asked.

"Somebody definitely is," Holly mumbled. "And are we sure they are love tokens? Could they be part of a game?"

"Are you saying she doesn't like me?"

"You're both young. You're both beautiful," Holly said. "It would make sense for you to spend time together."

The Defender jerked to a stop outside of Black Rock Manor. The door was open and they scurried out of the rain, shaking water from their clothes.

"My dad taught me about tracking and shooting and how to fix roofs," Callum said. "He said nothing about... courting."

Holly bit down a laugh. "Firstly, it's not called courting anymore and secondly— "

"Are you two bickering again?" Mrs Masterly asked as she swept into the reception room. Her hair was drawn into a ponytail trailing around her neck. "Because if you are, it will have to wait. We have bigger problems."

Holly and Callum fell silent, and Mrs Masterly led them into the kitchen. The surfaces gleamed with a shimmer reminiscent of an oasis in the desert. The floor was swept, hoovered, and polished. The glass cupboards were fingerprint free and there was a strong smell of bleach.

Mrs Masterly caught Holly's amazed stare.

"I clean whenever I get nervous," she said as way of explanation.

Her eyes went to the floor where Holly and Callum had left muddy footprints. Mrs Masterly stiffened and reached for a mop.

"I got a call from Mr Xavier," she said. "He's in the area and couldn't wait to see Greyston's cabinet any longer."

"We don't know where it is," Callum said.

"A fact I was forced to omit," Mrs Masterly said.

"Well, you can't let him in here," Holly said.

Mrs Masterly swiped the mop over Holly's dirty shoes. "Yes, I know that, dear."

"No, I really mean you can't let him in here." Holly detailed her visit to Charleston Collectibles and the information she'd discovered about Mr Xavier.

"Did you know how obsessed he was with the cabinet?" she asked.

"Obsessed?" Callum asked.

Mrs Masterly held her mop tightly. "I knew he was an amateur historian. Are you saying he's dangerous? Are you claiming he is the thief?"

"He might be both," Holly said, pacing the floor, inadvertently spreading the mud from her shoes further.

"But that doesn't make sense," Callum said. "If he stole it, he knows it's not here. Why arrange to come and see it?"

Holly shrugged. "To maintain his innocence? To provide a reason to disapprove the grant application? Maybe his plan isn't finished yet? Whatever the reason, we need him in Little Belton."

The colour drained from Mrs Masterly's face. "What? I thought you said we should keep away from him."

"The closer he is," Holly said, "the better we can keep an eye on him."

"But what if you're wrong?" Callum asked.

Holly opened her mouth to speak. It hadn't occurred to her she might be wrong. Seconds before, she'd been sure. A man like Mr Xavier had prime suspect written all over him. She was still sure, but the consequences of bungling this were horrendous.

"It's the only answer," she said. "We need to keep Mr Xavier in Little Belton."

"But away from the manor," Mrs Masterly said. "That way he can't do whatever it is he plans to do. I'll stand guard. Defend the perimeter."

Holly ceased pacing the floor and the squeak of her boots died to nothing. "How do we keep him away from the manor, though?"

"I have an idea."

All three of them turned to the voice behind them.

Simone was leaning in the doorway.

"Has anyone heard of the Bathing of the Green Man?" she asked.

Chapter Twenty-Seven

When it came to organising party supplies, there was only one man in the village to contact, and after twenty-four frantic hours, it was done.

The heat in The Travelling Star came less from the roaring fire and more from the bodies packed inside. Paul and Saul knocked tankards together, showering themselves in foamy beer. Mrs Winnow was behind the bar dispensing drinks, her lacquered beehive hair as hard as a crash helmet. As Holly squeezed into a corner, she saw Old Jack, the former owner of the Little Belton Herald drinking with Regina Foxglove, a woman who despised the cold.

In the far corner was a Northumbrian Pipe band fighting for enough space to play their bagpipes.

Big Gregg, his face ruddy from the sound of his ringing till, pirouetted through the crowd, his size and false leg no impediment to grace.

"Thanks for doing this," he said to Holly, handing her a vodka and tonic.

"It wasn't my idea," she said. "It was Simone's."

Big Gregg cocked an eyebrow. "Is this the fresh face in the village everyone is talking about? Rumour has it she's been seen with young Callum."

"Aren't you too old for gossip?"

"So it's true," Big Gregg said with a smile. "I hope you're not too upset."

"I'm fine with that," Holly said, batting away the gossip she'd been subjected to since her return to the village.

"Well, whoever she is," Big Gregg said. "I owe her a debt of thanks. Where is she?"

Back at Black Rock Manor, the atmosphere had turned frosty at Simone's sudden appearance. Like the rest of Little Belton, she clearly still thought Holly and Callum were a thing. Holly had been in no mood to correct her for the umpteenth time. They'd discussed strategies and details, but in between the talking were silences pointed enough to skewer an olive.

Callum had invited her to the party, but she'd declined.

And Holly was fine with that, too.

"Best if I stay out of the way," Simone had said, looking directly at Holly.

The piper's band finished their song to rapturous applause. When it died down, they were already bickering over their next song choice. Stumbling over a bagpipe, Mr Winnow forced his way through the crowd.

"Everything is set up," he said, taking a sip from his pint of beer. "But why are we putting on such a show?"

"Have you fixed my window yet?" Holly asked.

"I haven't had time," Mr Winnow said. "You called me away to organise this, remember?"

"He's coming," someone shouted from the crowd.

The band grabbed their pipes and working their elbows with renewed vigour, burst into song. The rest of the villagers rummaged under their seats, producing felted hats adorned with heather.

"Where did you get those from?" Holly whispered.

"I'm a one-man Amazon," Mr Winnow said. "Wait until you see what's outside."

CHAPTER TWENTY-SEVEN

As he made to escape the excited crowd, Holly latched onto his arm. "And I want a word with you about these silly straw dolls."

"Right. I'm on," Big Gregg said, jamming the heather hat over his head. "Exit. Stage left."

He moved through the crowd like water, stationing himself by the entrance.

Mr Winnow used it as an excuse to free his arm from Holly's hold and disappear.

"Welcome," Big Gregg shouted as he opened the door, "to Mr Xavier."

The crowd cheered and a man jerked to attention in the doorway, his mouth opening like a faulty trapdoor. He was in his early fifties and of average height with dusky skin and a dark beard trailing to his chest. He was dressed in a camel hair overcoat with a rucksack of black and yellow over his shoulder.

Big Gregg snatched a spare heather hat and pressed it onto Mr Xavier's head. "You're in luck tonight, sir because we are bathing the Green Man."

Mr Xavier removed the hat and studied it in horror. "You're doing what?"

"An age-old tradition in these parts," Big Gregg said, shepherding his guest to the bar. "It's how we greet strangers who we'd like to make our friends."

"I've never heard of it," Mr Xavier said.

"That's probably because you don't come from Little Belton."

"Actually, I do."

"What will you have to drink?" Big Gregg asked, ushering Mr Xavier forward.

Mrs Winnow had prepared a row of beverages on the bar, each brimming with something strong.

"I'm not much of a drinker," Mr Xavier said, "and I've got an appointment tomorrow that I can't miss."

"Then have a beer," Big Gregg said. "Just to be sociable, like."

"And it's the bathing of the Green Man?" Mr Xavier asked.

"Absolutely."

Mr Xavier stroked his beard. As he reached for a glass, the villagers cheered and raised their own. He took a sip, white froth collecting on his moustache.

"You're one of us now," Big Gregg said.

"I've never had a greeting quite like it."

Big Gregg wrestled the rucksack from Mr Xavier's shoulders. "Let me take this upstairs to your room. We've booked you in for the next few nights."

Mr Xavier reached out his hand. "Stop. That has important documents in it."

"It will be perfectly safe," Big Gregg said, giving the bag to Holly, "and while that's being done, I'd like you to meet some of my patrons."

Holly scuttled to the door leading to the hotel above them. She cast a backward glance at Mr Xavier as he was swallowed by the crowd, like a raft in a storm succumbing to the waves. There'd be drinking and chatter to delay his bedtime by several hours. If the residents of Little Belton knew anything, it was how to talk and get drunk.

Racing up the stairs, Holly found Callum lurking in the shadows.

"This is so bad," she said, giving him the rucksack.

"No one is crowning themselves in glory tonight," Callum said. "Least of all, Mr Xavier. All we're doing is taking a little peek."

Callum undid the straps of the rucksack with a single snap.

"Hurry up, will you?" Holly asked, chewing on a fingernail.

Callum emptied the bag's contents on the floor and searched through them.

"Well, all his clothes are clean," he said.

"That's a good thing, isn't it?" Holly asked. "Unless you like digging through dirty underwear."

"But there are so many of them. How long is this guy staying?"

Holly peered over Callum's shoulder. "I can't imagine he'd be staying that long. What if he stayed somewhere else first? It would place him in the area at the time of the theft."

"What's this?" Callum retrieved a stack of papers bound with twine and handed it to Holly.

Holly scanned the document, her eyes widening with every word. "It's Mr Xavier's research on the cabinet."

"What kind of research?" Callum asked.

Holly shook her head, unable to comprehend what she was reading. "Alistair Greyston wasn't the God-fearing man we thought he was."

The music from downstairs reached a crescendo followed by the sound of clinking glasses. The villagers sounded happy.

"The markings on the cabinet. They were supposed to be part of some devout symbolism. According to Mr Xavier, that's not true. The etchings are an ancient Northumbrian language. The cabinet wasn't raised to the glory of angels. It was an altar to demons."

"Demons?" Callum asked. "In Little Belton?"

Holly wiped her brow. "I'd need to read all of this to understand it properly, but apparently after Greyston disappeared, he returned as a follower of dark sorcery. He was an occultist. The cabinet is an ode to the occult."

Mr Charleston was right to doubt which god Greyston worshipped.

The party's noise had abated and Holly heard her own breathing over the silence.

"We've invited Satan to our door," Callum said.

Holly carefully placed Mr Xavier's belongings into his rucksack. "I wouldn't go that far, but why would a grant assessor be involved in the occult?"

Zipping the bag tight, Holly ran a hand through her hair. "Look, we stick to the plan until we figure this out."

Pacing the floor, Holly waited until Callum retied the straps on the rucksack.

The low hum of laughter came to them from outside.

"Sounds like we're at stage two," Holly said. "Tomorrow, Mr Xavier will be so hungover, he'll barely know up from down and then Mr Winnow is taking him on a boating trip."

"By the way Mr Winnow sails, Mr Xavier will be so seasick, he'll be wishing he was still hungover," Callum added.

"That should buy us a couple of days," Holly said, "but after that, we're in trouble. He'll go looking for the cabinet."

Callum threw the rucksack over his shoulder. "I'll put this in his room. Do you want me to stay with you?"

Holly grimaced. "I'll stay with Mr Xavier. Make sure he doesn't get into any real trouble. Why don't you go home and we'll start in the morning?"

"What if Simone turns up?" Callum asked.

Staring at the hope in his eyes made Holly's heart sink. She was reminded of all her petty thoughts and jealousies, her insecurities regarding her age and appearance. Holly disliked Simone for the most superficial of reasons.

"You could stay, if you'd like," she said. "I'll go home instead."

The expectation of seeing Simone made Callum's face glow, but presented with the reality of it actually happening, it lost some of its sheen.

"What would I say?" he asked. "We've been seeing a lot of each other, but I'd like to kind of make it official. I'm thinking of asking her to step out with me."

Holly shook her head in disbelief. "Bloody hell, Callum. It's not the nineteen-thirties anymore. No one 'steps out' anymore. Just ask her to the cinema. If it makes you feel more comfortable, you can call them

CHAPTER TWENTY-SEVEN

'the talkies.'"

Licking his lips, Callum looked left and right. "Well, how should I ask her, then?"

"You've spoken to her before, Callum. It's not that hard," Holly said, giving him a smile. "Offer to buy her a drink and then get to know her better, but don't talk about the cabinet, the theft, or the manor. Please don't mention the dolls and don't mention what we're doing here. Also, don't mention the plan. The bar is filled with gossipers. We don't want them to know the truth. After that though, ask her out on a date, but be sure to be home by eleven. We still have a cabinet to find and I need you fresh."

"It's because of the dolls, I feel so sure about her," Callum said. "Why wouldn't I mention them?"

Because I'm the one who is sending them.

Because I'm an idiot.

Because I haven't plucked up the courage to tell you yet.

Holly took a long breath before speaking. "Forget about the dolls. She likes you regardless."

"But that's how it all started," Callum said. "They're important."

"I think maybe it's best if we concentrate on one thing at a time," Holly said. "We concentrate on the cabinet and then there'll be plenty of time to discuss the dolls, okay?"

Callum's shoulders slumped. He opened a nearby door and pitched Mr Xavier's rucksack onto his bed. "I think I'll just go home."

"She said, she wasn't coming tonight anyway," Holly said. "You'll have other chances to get her alone."

Callum traipsed by her, looking unconvinced. His heavy boots thudded down the stairs to the outside world.

"She's beautiful, you know?" Holly said, lingering on the top step. "Simone, I mean."

"Are you jealous of her?" Callum asked.

As Holly was about to answer with a lie, Callum disappeared through the door, slamming it shut behind him. She got the impression he'd already guessed her response.

Holly imagined him in the high street, stooping against the braying rain of Long Robert until he reached his Defender. Wet and alone, he'd return to an empty cottage and wait for the morning. What good were his love tokens if Callum had no one to love?

The world could be an unfair place for gentle souls like her friend. Luckily for Holly, gentility wasn't in her wheelhouse and she willed herself into action.

Downstairs, the crowd had moved to the beer garden at the rear of the pub. The night air hit Holly in a dizzying whirl as she stepped into a barrage of lights. Strings of green bulbs swung above her, painting the beer garden in lime. The air was filled with beer and the astringent tang of something burning. As Holly searched for the source, Mr Winnow sidled up close.

"What do you think?" he asked, sour whisky on his breath. "I got a bargain on the bulbs."

A stage had been constructed from a pile of teetering wooden pallets. Suspended above it was a papier mâché head of the Green Man. His face was stern and fringed with leaves and berries. His beard was made from moss. Holly remembered Callum's description of the woodland god; a persona he swore he'd seen in person.

"Where is that burning smell coming from?" Holly asked, wrinkling her nose.

"That's going to cost you extra," Mr Winnow said.

Holly forced her way through the crowd with sharpened elbows, frustrated that she was sober and they were not. She came to a clearing where smoke billowed in clouds. Shielding her eyes from the flames, Holly saw a bale of hay on fire, despite the rain.

"The Bathing of the Green Man is an ancient rite of passage," Big

Gregg said, stumbling onto the makeshift stage, "but one we must honour in this Little Belton village."

"Here, here," laughed Mr Xavier.

The grant assessor was as drunk as the landlord. Maybe more so, given Big Gregg only had one leg and Mr Xavier was struggling to walk on two.

On one side of the burning bale were metallic steps leading up. On the other side were steps leading down.

Holly rubbed her stomach, attempting to quash the ill-feeling inside.

"So now is the time to bathe, dear Green Man," Big Gregg said, raising a beer glass in the air. "Bathe our new friend in the flames of your warm welcome."

Feet stomped on the ground. Chanting echoed off the walls. The pipers began a slow, sonorous note, which grew in volume.

"Okay," Mr Xavier shouted. "Here I go."

He started at full tilt, running toward the fire.

"Bloody hell, no," Holly said.

Mr Xavier pelted up the steps and leapt into the air, his head becoming wrapped in a string of bulbs. His legs swung from under him as he somersaulted over the fire, mercifully clearing it before he came back down to earth with a crash.

The villagers grew silent.

Holly rushed forward, skidding to a halt at Mr Xavier's prone form. She quickly extinguished the flames crisping his beard. "Are you still with us?"

When Mr Xavier didn't answer, Holly checked for a pulse.

It was erratic, but strong and Mr Xavier's eyelids fluttered open.

"Did I make it?" he asked.

The crowd cheered and the Northumbrian Pipe band struck up a song.

Barely, Holly thought, but at least there wasn't any damage.

Roused by Little Belton's support, Mr Xavier attempted to stand, but he collapsed, his face stricken in pain.

"Hey, what happened to my leg?" he asked.

Chapter Twenty-Eight

"One night," Holly said. "I had to keep him safe for one night."

"He didn't break anything," Callum said. "It was a sprain."

It was a minor victory, she thought, and if she was being honest, Mr Xavier's injury bought them more time. She didn't wish him any harm and now that it had happened, Holly wasn't going to lose a lot of sleep over it.

She didn't have the time. It was a new day and Holly needed to make the most of Mr Xavier's injury to find the cabinet. With no sign of Hector, they'd decided to leave the village for a while.

Holly and Callum sat at a desk in a library in Amble, a small village on the north-east coast of England. The library was a red brick building with a revolving glass door entrance. It had also once housed a hairdressing salon as a way of generating enough income to keep the library open, but it had gone bankrupt. In its place was a pottery studio. When Holly had walked by the empty shop and the glum-looking potter, she sensed there'd be another change of ownership soon.

The books in Amble's library had been digitised to save space and Holly scanned through the catalogue on a computer.

A single male librarian watched from afar. With no books to stamp or shelves to rearrange, he spent his time glowering at Holly and Callum.

"The weather is getting worse at home," Holly said, searching through possible book titles.

"If you're right about the cabinet being dark magic," Callum said, "it will rain until we find it."

"You think Long Robert is punishing Greyston?" Holly asked.

"Or the person who bought it."

Callum was wrong, of course. Supernatural entities didn't plague the living. They existed in the imagination, but if people believed in them, as Callum did, it made them real, which was why they were at a library.

"There aren't any books on Alistair Greyston," she said, "but there are plenty about the occult."

"Try that one," Callum said, pointing at the screen.

Holly double-clicked on *The Magickal World of Northumberland* and used her finger to flick through the pages. "It's just nonsense. For instance, did you know there is a creature called a bluecap living near Little Belton?"

Callum nodded. "They were spirits who worked down the mine, guiding the miners to rich seams of coal."

"Of course you knew that," Holly said. "Do you know what they look like?"

"A little blue flame. I saw a bluecap once."

Holly heaved a sigh. "You didn't, Callum. At best, you saw a blue flame. Maybe someone turned on a gas hob, but you didn't see a magical spirit."

"Well, what are we doing here if you don't believe in the underworld?" Callum asked.

"We're here because other people believe in it," Holly said. "Not us. If we can find out what makes the cabinet so special, maybe we'll figure out who took it."

But *The Magickal World of Northumberland* didn't appear to be the best place to look. Holly trawled through the chapters on spirits and ghouls. Each was more ridiculous than the last and she struggled to contain her frustration. She believed in facts, in both her role as a journalist and as a rational human being. Mythical legends may have explained the inexplicable in the Dark Ages, but not in a time of digitised books and internet connection.

"Look at that," Callum said, leaning closer to the screen.

Holly had stumbled onto a chapter about devil worship. The pages were filled with pictures of imps and demons cavorting in forests. Some danced with witches. Others stared menacingly out of the page. There wasn't much text to accompany the images, presumably because there was little to discuss. None of it was real.

"It says here," Holly read, "that to make a pact with Satan, a sacrifice is needed. In sixteenth-century Romania, sometimes whole villages were wiped out in his name."

"Villages like Little Belton?" Callum asked.

Holly continued reading. "More usually, a virgin or an innocent was chosen."

Her eyes returned to the pictures and one picture in particular. A man with horns and a ragged beard stood over an altar. His face was goat-like and he was holding a dagger.

"Does that look like Mr Xavier to you?" Holly asked.

"Never mind that. Have you seen that altar?" Callum asked.

The altar wasn't made of stone. It had been constructed from a dark wood. Its surface crawled with intricate insignia. At its centre was a partially open door from which a snake appeared.

"It looks more like a cabinet to me," Holly said, her palms sweating.

"And have you seen who's on top of it?" Callum asked in a whisper.

A woman dressed in sheer lace writhed under the devil's blade, as if caught in the middle of a hypnotic trance. She faced outward from the page, her mouth contorted in pain.

Holly pressed her fingers to her lips. "My God. She looks like me."

Her phone started ringing and Holly jumped. Taking a moment to compose herself, she heard the librarian tutting at her and she waved him away before answering the phone.

"Who is this?" came the voice from the other side.

"Er, you called me," Holly said. "Can I help you?"

"Can't work this blasted phone," the voice said to itself. "Is anybody there? Over."

"This is Holly Fleet," Holly said. "You're coming in loud and clear. Can I help you with something?"

She listened to the sound of fumbling before the voice spoke again.

"Yes, hello, dear. This is Roland from Roland's Hardware. I can hear you now."

Holly covered the receiver with her hand, mouthing the name Roland at Callum and pointing at her phone.

She returned her attention to the caller, secretly grateful to be back in the normal world of Northumberland.

"Hi, Roland," Holly said, placing the phone on speaker so Callum could hear. "I wasn't sure if I'd hear from you again."

"Sorry about that," Roland said. "My grandson bought me a newfangled iPhone. I can barely work my oven, never mind this monstrosity."

"And how is your grandson doing?" Holly asked.

"Oh, he's grand. What a gifted boy he is," Roland said, his grandfatherly pride oozing down the line. "He'll never get a girlfriend, though. Not with that nose."

"Did you ask him to trace those receipts for the brass handles?"

"Absolutely."

Holly waited, expecting an answer. When the minutes ticked by and it still didn't arrive, she decided Roland needed a prompt.

"Could you tell me, please?" she asked.

"Yes. Where are we?" There was rustling and cursing down the line before Roland spoke next. "It was Mrs Masterly from Black Rock Manor."

CHAPTER TWENTY-EIGHT

"What was that?" Callum asked.

Holly's heart sank and she cupped her hand over the phone.

"We already knew Mrs Masterly had an account with Roland," she said to Callum. "She was buying supplies for the renovations."

"Yes, but she wasn't buying handles for a replica cabinet so she could burn it at the Witches' Hall, was she?" Callum asked.

Holly returned to the phone.

"Are you saying Mrs Masterly bought those handles?" she asked.

"And a ratchet hoist," Roland added.

"That's impossible," Callum said. "Mrs Masterly isn't involved in this. She would have said something."

"Would she?" Holly asked. "She's pretty good at keeping secrets. I mean, she kept the purchase of the cabinet from us."

She heard Roland's muffled voice and lifted the phone closer to her ear. "Pardon?"

"Mrs Masterly holds the account," Roland said, "but it wasn't her who bought the handles. Someone used the account in her name."

There was another pause and more rustling.

"It was a man called Hector," Roland said.

And Holly ended the call.

Chapter Twenty-Nine

They hurtled to Little Belton and The Travelling Star. Before reaching the outskirts of stone buildings, Holly finished another phone call and settled into her seat. She watched the scenery blur as it whizzed past her window.

The Travelling Star was empty, save for the mess, which was everywhere. Chairs were upturned. Tables were littered with empty glasses and heather from the felt hats covered the floor like a sponge carpet.

The only occupant was Big Gregg, who was lying on the bar, pressing a cool rag to his forehead.

"How's your hangover?" Holly asked.

Big Gregg peered at her through puffy eyes. "Pardon?"

"I said, how is your head?" she shouted.

Big Gregg jumped at her voice and rolled off the bar into an ungracious heap at Holly's feet.

"That was uncalled for," he said, pulling himself up.

"Uncalled for? This was supposed to be a distraction," Holly said. "Not some Bacchanalian orgy. How is Mr Xavier?"

Big Gregg mopped the alcoholic sweats from his ruddy cheeks. "Worse than me."

"That bad?" Callum asked. "Where are Paul and Saul the decorators?"

CHAPTER TWENTY-NINE

"How do I know? I'm not their mother."

Holly took the rag and filled it with ice cubes from behind the bar.

"If you were," she said, offering Big Gregg the rag, "I'd be calling Social Services."

He clung to the bar, stabilising himself with his meaty arms.

Callum cleared his throat. "You're missing a leg."

"How observant of you," Big Gregg said, rolling the ice cubes around his temples.

"No, I mean, your prosthetic is gone."

Glancing at his feet, Big Gregg grimaced when he found only one. "Please tell me I didn't lose it in a bet again."

Callum searched the pub, pushing back the furniture and checking the fireplace. When he discovered the false leg in an umbrella stand, Callum's face twisted at the smell.

"This thing needs a rinse," he said. "Someone didn't make it to the bathroom in time."

Big Gregg thanked Callum and placed his leg at the furthest reach of the bar. "What did you want to know about those Spectre brothers again?"

"Did they say anything about where they were going today? We need to speak to them about their brother."

"They said, they were going to make the worst of a bad situation," Big Gregg said.

Five minutes later, Holly and Callum were back in the Defender and driving through the village.

"Do you know where it is?" Holly asked.

When Callum didn't answer, she knew it was a foolish question. There wasn't a blade of grass Callum didn't know about on the estate. She let him drive while she lost herself in her thoughts.

The Travelling Star had looked like it had been ransacked by angry toddlers and a man had been hurt. Not seriously, thankfully, but enough for her to feel a sense of doubt.

Were they doing the right thing?

Were they tracking the right people?

And what would happen when they found them?

They stopped at Bimpton's sandstone quarry. It was a bowl of craggy cliff faces blocking out what remained of the sun. The floor was amber-coloured where the stone had been crushed to dust. Skeletons of old machinery had been left to the elements, their bodies pockmarked by holes as they broke down into metallic lace.

Callum pointed to a path descending into further darkness.

"Down there," he said.

A path littered with yellow rocks led to a lower ground level where the cliffs grew in height. Holly paused at the edge of a puddle so big it could have sustained life. She heard voices and laughter from up high. Craning her neck, she saw Paul and Saul climbing the cliff like gibbering monkeys. They were topless again, despite the drizzle. Their skin glistened in the damp and Holly forced herself to blink.

"Where the hell are their ropes?" Callum asked.

Distracted by their nakedness, Holly hadn't noticed their lack of safety equipment. They wore rock-climbing helmets and very little else, but helmets would not save their lives if they slipped.

"Hey," Holly shouted.

Even though the quarry magnified her voice, the brothers didn't hear her.

"Hey," Holly shouted again, but to no avail.

"We need to speak to them before they get to the top and vanish," Callum said.

Holly snorted. "Or fall to the ground and die, but if you think I'm climbing this cliff, you've got another thing coming."

"I wasn't suggesting you do." Callum pointed up the path. "Go back to the jeep and hang a right. Circle around and I'll meet you at the top."

CHAPTER TWENTY-NINE

"What are you going to do?"

Callum's fingers squirrelled into a gap in the rock face. They became like steel and he dragged himself up the cliff, his feet scrambling for purchase beneath him. Stretching out an arm, he found another handhold and another, his jaw as hardened as the rocks in his fist.

"What are you waiting for?" he asked between gritted teeth.

"Aren't you coming with me? It seems like an easier option."

She watched as Callum looked upwards at the heels of the younger men. His face stiffened and he searched for another handhold.

Envy was catching, Holly thought. Callum had something to prove.

She bolted along the path, determined not to be the last to the summit. Skidding around the Defender, she dashed out of the quarry and along a soggy field. Her lungs burned and pain stabbed in her thighs, but she kept going, only slipping twice on her race to the top. Rounding another corner, she saw Paul throwing his arms over the cliff edge, kicking his legs as he dragged himself onto the horizontal ground.

Pumping her arms and ignoring the sweat in her eyes, Holly reached him before he got to his feet.

"What are you doing here?" Paul asked.

Bending over, Holly shook her hand at him as she caught her breath between rasping coughs.

Saul appeared over the edge, grabbing handfuls of grass to pull himself forward. As he stood, brushing himself down, he looked at Holly with a frown.

"You look like you might throw up," he said.

The coughs turned to spluttering and Holly swallowed repeatedly to moisten her mouth.

"Drink this," Paul said, giving her a water bottle he had tucked into his shorts.

Holly glugged at its contents. Finally able to speak, she straightened, grabbing at the stitch in her side. "I wanted a word."

The brothers smiled and waited.

"Hang on," Holly said. "Where's Callum?"

She rushed to the cliff edge, peering into the quarry below, but Callum was nowhere to be seen.

Hands grabbed at her shoulders and she was pulled backwards. She fought free and turned to face her attacker.

Callum shook his head. "You could have fallen off that cliff. How would you feel after that, mmm?"

His face was bright. Where the brothers were covered in muck from their climb, Callum remained clean and fresh.

"How did you get up here so fast?" she asked.

Paul slapped Callum on the back. "He totally free-styled it. He was awesome."

"No safety ropes," Saul said. "No nothing. He was like Tom Cruise in that film."

Callum shrank under their praise, but Holly thought she detected a slight arch to his eyebrow, telling her he was not immune to it.

"Why weren't you using safety ropes?" Holly asked the brothers.

"We were just having a laugh," Paul said.

"Climbing is dangerous. You could have fallen."

"But— "

"No buts," Holly said. "I'm very disappointed in you."

The Spectre brothers kicked at the grass.

"Sorry, Mrs Fleet," they said together.

"And most of the time we do use our equipment," Paul added. "We have the ropes, the belays, the cams. We were in such a hurry to get out, we forgot it today."

Neither of them would look Holly in the eye and she got the impression they were lying.

"You ever use a ratchet hoist?" Holly asked, remembering the second item Hector had bought using Mrs Masterly's account at Roland's

CHAPTER TWENTY-NINE

Hardware.

The brothers looked at each other for an answer.

"No," Paul said.

"Maybe you tie it to a tree?" Holly asked. "Use it to pull yourself up?"

Paul grinned. "That's not rock climbing. That's taking the stairs."

Callum stretched his arms above his head and pretended to yawn. "I suppose you could also use a hoist to lower a piece of furniture from the first floor to the ground floor, couldn't you?"

"Definitely," Paul said. "We've done that before, but the one we had broke."

"Did you replace it?" Callum asked.

Paul shook his head. "Nope."

"Did Hector?"

Paul and Saul pressed together, closing ranks. "He said nothing to us, if he did."

Holly took Callum's cue and tried to appear casual. She didn't want the brothers to feel like they were being interrogated. They were simple men and there was a chance she'd scare them into silence.

She picked a blade of grass from the ground and teased it between her fingers. "What about brass handles? Did Hector buy any brass handles?"

Paul consulted his fingers, counting them down. "Yes. Fifteen. He bought fifteen to replace the handles on a set of wardrobes Mrs Masterly had. Just to make them look a bit older, but they went missing."

"Someone stole them?" Holly asked.

"Hector said, they hadn't arrived with the rest of the order," Paul said, "but they could have been stolen, I guess."

Holly rubbed a finger across her chin. "And Mrs Masterly can confirm the handles were for a set of wardrobes? Not for a cabinet?"

"I guess so," Paul said. "Mrs Masterly doesn't have a cabinet, does she?"

145

Once again, the brothers' ignorance shielded them from Holly's suspicions, but it didn't protect Hector from them.

"I heard you've done work at Charleston Collectables in Berwick," she said.

"You're asking a lot of questions," Paul said. "How did you know we were there?"

"The owner told me his office had recently been decorated. I called Mr Charleston on the way here," Holly said, "and he gave me your names."

"We were working there when we got the job for the manor," Paul said.

"Was Hector working there too?"

A rock, loosened by its recent tussle with three grown men, fell from the cliff, tumbling to the quarry below.

"Yes," Paul and Saul said together.

"Hector seems to be a very busy man," Holly said. "We never see him around. I take it he's not with you today."

"He sometimes takes extra jobs," Paul said.

His brother jabbed him with a sharp elbow and pursed his lips.

"If he's doing extra work, why would he leave you behind?"

There must have been something very special about their climbing shoes because Paul and Saul studied them intently.

"Your van isn't parked in the quarry, either," Callum said. "It's a long walk from Little Belton."

"A wet one too," Holly added, eyeing the rain clouds above. "Does Hector use the van?"

Paul tucked his chin into his chest. "Yes."

"He leaves you to walk in the rain?" Holly asked.

"It's not his fault," Paul said. "Hector, I mean."

Saul cast his brother an accusing look, but it quickly slipped from his face.

"We mess around a lot," Paul continued, "and he says his extra work is too important for mistakes."

"Did he say what this extra work was?" Holly asked.

Paul shook his head. "He doesn't like to talk about it."

"Why?"

Paul picked grit from his palms. He sprinkled it like fairy dust, entranced by its fall to earth.

"We don't want to get anyone into trouble," Holly said.

"I know that, Mrs Fleet," Paul said. "It's just our Hector has a gambling problem."

"*Had* a gambling problem," the other brother said, emphasising the past tense.

"He doesn't do it now," Paul said with a gulp, "but he owes money to people. We don't like anyone to know about it in case they won't employ him."

Callum folded his arms, bunching the muscles in his biceps. "What kind of people does he owe money to?"

"You don't have to worry. They're not from around here. I think that's why Hector wants to stay for a while. To keep us out of harm's way."

Paul and Saul were boys to Holly then, children who had accidentally slipped the anchor of their family. They'd been abandoned by a brother who should have been looking out for them.

She took a handkerchief from her pocket and used it to wipe dirt from Paul's face. When she had finished, he smiled through his blushes.

"Is Hector trying to pay off his debts?" Holly asked.

"They're not patient men," Paul said. "People like that rarely are, but we don't need to worry. Hector says, it's almost over."

Holly held Paul by the shoulders, fixing him with a stare. "Did you do something, Paul? Something to help your brother?"

Paul frowned, a look that was mirrored in his twin. "What do you mean?"

"You said, it was almost over. What did you mean by that?"

"That's what Hector told me," Paul said. "He said, he had something in the pipeline and I thought that was funny because we usually get a plumber to lay all the pipes. And Hector said, I was stupid. So I said— "

Holly held up a hand, halting a story she sensed would never end.

"Listen, I need to ask you something important," she said, swallowing the apprehension wedged in her throat. "This isn't easy, but did you help Hector take anything from the manor? Something valuable you could sell?"

The look of horror on Paul's face forced Holly back a step.

"Of course not," he said.

"We really like Mrs Masterly," Saul said.

Paul sucked the rest of the water from his bottle and tucked it neatly away in his shorts when he was finished. "We would never do that. Stealing is a terrible thing."

"That sounds like something Hector would say to you," Callum said. "As a big brother, like."

But Paul shook his head. "I know stealing is bad. I don't need anyone else to tell me that."

"When Hector said, it was almost over, do you think Hector might have stolen something from the manor?" Holly asked.

"We have to go now," Paul said.

"Go where?" Callum asked.

"Hector only has one more job to go," Paul said, "and he's debt free. I don't know what it is. I'm sure it's not stealing stuff, but after that, we're leaving and never coming back. He said, we could never come back to Little Belton."

Chapter Thirty

Holly and Callum searched the lower levels of Black Rock Manor and found them empty. Climbing the staircase, they heard scuffling behind the door to the servants' quarters. Callum grabbed the handle, swinging open the door to be greeted by a broom shank swinging back at him. He ducked and the broom swept through the ceramic vase stationed outside, obliterating it into pieces.

"What are you doing?" Callum asked from a crouched position.

"Tidying up," Mrs Masterly said, lowering the broom. "Sorry, dear. I'm a little on edge. I thought you might be another intruder."

Her eyes went to the shattered vase. "At least, no one will steal that, but I have to ask - how did you get in here?"

"We came through the door," Holly said. "Same as always."

Mrs Masterly leaned on her broom, her face falling. "Really? I thought I'd locked it."

"Are you okay?" Holly asked.

Mrs Masterly lifted the broom, but rather than launch a second attack on Callum, she began sweeping the vase into a tiny pile of fragments.

Callum took the broom from Mrs Masterly. "Let me do that."

Holly looked over Mrs Masterly's shoulder. The servants' quarters were empty, save for the cold air seeping under the edges of the Raquel Welch poster. Holly heard the ivy leaves rustling outside, but there was no birdsong, no robin to fill the room. Mrs Masterly was existing in a vacuum and if they didn't find the cabinet, Holly worried she always would.

"We have some news," Holly said and related their encounter with Paul and Saul. "Hector worked in Charleston Collectables. He may never have seen the cabinet while it was here, but I'm guessing he knew it was arriving."

"It's important we find him before he finishes this last job," Callum said, "or he'll be gone forever."

Mrs Masterly grew rigid. "I hope you're not saying what I suspect you're saying."

"We just want to speak to him," Holly said. "He's never at The Travelling Star. I was wondering if you had his business card or a phone number for him."

"Sorry, it all happened so fast," Mrs Masterly said. "I didn't write it down."

Holly frowned. "Well, how did you contact him about the renovations?"

"He called me," Mrs Masterly said.

"Out of the blue?"

Mrs Masterly strolled to the poster, pressing down the flapping edges in an attempt to halt the dropping temperature. "He said, he was working in the area. That he was a restoration specialist and he wondered if I needed his help. I believe in fate and fate brought me Hector. He was so much cheaper than the other quotes I'd received. I honestly thought he was a godsend. Hector was so understanding when the money ran out. He's not even suing me like the rest of my suppliers."

"We know why," Callum said. There was a crack as the broom handle snapped in his hands. "He has a cabinet worth forty thousand pounds. He doesn't need any more money."

CHAPTER THIRTY

Holly held up her hands. "We don't know anything yet, but it looks like Hector knew about the cabinet and planned to be here when it was delivered."

"He has a van," Callum said, "and all the equipment he needs to move the cabinet by himself."

"Are you saying Hector, a man I invited into my home, a man who - " Mrs Masterly paused, placing a hand on her chest. " - flirted with me, was only there to steal?"

Holly shuffled on her feet. She'd been thinking about something on the journey there and the more she thought about it, the more it became an unattractive fact.

"Maybe he was flirting with you for a reason," she said.

"Isn't there always a reason behind flirting?"

"A different reason, I mean," Holly said. "You're a beautiful woman. Any man would be attracted to you, but what if he was trying to get close to you to learn about your night-time habits?"

Callum turned into the corner and studied his fingernails.

"Wait, I'm not explaining myself properly," Holly said, her cheeks flushing. With a sigh, she started again. "You were drugged. Hector had to know you took vitamins before sleeping. Did he have access to your bedroom?"

Callum coughed into his hand.

"Oh, grow up," Holly said to him.

Mrs Masterly grew wan. "I often left them alone in the manor. They had free rein to explore wherever they wanted. I trusted them."

"If it makes you feel any better," Callum said. "Paul and Saul worship the ground you walk on."

Judging by the look on Mrs Masterly's face, it didn't and Holly didn't blame her.

"The good news is we think he is still in the area," Holly said.

"How do we know that?" Callum asked.

"Paul and Saul," Holly said. "Hector doesn't involve them in his extracurricular activities. He's too protective, but he's not about to abandon his brothers in Little Belton. He'll come back for them."

"And what about the cabinet?" Mrs Masterly asked with an expectant glimmer. "Will we get it back?"

Holly rubbed her chin. She was less sure about that. She was hoping Hector was smart enough to know selling the cabinet might draw unwanted attention. It was a unique piece and she imagined black marketeers would be nervous about the association. If that was the case – and there were a lot of *ifs* in her theory – Hector might have been forced to hold on to the cabinet until the heat died down.

Unless he had already arranged a buyer. Hector had burned a second cabinet as a distraction. A man smart enough for that was smart enough to think ahead.

"I'd like to take another look around, if that's okay?" Holly asked. "I want to see if Hector left anything we could use to track him down."

Mrs Masterly raised her eyebrows. "You want to look around my house?"

"We won't touch anything, I promise."

"And we won't go into your bedroom, either," Callum said in a low voice.

Mrs Masterly looked uncertain, but eventually gave a nod.

Callum returned her broom.

"Try not to hurt anyone with this," he said.

Holly and Callum walked down the creaking staircase and stepped inside the ballroom that had once been muted as a gift store. When Holly had first visited, she'd felt excited, intrigued by the possibilities. Standing there now, all she felt was hollow and filled with echoes.

"She's been cleaning in here as well," Callum said.

The scaffolding remained, but the dust sheets had been folded away into a neat pile. What was left of the brothers' tools were now in Perspex

CHAPTER THIRTY

boxes, labelled and stacked in a corner. There was a scent of lemon tickling Holly's nose, suggesting not only had the floor been swept, but scoured with detergent.

Mrs Masterly had done a thorough job in eradicating the presence of the intruders in her home and if there were any indicators to Hector's current location, they were also gone.

Holly strolled around the room, her hands clasped behind her back. "Did Hector strike you as a man who knows about antiques?"

"Not sure," Callum said. "Never met the guy."

"It's possible, I suppose," Holly said, "but if he wasn't, how would he find a buyer for the cabinet?"

"Like I say, I've never met him."

Holly went to the window and closed her eyes while thoughts tumbled around her head. "People who like antiquities, they live and breathe that stuff. They research it. They go to antique fairs and things. How would he know someone like that?"

Callum sighed. "You're talking to yourself, aren't you?"

"We can tie Hector to Mr Charleston, but he wouldn't buy back a cabinet he just sold, would he? He wanted to get rid of it."

"And who would buy an antique from a decorator without being suspicious?" Callum asked.

Holly spun on her feet and opened her eyes. "I mean, who would buy an antique from a decorator without being suspicious?"

Callum shrugged his shoulders, a pained look on his face.

"You're being quiet," Holly said. "Don't you have anything to contribute?"

"The buyer would have to be someone who wanted the cabinet no matter what," Callum said through his teeth.

Holly raised a finger to the ceiling. "Someone who saw the cabinet's value to be greater than their moral compass. Someone who would harangue Mr Charleston for the smallest of details. They would be so obsessed with the cabinet, it wouldn't matter to them if it had been stolen, as long as they had it in their possession. So they could study it. So they could continue their research."

With Hector still missing and seemingly untraceable, Holly's thoughts turned to Mr Xavier and she jammed her hands onto her hips.

"Now where could we unearth someone like that?" she asked.

Chapter Thirty-One

It was easy to find Mr Xavier.

Holly and Callum lingered in the doorway of The Travelling Star watching the rain-washed high street of Little Belton. The village green was under an inch of water. Blades of grass poked through the puddles, desperate for daylight on their yellowing skin. Quiet ravens sat hunched on the rooftops, rain trickling down their oily, black feathers. They watched the bubbling water flow down the pavements and pool around the drains already fat with liquid.

Only one other living creature braved the weather. Plunging through it all was Mr Xavier. He lay prostrate in a shopping trolley, a bandaged leg sticking in the air like a ship's mast. The wheels of the trolley squeaked madly as he propelled himself along with a walking cane, as if he was punting along a Venice canal.

Despite his awkward manoeuvres, he was approaching Holly and Callum at speed.

Callum stepped into his path, skipping around Mr Xavier as he skirted by. He grabbed the trolley's handle, bringing it and Mr Xavier to an abrupt halt.

"What do you think you're doing?" Mr Xavier said, brandishing his walking cane like a sword. "Have I not suffered enough?"

If Holly had to answer that, she'd probably say no.

"First, I sprain my ankle," Mr Xavier continued, "and thanks to Little Belton's inadequate patient care, I'm forced into using a shopping cart instead of a wheelchair."

Callum loomed over him. "Don't forget to return it or you won't get your pound back."

Mr Xavier waved the cane around his head, forcing Callum to hop out of its reach. "I don't appreciate being manhandled, young man."

He gave Callum a hard stare, which suddenly softened. "Don't I know you?"

"You might have seen me at the Green Man ceremony," Callum said. "Briefly."

Colour flooded Mr Xavier's cheeks. "I'll be the first to admit, I made a bit of a fool of myself. Luckily, I can't remember much of that. I'm paying for it now, of course. If I need to get around, I have all the dignity of a bag of groceries."

"How is your leg?" Callum asked.

"Just need to stay off it for a while," Mr Xavier said, studying Callum closely. "I was so drunk, I wouldn't have recognised you from the so-called Bathing of the Green Man, but you look familiar."

"Maybe I have one of those faces."

"Maybe," Mr Xavier echoed. His eyes scanned Callum, travelling from his muddy boots up to his dark locks. When they stopped at Callum's face, Mr Xavier leaned forward. "Is your second name Acres, by any chance?"

Callum grabbed at his jacket's lapels and jutted out his chin. "It is."

Mr Xavier slapped the side of the shopping trolley and laughed. "It's a pleasure to see you again. I'm your uncle."

* * *

Mr Xavier eased himself out of his trolley while Holly and Callum

CHAPTER THIRTY-ONE

watched on. They sat around a circular table in The Travelling Star. The fire had been lit and Big Gregg poured them mugs of coffee before returning to the bar.

Callum pushed his drink out of reach while Holly sipped quietly.

"Your father and I went way back," Mr Xavier said. "We were inseparable at one point. We'd hunt rabbits together, collect bird's eggs, track deer. It was the perfect childhood in many ways. How is the old rascal, by the way?"

Callum chewed on his thumb. "He's dead."

The fire crackled, spitting ruby-red embers onto the hearth.

"I'm sorry to hear that," Mr Xavier said into his coffee.

"I take it you're not Callum's real Uncle?" Holly asked, unable to resist her curiosity.

"No, no, but we were like brothers. We grew up in neighbouring cottages."

Holly took another sip of her drink. "You said, you were inseparable at one point. What happened?"

"We'd chat for hours about travelling the world. We'd make such elaborate plans, but I could tell his heart wasn't truly in it. And then he had a son." Mr Xavier turned his attention to Callum, his face grave. "He wanted you to have the childhood he'd had. I suppose, he'd hoped his memories would become yours."

Callum lowered his head. "He'd take me around the estate. Teach me about birds and plants and animals. It was kind of perfect, actually."

"Meanwhile, I had my own life to live," Mr Xavier said, "so I left without him. That was over twenty years ago. I barely recognise the faces around here now, and no doubt no one recognises mine, but your face, Callum... you look just like your father."

The grief burned deeply in Callum's eyes. It was fresh and bright, as if Mr Xavier had inadvertently taken Callum back to the day his father had died.

Holly placed a gentle hand on Callum's shoulder where she felt it shaking.

"It is odd to be back, though," Mr Xavier said. "So much has gone. There used to be a butcher, a tailor, a hardware store. There was the school, of course..."

He trailed off and watched the fire burn. "Such a terrible accident."

"There were rumours it wasn't an accident," Callum said. "That it was arson."

Mr Xavier bristled, like a peacock ruffling its feathers. "A village this small is full of rumours. It's nonsense, just like the Bathing of the Green Man. No basis in reality at all."

"How do you know?" Holly asked.

"It's an area of my expertise. I specialise in folklore and mythology. The Green Man is real, of course. There are depictions of him as a fertility god throughout history, but never has there been a celebration of him taking a bath. I mean, who comes up with this foolishness?"

"No, I meant, how do you know it wasn't arson?" Holly asked.

Mr Xavier tugged on his beard. "An educated guess."

"And by the way," Callum said, his voice like a growl, "it was our friend who told us about the bathing of the Green Man and I don't like my friends being mocked. You weren't so sceptical while you were leaping over a flaming bale of hay."

"I was swept along by the hospitality."

Holly left her hand on Callum's shoulder, but tightened her grip. His grief was spilling into anger and Holly needed him to stay calm. Mr Xavier's insensitivity was startling, but it was also to be expected from a man who had repeatedly harangued someone in a wheelchair.

"As an expert in folklore, how much do you know about the occult?" Holly asked him.

"Nothing."

"Are you sure?" Holly asked, not quite believing her ears.

CHAPTER THIRTY-ONE

Mr Xavier finished his coffee. "I know my own mind, dear, and the occult is far too dark for me, thank you."

The door to the pub flew open and rain lashed inside. In seconds, the carpet was as sodden as a marsh. Holly and Callum expected to see a weary traveller stumble through the doors, clothes so wet they were like a second skin, but no one appeared.

Big Gregg hurried forward, poked his head outside to check the high street. When he retrieved it, his hair was wet and there was a confused look upon his face. Snapping the bolts shut, he returned to the bar.

"Bloody Long Robert," he muttered before glancing at his customers. "Can I get you anything more to drink?"

When they didn't answer, he rustled his newspaper despondently and peered at them over the pages.

"How well do you know Hector? The decorator working at the manor?" Holly asked.

"Mrs Masterly is refurbishing the manor?" Mr Xavier asked, looking perplexed. "That seems a little foolhardy. Her grant has yet to be processed."

"So do you know him or not?" Callum asked.

Mr Xavier gathered his coat and walking cane. "I can't say that I do, but if you're looking for a tradesman, visit the nearest building site. You'll find plenty there."

The fire did little to warm the cold sensation creeping down Holly's neck.

"Hector was working at Charleston Antiques around the same time you were harassing its owner," she said. "You knew him. Admit it."

"Harassing? Is that what the old fool told you? Did he also tell you how he ended up in his wheelchair? Crushed by his own furniture." Mr Xavier thumped the folds of his coat. "I admit I called Mr Charleston and attempted to gain entry to his shop on many occasions."

"Why?" Holly asked.

"I was protecting the Greyston cabinet," Mr Xavier said. "What if something had fallen on top of it? Or it was scratched by that imbecile in his wheelchair? It is a valuable work of art. I had to let Mr Charleston know there was someone nearby who cared."

"Is that why you're in Little Belton," Holly asked. "To do the same to Mrs Masterly?"

"I'll do whatever it takes," Mr Xavier said, shaking his coat and climbing to his feet with a wobble. "I take it you're friends with her?"

"What of it," Callum said.

"Well, perhaps you can pass on a message. Tell her I'm coming for the cabinet. I want to be part of its history. It's important to me and she should understand that." Mr Xavier hobbled through the pub, pausing at the door leading to the rooms upstairs. "I don't know this Hector person, but I have an arrangement with Mrs Masterly. It's a simple transaction and if I don't get what I want, she won't get what she wants."

"And what is it you want?" Callum asked.

But the door had closed and like the butchers, the tailors and the rest of Little Belton, Mr Xavier had vanished.

Chapter Thirty-Two

Derek stood with his hands on his hips, staring at the hole in the roof. He was dressed in a makeshift cowl fashioned out of black plastic bags. On his head sat a limp bobble hat soaking up the rain.

"Will you come inside?" Holly shouted from the front door.

"I think it's getting bigger," Derek said. "The hole, I mean."

Holly didn't need to stand in the rain to realise that. All she had to do was count the number of buckets catching drips in her home.

"Perhaps you should go to the village. Get some supplies," Derek said.

"What kind of supplies?" Holly asked.

"I don't know. Things to fix a roof."

"Will you get in here before you cause any more trouble?" Holly asked.

Derek stepped inside, shaking like a wet dog. "I know where the problem is."

So did Holly and he'd cut up her plastic bags to fashion a ridiculous coat.

"If you go get some tiles and stuff, I could fix it this afternoon," Derek said.

"The kettle is on," she said. "Come and get warm."

They heard an engine groaning up the hill. Mr Winnow's olive-green delivery truck stopped at their cottage with Mr Winnow beaming from the front seat.

"I've got the glass for your window," he said, hopping from the truck. "Made a deal with a guy in Amble so I saved you some money."

Callum jumped from the truck, fastening the buttons on his wax jacket.

"What are you doing here?" Derek asked.

"I promised to fix your roof, remember?" Callum said, untying a set of ladders.

Holly looked at her husband, her eyes narrowing. "Is that why you wanted me to buy supplies?" she asked. "You wanted to fix the roof before Callum got the chance?"

Callum clambered up the ladder, his assured feet moving swiftly.

"I'm sorry, hun," Derek said, peeling off his plastic bags. "Mr Winnow called to say he was on his way with Callum. I wanted one last chance at fixing the roof, but I guess I'm better with spreadsheets than actual life."

Holly folded the bags, hoping she could reuse some of them. "And that's fine, Derek. Some people aren't cut out for this sort of thing. Listen – Hey, wait a minute. What are you doing here?"

Simone dropped from the truck. Gone were the lace dresses and flowing gowns. She wore a set of denim coveralls splattered with paint and plaster, though Holly noticed they'd been taken in at the waist to accentuate her bust.

"I'm here to help Callum," she said. "I've fixed my share of roofs. I can show you how to do it, if you want?"

Holly forced a smile, feeling the same way Derek must have felt whenever Holly patronised him.

"I'll stick with making the teas," she said.

Mr Winnow donned a pair of rigger gloves and heaved the glass from his truck. It was wrapped in cardboard sporting the logo of a local

CHAPTER THIRTY-TWO

reclamation yard.

"I got you a bargain here," he said with a grin. "Cheap as chips, and as my old dad used to say, *a penny saved is a penny taken from the taxman's pocket.*"

Holly pressed in close to Mr Winnow, bringing her lips to his ear. "Did he say anything about that game you sold me and the note I found?"

The grin slipped from Mr Winnow's face. "What about it?"

Callum skated down the last rungs of his ladder.

"We'll have your roof patched up in no time," he said before frowning at the look on Holly's face. "Is everything okay?"

Holly quickly stepped away from Mr Winnow. "Yep, it's great. Just discussing the new window."

She couldn't let Callum find out about the dolls. Not like this, anyway. Not in front of an audience. He'd be crushed and Holly wanted to protect him from that for as long as she could.

She turned to Mr Winnow. "Will the window fit?"

"Measured it twice myself. Don't worry. You're going to be thrilled," he said.

Mr Winnow stripped the cardboard away with a flourish.

Holly scratched her head. "What's that?"

Running a tongue over his teeth, Mr Winnow appeared lost for words. He studied the window as if it might metamorphose into something more suitable.

"You got this from a reclamation yard?" Holly asked. "Did you ask where it had been reclaimed from?"

"I just gave him the size," Mr Winnow said, "but at a guess, I'd say it came from a pub."

Water rolled down Holly's new window and over the etching of a bull's head. Rain collected in its horns and pooled in its nose ring.

"At least we know why it was so cheap," Holly said.

Mr Winnow smiled. "It's rather fetching."

"You would say that." Holly imagined sunshine flooding through the window, casting an image of a bull's face onto her carpet. It would be a talking point, she supposed and it might mask some of the threadbare portions. "Okay. Anything is better than chipboard."

"With a fancy new window like this," Mr Winnow said, "you'll be the talk of the village."

For all the wrong reasons, Holly thought, but she didn't have the energy to complain. She left the workers to it and found Derek nursing a cup of tea in the kitchen.

"Replacing tiles isn't as easy as I thought," he said.

"Why would you think it was?" Holly reboiled the kettle and made her own cup of tea. "Callum will take care of it. And Simone, of course."

The teaspoon clinked inside the mug as Holly stirred, turning the liquid darker. "We should know our limits."

"Do you think we fit in here?" Derek asked.

Holly ran the Little Belton Herald. It wasn't full of risky exposés or shattering news, but it was at the heart of the village. She had lots of friends, people she could easily pass the time of day with, and she had their support, as evidenced by the team currently working on their house.

Derek rarely visited the village. His work was with spreadsheets and Gantt charts, keeping him confined to an office. He didn't have friends or people he could rely upon. He tried to ingratiate himself with the locals, but there was always a divide. With Derek, it was always them and us.

"I can't fix a roof," Holly said, "and I can't climb mountains, but I'm still a part of this community."

"What about me?" Derek asked.

Holly stood over him, placing a hand on his shoulder. "You have other skills."

"Like what?"

CHAPTER THIRTY-TWO

With a long breath, Holly explained about the cabinet and its disappearance. She listed suspects and their motivations. She spoke at length about Mr Xavier's threat and his lies regarding his research, and voiced her concerns over Mrs Masterly's health.

"What can I do about it?" Derek asked.

"You can get involved," Holly said, remembering how it felt to be patronised. "What I mean is, you don't know how to fix a roof, but you're good with computers and things. You can do background checks on people."

"I found out about Mrs Masterly's accounts because I have access to them. I'm not a private detective."

"The village is relying on me to figure this out," Holly said, "whether they know it or not. I need to be able to rely on you."

They listened to Callum's footsteps on the roof and the sound of tumbling slates. Simone called out, though they couldn't hear her words over Callum's laughter.

"I must use the internet," Derek said, "which means leaving the village to find somewhere in the twentieth century."

"So you'll help?"

"Might have to stay over, though. Are you okay with that?"

Holly paced the floor, tapping her finger against her chin. "That's great. It will really save time. We'll have access to everything."

Getting to his feet, Derek finished the last of his tea. "I take it you want some information on this Mr Xavier?"

Holly leaned over the sink, catching her reflection in the window in front of her. She needed sleep. There were hollows under her eyes and her skin was sagging. Even if Mrs Masterly had magic beauty pills, Holly was beyond that now. It was as if she'd left her youth behind in London, and there was no getting it back.

She raised her face to the ceiling, listening to Callum and Simone laughing on the roof. Their happiness drowned out the hammering and the drilling. Slates fell with a crash. Someone turned a radio on, tuned to loud, tinny music.

"I can't complain about going out of town, I suppose," Derek said. "It's going to be like living on a building site around here."

Holly turned to her husband and pressed a kiss on his surprised face.

"Something I said?" he asked with a grin.

Yes, it was, thought Holly.

If Holly was looking for a builder, she'd need to go to a building site and Holly knew where she could find one.

Derek had given her an idea.

Chapter Thirty-Three

With the roof fixed and her carpet finally able to dry out, Holly decided to search for Hector.

"Remember what Mr Xavier said about finding tradesmen on a building site?" Holly asked Callum, as he steered the Defender along a country lane.

Coming to a junction, he turned right onto what Holly had heard Callum call *a grown-up road*. There were no potholes, no wandering sheep. Just smooth tarmac heading toward the horizon.

"I don't like that guy," Callum said. "I try not to listen when he talks."

"What if Hector had heard of an opportunity to find work?" Holly asked. "He needs the money."

"He's stolen a cabinet worth forty thousand pounds. Isn't that enough for him?" Callum asked.

The grown-up road took them through a patchwork of fields. Combine harvesters and tractors buzzed about them, like bees to flowers, collecting grass for the winter silage. Holly watched them strip the fields bare before moving onto the next one.

"This could be Hector's routine," she said. "He calls around and finds work at historical buildings like Black Rock Manor. He does a bit of decorating, but really he is looking for valuables to steal."

Callum tipped his head as he considered the notion. "Okay, I agree. He's casing the place, but that doesn't explain why we're going to stupid Crockfoot."

"Their town hall spire is being renovated. I was writing an article about it before all this started. It's the nearest building site to Little Belton and there'd be plenty of things to steal at a town hall. It's worth a shot."

Callum's face twisted.

"Bloody Crockfoot," he mumbled.

He was silent for the rest of the journey, but it was a quick trip and they were soon walking down the high street toward the town hall. Holly had a grudging respect for Crockfoot. Unlike Little Belton, it was thriving and it was partially down to their cosmopolitan outlook.

Where Little Belton had a convenience store, Crockfoot had a delicatessen, an artisan baker and a vegan smoothie café. Callum paused by its window, studying their menu on a chalkboard.

"What on earth is a cress and goat's cheese milkshake?" he asked.

Crockfoot had a mocktail lounge, a cutlery store dedicated entirely to the left-handed and a pop-up cinema showing early East German films. It drew in tourists and the city folk who liked the countryside, but didn't like to leave behind the trappings of their sophisticated lives.

Callum paused again, this time pointing at something in a craft store. "They've glued wobbly eyes on a rock and expect me to pay ten pounds for it? You can forget that for starters."

Holly dragged him away by his coat. "Come on. The town hall is down here."

It was situated along one side of a cobbled square, its spire casting a triangular shadow over the stones. A statue of Sergeant Culpepper guarded the entrance. According to the plaque Holly read, he'd fought off an advance from the Scottish Covenanters in sixteen thirty-nine, thus keeping Crockfoot for the English Royalists. He was a dour-faced

CHAPTER THIRTY-THREE

man with an air of imperiality that fitted the village well.

The building itself was just as dour and was surrounded by the white vans of bricklayers, plasterers and electricians. Holly had never seen Hector's van so couldn't be sure if it was there, but at least they were in the right place.

"All right, beautiful?"

The catcall came from a gang of workers in overalls leaning against a wall, smoking cigarettes.

Holly continued walking. She only realised the call was meant for her when Callum disappeared from her side, storming over to confront the rough-faced men. He squared off against the biggest man, who had a spider tattoo on his neck and wore a sarcastic smile.

"What's the matter, mate?" the man asked. "I was only paying her a compliment."

"You don't speak to women like that," Callum said, jutting out his chin.

The man sneered. "Are you her toy boy or something?"

Callum's face drained to a cool white glow.

Holly rushed over, her heart in her mouth, hoping to avoid a bloodbath.

"Let's get inside," Holly said to Callum.

The man led his friends in a chorus of laughter. "That's it, mate. Do what the little lady says. Is she your wife or your mother?"

Callum swung back a fist. Holly grabbed his arm in time, diverting the punch in a fruitless arc.

The man reared, spitting out his cigarette. "If you wanna try that again, I'll slap that girly face of yours so it's sitting at the back of your head."

Before she knew what she was doing, Holly had punched the man in the eye. His head rocked backwards and he staggered. His co-workers fell silent in shock.

Callum looked at her, his mouth hanging open.

"Come on," Holly hissed. "It's time to go."

They scurried into the town hall and down a corridor lined with aerial photographs of Crockfoot.

"What was all that about?" Callum asked.

Holly nursed a hand pulsating in pain.

"He shouldn't have said you had a girly face," she said.

"Remind me not to annoy you," Callum said with a smirk.

"I do. All the time, but you don't listen." Holly stared up and down the corridor. "Let's see if we can find Hector before I get arrested for assault."

They followed the sound of machinery, taking the stairs to the upper levels to where the walls were covered in protected plastic sheeting. Dust caught the back of Holly's throat and she coughed into the crook of her arm.

"Can I help you?" A thin-boned man in a high-vis jacket who carried a clipboard waved them over. Written on his jacket in black marker was the name Nigel.

"I'm sorry. You can't be here. Health and Safety," Nigel said.

"We're looking for someone. We really need to speak to him," Holly said, attempting to make her eyes as big and as appealing as possible.

"What's he called?"

"Hector," Holly said. "Hector Spectre."

Nigel burst into laughter but stopped, noticing Holly's hard stare.

"Oh, you were being serious," he said, checking his clipboard. "There is a Hector here. He's working up by the spire, but like I say, you can't go in."

"This is Holly Fleet," Callum said, pointing at her. "Editor-in-chief of the Little Belton Herald. She is writing an article about how you're employing criminals here. Do you have anything to say about that?"

Judging by the constipated look on Nigel's face, Holly thought not.

CHAPTER THIRTY-THREE

"Do you complete background checks on your employees?" she asked. "Are they registered with professional bodies of accreditation? How are they paid? Digitally or by cash?"

Nigel threw up his hands in surrender. "Bloody hell. I don't know. This is my first day."

"Hector has agreed to go on the record for the Herald, offering to defend the working practices here. If we don't get to speak to him, it will not look very good for you, will it?"

Nigel quivered.

"Can we go?" Callum asked.

With a brief nod, Nigel turned and bolted for the nearest exit.

Entering the next room, the noise met them with a deafening whoosh. Tools clanged and screamed. Workers in overalls shouted over the cacophony, adding to it with their conversation and laughter. And it was hot. Sweat gathered in Holly's armpits. The dust that had tickled her throat earlier now hung like smog, stinging her eyes.

Callum wrapped an arm around her and guided Holly toward a woman in a hard hat.

"We're looking for Hector," Callum shouted.

"Who?"

"He's working in the spire," Callum shouted, trying to make himself understood.

The woman wiped her face with a dirty handkerchief. "The spire? Over there, mate."

Callum followed her directions, dragging a sputtering Holly with him.

"Are you okay?" he asked.

"I will be when we get out of here," Holly said.

They fought their way through the dust and the heat, finding a rickety metal staircase winding up to a hatch in the ceiling.

Callum went first and Holly followed, holding tightly, hoping the stairs could take their weight, particularly hers.

Pushing open the hatch, Callum scrambled through, extending a helping hand to Holly as he pulled her up.

The spire opened above them, church-like and replete with the ghostly echoes of the noise below. Electric lights hung from grey cables, fastened haphazardly to the walls, shedding an orange glow. Stone arches and warped wooden beams interconnected, holding the spire's roof in place. There were plastic sheets and tools, but there was only one man. He was balancing at the top of a ladder, his back to them, chipping away at broken plaster.

"Hector?" Holly shouted.

The man turned in fright.

"You're not Hector," Holly said.

"What are you doing up here?" the man asked, tugging nervously on his moustache.

"We're looking for Hector," Callum said. "We were told he was working in the spire."

The man shook his head. "He was working here. He left. Shot off like a whippet."

"Where did he go?" Holly asked.

But the man shrugged. "No idea. Said it was some sort of emergency. Must have been bad, though. He left without taking any of his kit."

The man pointed to a bundle of clothing and tools tucked under a wooden bench. Without waiting to ask if she could, Holly riffled through them.

"Looks like it's his work gear. Some chisels. Safety gloves. And what's this?"

Holly presented Callum with a jar filled with a dark oil. There was no label and the jar looked as if it had been used many times over.

Callum unscrewed the lid and sniffed. "Ah, that stinks."

The man laughed from the top of his ladders. "That's his magic cream, he says. Uses it for his aches and pains. It's got herbs in it or

CHAPTER THIRTY-THREE

something. I said, have a hot bath like the rest of us, but he wouldn't have it. Said it was one of them all-natural remedies."

"What do you think is in it?" Holly asked Callum.

He shrugged. "No idea and Hector isn't around to ask. Again."

"Well, I doubt he's coming back soon," Holly said. "Let's get out of here. It's too hot and dirty, and I might have to go on the run from the law soon."

"I know someone who could tell us what's in this jar," Callum asked, looking at Holly expectantly, "and so do you."

Holly groaned. It was only fair, she supposed. Holly had convinced Callum to drive to Crockfoot, a place he loathed and hated in equal measure. It was only right she suffered a little irritation in return.

"Fine," Holly said. "We'll visit Simone, but I'm not going to pretend to enjoy it."

Chapter Thirty-Four

"Are you sure this is a good idea?" Callum asked.

The following morning, Holly had trapped her foot in a nest of tree roots. She wriggled her toes, feeling water soaking into her boots.

"You came up with it," she said.

They were skirting the outliers of Crair's Wood. As usual, Callum insisted it was haunted, this time by the hanged descendants of a Saxon king. Holly ignored him, preferring to concentrate on where she placed her feet. Startled by a sudden shadow, she'd slipped and concentrated on maintaining her composure instead.

Callum hurdled over the roots and took hold of her ankle. "What will we talk about?"

With a gentle twist and yank, he freed Holly's foot.

"Ask her about the jar we found," Holly said. "Maybe pry out some more information about Hector and if there's time, get to know her better. Ask about her favourite colour or something."

Callum shot her a look.

"Okay. Don't worry. I'll be your wingman," Holly said, "and I won't interfere. I promise."

And Holly had made a solemn vow not to do so. Despite her misgivings about Simone, she recognised Callum's infatuation with her. Hector's mysterious potion had given him the perfect opportunity to spend

CHAPTER THIRTY-FOUR

time in her company. The tiny village of Little Belton offered few opportunities for young people to "court," as Callum had phrased it. She couldn't stand in his way, no matter what the nagging voice inside her head told her.

Holly shook her wet boot, failing to release the dampness inside. "It was time we all became friends."

They moved quickly and Holly did her best to meet Callum's brisk pace without complaining. Scrambling up a stony outcrop, they paused by Juniper Falls, watching ravens fly in lazy circles around Simone's bothy.

Callum approached and knocked gently, lowering his head while he waited for an answer.

"What if she doesn't like me the way I think she does?" Callum asked in a whisper.

"You're going to have to knock harder than that," Holly said.

Callum tried again, more firmly this time.

There was still no answer.

"Perhaps she's in the garden," Holly said.

They trailed around the bothy and wandered into the ruins of an old building. The remaining sandstone walls were reduced to a foot high, picked apart by the Northumbrian weather. Gelatinous fungi sprouted from crumbling wooden supports lying like fallen matchsticks.

"What is this place?" Holly asked.

"A second bothy?" Callum offered as an answer. "A lot of these places are abandoned. They aren't needed as much and it's costly to maintain them."

"Like the manor," Holly said.

Callum ran a hand through his hair, his eyes narrowing. "It's hard to see our history reduced to rubble like this."

It may not be a home anymore, thought Holly, but thanks to Simone, it continued to be occupied. Out of the ruins sprung forth a garden. In what appeared to be a doorway were canes supporting climbing pea shoots. In the square of a small bathroom were carrots and beetroot growing in regimental lines. The main sitting area was host to an explosion of herbs.

"Where have all these come from?" Callum asked. "The herbs? I don't recognise any of them."

Holly pinched a leaf between her fingers, recoiling at the pungent smell it released. "I thought you knew all the plants on the estate."

"This doesn't feel like the estate to me," Callum said. "This feels like Simone."

By the herbs was a charred metal pot sitting on a pile of ash. There was also a ladle for stirring the pot's contents and a pestle and mortar for preparing them.

"I'd be surprised if we didn't find *eye of newt* here somewhere," Holly said.

Callum pointed at a mass of flattened grass.

"Footprints," he said, "and they lead out of the garden."

"Do they belong to Simone or Simone's stalker?" Holly asked, biting the inside of her cheek.

"She said her stalker wore size ten boots," Callum said, inspecting the prints. "These were made by bare feet."

They followed the track marks and descended into a buckwheat meadow where the prints disappeared.

"What if she's in danger?" Holly asked. "We have to find her."

"Look," Callum said, dropping to his haunches. "The stalks are bent. Someone passed through here."

Following an uncertain path, they picked their way through the field, feeling the first drops of rain on their faces.

The buckwheat waved in the breeze as they waded toward a wooden stile set among the stones of a boundary wall. Callum clambered over, but Holly took her time, fearful of slipping on the wet steps. She held

CHAPTER THIRTY-FOUR

out her hand for Callum's assistance, but he had marched onward, propelled by the hunt.

Or the thought of Simone in peril.

Holly hurried after him.

"She could be anywhere," she shouted.

Callum turned, pressing a finger to his lips. As Holly reached him, he pointed to the horizon.

Simone's silhouette was caught between the bridge of a hill and the rolling grey clouds.

Holly leapt up and down, waving her arms. "Simone. Simone."

Callum grabbed Holly and wrestled her to the ground.

"We've found her," he said, "but what if her stalker is out here too?"

"Then we should warn her," Holly said.

"Or we could wait," Callum said, "and see if we can draw them out."

His stony face was in profile, his green eyes trained on the sky and the land, waiting for his prey to emerge.

Holly observed him carefully. "Simone could get hurt."

"I know."

"So we should help her."

"I am."

Rain washed down Holly's face, freezing it from her forehead to her chin. "By using her as bait?"

Callum shifted. Not by much. A tilt of the shoulder. An arch of the foot.

"I'm helping," Callum said, "by eliminating any and all threats to her."

The clouds rolled in darker and the birds fled to shaking boughs in the trees.

"Because I don't know what else to do," Callum added.

Holly had seen Callum like this before. He was an arrow with a target and nothing would get in his way. His aim was to protect; an instinct inherited from generations of his family. She hoped whoever was stalking Simone was ready for a fight.

Callum stiffened, the hairs on the back of his neck standing proud.

"What is it?" Holly asked.

The clouds sashayed over the horizon, like the curtains of a theatrical play in its final act.

The air grew colder.

Holly's breath crystallised in front of her.

Simone waited on the horizon, her lace dress floating on the breeze. She seemed unaware of the second figure. Her back was turned to his approach. It was a man with broad shoulders and a troubled face. He crept toward her, his pace quickening as he closed in.

"Get ready," Callum said, shuffling forward, his arms and legs braced for a sprint.

Holly's heart pattered with the irregular beat of the rain.

The stalker grew nearer, his arms stretching toward for her.

Unable to contain her panic any longer, Holly shouted. "Run."

But her voice was swallowed by the rain.

Unheeding, Simone spun toward the stranger.

Holly got to her feet.

"Run," she shouted again.

A shaft of light illuminated the stalker's face. Hector jogged to a stop in front of Simone. They embraced and he buried his face into her neck. Their arms found purchase in each other, their silhouettes melding into one.

Holly turned to Callum, her heartbreaking for him. "She's not as alone as we first thought."

Callum, as taut as a crossbow's string, hissed as the tension left his body. He shook the rain from his hair and buttoned his wax jacket tightly to his throat.

"I guess I waited too long to ask her on that date," he said.

Chapter Thirty-Five

"Why are you sitting out here?" Holly asked. "We said, we'd go to the pub."

The rain flattened her hair, plastering her wonky fringe to a troubled forehead.

Callum seemed immune to the latest deluge. He sat at the picnic table on the village green. The warmth of The Travelling Star was metres away and yet moving him toward it felt like rolling a rock uphill.

Rain trickled down his neck, soaking the collar of his shirt. His hair fell in choppy locks over an unhappy face.

"You're right. I'm being too emotional," he said, staring at the puddles gathering around his boots.

"We don't know what was happening on that ridge," Holly said. "It might be a friends thing."

"We meet up on the estate a lot, don't we?" Callum asked without looking at her. "And we both know what the village has to say about that. Most of them are waiting for a marriage proposal. Well, a divorce proposal first and then a marriage one."

"It doesn't mean they're right." Holly wiped her face dry, only to feel it dampen seconds later. "The point is, we don't know anything yet. We need to speak to Hector."

"About being Simone's boyfriend?" Callum asked. "Or are you more interested in his whereabouts on the night of the theft?"

Callum's words landed heavily and Holly felt each one. Of course, she was preoccupied with finding the thief. Mrs Masterly was relying on her. So was the village. Why would Callum throw that in her face?

"It makes you wonder though, doesn't it?" Holly asked no one in particular. "Why would they meet in such a desolate spot?"

"Why would anyone?" Callum asked. "To hide their relationship."

He retrieved a love token from his pocket. The doll was battered, its straw unwinding so what had once looked like Callum now looked like a mouse's nest.

"I thought this meant something," he said.

"What are you two doing out here?"

Mrs Winnow waded through the sodden village green, huddled under a polka dot umbrella.

"You'll catch a cold," she said.

Callum ran a finger around his wet shirt collar. "I've been out in worse."

"He's feeling down on himself," Holly said to Mrs Winnow.

A raven landed at Callum's feet. It hopped out of striking distance, but stared at him with its beady eyes.

"How did you and Mr Winnow meet?" Callum asked.

Mrs Winnow smiled, a faraway look in her eyes. "Oh, you don't want to hear about that, do you?"

Callum nodded, managing a smile himself.

"It wasn't long after the primary school burned down," Mrs Winnow said. "The place was a shell. They said it was an accident, but no one believed it. My dear husband-to-be was there as part of the clean-up crew. Of course, I liked the look of him the moment we met. Who wouldn't be attracted to a hunk like him? But it wasn't until later on that I knew he was the man for me."

"What were you doing there?" Callum asked.

CHAPTER THIRTY-FIVE

"I was running a mobile sandwich van," Mrs Winnow said. "I was selling egg and cress to the crew. They were a hungry bunch. I made a fortune. Anyway, one afternoon, I caught the love of my life loading school desks into the back of his van. They were only slightly singed. He said he could get good money for them."

"Kindred spirits, eh?" Holly asked.

"That, and he had a back end like two avocados in a bag," Mrs Winnow said.

Holly wasn't sure if that meant Mr Winnow's bum was green and dimply or if it was overpriced. It didn't matter, she supposed. They had found each other.

Mrs Winnow was lost in her smile as the rain beat against her umbrella, sounding like a roar of applause.

"Affairs of the heart," she said. "When they work, they work, but they're not easy to navigate."

"Especially for someone who has avoided them his entire life," Callum said.

"Come to the shop, dear. I'll make you a nice cup of tea."

Callum checked his pockets, finding them empty. "I'm sorry. I don't have any money."

Mrs Winnow brushed the hair from his eyes and tenderly cupped his chin in her hand.

"Don't be so silly, dear," she said. "I can see you're hurting. You can pay me later."

Inside the convenience store, Mr Winnow sat behind his counter, his fingers laced over a round stomach. His wife whispered into his ear while stealing glances at Callum.

"I'm going to disappear upstairs," Mrs Winnow said. "I need to touch up my roots and this feels like a man-to-man conversation, doesn't it?"

Holly watched her go, wondering if she should touch up her roots too.

Callum joined Mr Winnow next to a stand selling out-of-date marshmallows.

"Now what's all this about a broken heart?" Mr Winnow said.

"It's my own fault," Callum said. "I was led down the wrong path."

Mr Winnow cocked his head to the side. "That's hard to believe, mate. You're the best tracker on the estate. You'd never go anywhere without a good reason."

Holly lingered by the doorway.

Opening a bag of marshmallows, Mr Winnow popped one into his mouth and chewed thoughtfully. "I've seen a new face in the village. Beautiful, young thing, she is."

"She's not just a pretty face. She knows all about folklore, about nature and about plants," Callum said.

Mr Winnow swallowed the remnants of his marshmallow and resealed the packet, putting it back on display to sell. "Well, she sounds great. You know, who else is great? Our own Holly here."

Twitching at the sound of her name, Holly faced the two men, suddenly nervous.

"She was in here the other day," Mr Winnow continued. "Looking for some way to - "

"I'm going to buy some biscuits," Holly said, louder than she'd expected. It drew Mr Winnow's attention and he thankfully shut up.

"Simone and I were getting on really well," Callum said, clearly lost in his own thoughts. "I even saved her life. I stopped her from eating a poisonous mushroom, but I blew it in the end."

Mr Winnow cleared his throat. "I thought you said she knew about nature and stuff. What was she doing eating a poisonous mushroom?"

"She - " But Callum faltered in his response.

Holly put down the biscuits and walked to the counter.

As her shadow fell over Callum, he gathered himself and sat higher in his seat. "Well, panther caps, I mean, they look like a lot of other mushrooms. The blusher mushroom, for instance. Angel parasols..."

Simone claimed to be an expert, Holly thought. She certainly behaved as if she was, but how reliable could she be when her knowledge stemmed from folklore and old wives' tales? Putting her scepticism aside, Holly had always struggled to take Simone seriously and here was the evidence.

Callum pushed from the counter and wandered the shop shelves. They were stacked with a collection of tourist oddities. Callum's fingers walked over the Northumbrian fudge, the cottages carved from coal and the sheaves of yellowed maps.

"Simone didn't know the mushrooms were poisonous. She hadn't even known not to eat something she couldn't identify," Callum said. "Everyone knows that. Even Holly."

"Are we sure it was a mistake?" Holly asked.

Callum looked up from the maps. "What else could it have been?"

Rubbing his temples, he looked as if he was suffering from the first pangs of a headache.

"Are you okay?" Mr Winnow asked. "Should I get the wife?"

"I'll survive."

"Listen, everyone drops a clanger from time to time," Mr Winnow said. "Maybe she was trying to impress you. Maybe she likes you more than you think."

Callum breathed deeply. "She wrote me some poems."

He took the straw doll from his pocket and placed it on the counter for Mr Winnow. "She hid them in these love tokens."

Mr Winnow's eyes went from Callum to the doll and finally to Holly, whose heart threatened to stop.

He burst out laughing. "Simone said this was a love token? I'm sorry, mate, but I don't think this girl is as bright as you think she is."

"Oh, no," Holly whispered to herself.

183

"Don't tell me she was wrong about that as well?" Callum asked.

Mr Winnow grinned at Holly. If he registered the rictus of terror on her face, he didn't show it. He had no idea he was about to drop a clanger of his own.

"Remember when I said our Holly was in here?" he asked Callum. "That she was a lovely girl?"

Holly panicked and grasped at her clothes. "This isn't the right time."

Chewing his lip, Callum let out a slight nod.

"She was writing a piece about how entrepreneurs were dealing with the downturn in business," Mr Winnow continued. "She did one with Big Gregg and his 'Mamma Mia' evenings. Anyway, she came to interview us."

"What's this got to do with Simone?" Callum asked.

"Nothing. That's what I'm telling you." Mr Winnow picked up the straw doll and examined its structure. "I made hundreds of these and Holly bought into the game."

"You made them?" Callum asked, the tone of his voice higher than usual. He turned to Holly. "You sent me poems?"

Holly held up her hands. "Not exactly."

"They're part of a treasure hunt, a game, that runs all over the estate," Mr Winnow said, grinning. "Good idea, isn't it? The first doll is posted to you and the clue is inside the doll."

"The poem?"

"No, the clue," Mr Winnow said. "I wrote them."

Callum rubbed his brow. "*Home is where the heart is,*" he said, quoting the first clue. "How does it work? Simone gave me the second doll."

"The first clue leads to the second."

Callum groaned inwardly. "She found it on my doorstep. At my home."

"Which leads you to the Witches' Hall, if I remember correctly."

"I found that doll," Holly said, remembering the *Holly Loves Callum*

CHAPTER THIRTY-FIVE

note inside. She had yet to discuss Mr Winnow's joke, assuming it was one. Why would he write something that could cause so much disruption?

Holly hadn't told Callum about the note and she wasn't going to do it now.

"All this time," Callum said to Holly, his voice low. "You knew about these bloody dolls all this time."

"It's a splendid gift," Mr Winnow said. "We even put cameras everywhere so we know people don't cheat. No expense spared."

Callum wasn't listening. He was focused on Holly and her increasingly red face.

"He said, it was a game," Holly said. Her words were impeding her breathing and she forced herself to calm down. "I thought you would appreciate it as a tracker and a huntsman."

"But I didn't know I was taking part in a treasure hunt, did I?" Callum answered slowly. "I thought I was receiving love notes."

"I didn't know, either," Holly said, raising a finger. "Simone said they were love tokens. Not me. I clearly stated otherwise. I thought you'd get a map and some clues. I didn't know Mr Winnow would use creepy dolls. I mean, one of them had a noose around its neck."

She turned to Mr Winnow, who withered under Holly's questioning glare.

"I found a spare bit of string," he said with a shrug. "Thought it might add a bit of drama, you know?"

"As if we need any more of that around here," Callum said, cracking his knuckles.

"I didn't make the link until Simone showed me the notes," Holly said. "By then, it felt like it was too late to say anything."

She lowered her head, unable to watch the pain in Callum's eyes any longer. It was the one thing she had tried to avoid, but things had spiralled out of control, as they often did when Holly tried to do a good thing.

Callum was her friend, her companion. He'd understand, wouldn't he? They'd be okay. All Holly had to do was explain. It was a simple mistake, something she could correct if -

The door to the shop opened and closed. When Holly looked up from the floor, she saw Callum marching down the high street without her.

Chapter Thirty-Six

"What's going on?" Holly asked, racing after him.

It seemed like a simple question, or so she thought.

Callum spun on his heel. A look flashed over his face. It darkened his eyes and there was almost a snarl to his lips. Holly remembered the first thing she'd ever heard about Callum. Before they'd met, she'd gone looking for him with a warning ringing in her head. He's half-feral, they'd said. He lived alone for a reason.

Holly had never believed it until now.

"If there's a problem," she said, "we can talk about it."

Grey clouds thundered over Little Belton, causing the windows to shake in the homes of its residents. They crept to their doors or parted their curtains for a better view of the disturbance. Holly felt their eyes on her and she folded under their gaze.

Callum didn't. He stood in the village green, up to his ankles in water, fixing Holly with a gaze of his own.

There was no lightning to the thunder, but Holly feared it was on its way.

Callum stamped the water-logged ground. "Am I a joke to you?"

"Of course not."

"Then why do you treat me as if I am?"

Callum threw a straw doll at Holly's feet. It splashed into a puddle, bobbing like a lifebuoy. The water soaked into its innards and if the doll had had arms, Holly was sure they'd be signalling for help.

He pointed at its struggling form. "We sat in your kitchen. We talked about those things and you never said a word to me."

A beady-eyed raven swooped down from the rooftop and snatched the doll in its beak. Hopping to freedom, it took to the air, taking Holly's mistake with it.

"What do you want me to say?" Holly asked, watching the raven disappear. "I didn't know the treasure hunt was inside the straw dolls. I mean, they're so creepy. It was supposed to be a kindness."

"You could have told the truth," Callum said, thumping his thigh with a fist. "You set me up. I looked like a fool."

Holly left the shadow of the buildings and entered the village green as if it was a boxing ring. The rain turned her hair into stringy ropes.

"I wasn't trying to hurt you," she said.

"I know exactly what you were doing." Callum circled her, the air around him gathering like a mini storm of its own. "You didn't want me to like Simone. You wanted me for yourself."

The words cut into her and suddenly Holly was circling Callum, taking on the role of a prizefighter as she looked to land her first punch. She didn't like Callum's tone and she didn't like his insinuation.

"That's ridiculous," Holly shouted. "You're believing your own gossip."

Callum raised himself up. "You never accepted Simone. You were jealous of her from the very start."

Holly's mouth fell open. She staggered to the edge of the green.

The crowd in their doorways waited, ready for a counterblow from Holly.

Mr and Mrs Winnow stood outside of their shop, arm in arm, their faces painted in worry. Big Gregg danced nervously by his open door, as if expecting to be tagged into the fight. Faces she didn't recognise grinned in anticipation. This was what they wanted. A juicy fight. A lover's tiff. Anything to add to the continued legend of Holly and Callum's relationship.

But Holly demurred. This wasn't what she wanted.

"I don't know what you're talking about," she said, clasping her hands, holding them as if she was about to pray. "I admit our relationship looks skewed from the outside, but we know what it is, don't we? I respect you, care for you and I only want the best for you."

"So why did you make me think Simone liked me?"

Holly swallowed, but the lump in her throat refused to budge. "She does like you. Anyone can see that. Including me."

Callum wiped his face and studied his wet hands. "Then why was she on the estate with someone else? I thought these dolls were love tokens. There were poems inside. I thought Simone gave them to me."

Holly fought down a sigh. "I bought the treasure hunt to amuse you. There wasn't much happening in Little Belton at the time. You're the world's best tracker. I thought you'd enjoy it. Honestly, I thought you'd have it wrapped up by lunch."

"But why didn't you say something?" Callum asked.

"Because events superseded my intentions. The village was suddenly plunged into potential ruin. We had to find a cabinet and rescue Black Rock Manor."

"It would have taken a simple word," Callum said. "Five minutes of your time."

The moral high ground shifted under Holly's feet. In an argument with Derek, she would have strived to regain it. With Callum, her friend, it was different.

"I knew what the dolls were and I knew they weren't important," Holly said, speaking into her chest. "At least not to me. I didn't realise how important they were to you. I'm sorry."

"Me too."

Holly approached Callum and held his hand. It was wet with rain, but warm in her grasp. "I disregard a lot of what you say because I think it's nonsense. The tall stories. The permissions. It's unfair of me, but do you think I'd stand in the way of your happiness?"

The thunder rolled by. The black skies were replaced with grey, promising a cessation in the rain.

Callum squeezed Holly's hand, forcing water through the gaps in their fingers. "I couldn't ask her out. Even though I knew - thought I knew - Simone liked me. It's like I don't want my own satisfaction."

"You were nervous. You have your insecurities in the same way we all do." Holly leaned onto her toes and lifted her face to Callum, kissing him on his cheek. "Which is nuts because you're gorgeous."

"But I'm also awkward, stilted and according to you, I come from the nineteen-thirties."

"You fell for the wrong girl, that's all, and just so you know, Hector isn't as handsome as you. Forget about him."

Holly recognised the cough of her car as it trundled along the high street. Derek was back and Holly was pleased to see him, although he could have timed it better.

Tumbling from the car, Derek got to his feet and stretched his back.

"Glad I'm back from my research trip?" he asked.

"Absolutely," Holly said.

With Derek's arrival, the Little Belton residents lost interest. They detected the fight had been postponed and the show had come to a close. And besides, *Antiques Roadshow* was about to start.

"What are you doing out in the rain?" Derek asked Holly and Callum.

Callum jammed his hands into his pockets. "Getting wet."

Derek hauled a rucksack from the boot of the car. "I thought you'd be on the estate. You know, searching for stuff."

"Why are you here? Why didn't you go straight home?" Holly asked.

"I'd heard the Winnows are selling a treasure hunt. I thought I might

CHAPTER THIRTY-SIX

give it a go. Sounds like fun."

Holly glanced at Callum, who had a pained smile on his face.

"Did you find anything out while you were away?" Holly asked.

He rummaged through his rucksack and produced a manila file. "It's all in there. Oh, and I bumped into Mrs Masterly on the way over here."

"Is she okay?" Callum asked.

He'd only been away for a night, Holly thought. Certainly not long enough to justify the rucksack full of clothes Derek was grappling back into the car.

"I also bought you a few gifts," Derek said, slamming the boot closed. "They're in my bag for whenever you're ready."

Holly glowed. "Thank you."

"Is Mrs Masterly okay?" Callum asked again.

Derek smoothed down the wet strands of his balding head. "No, I don't think she is."

"Come on," Holly said, waving the file at Callum. "We can read this on the way to Black Rock Manor. We better check on Mrs Masterly."

She made to move, but Callum stood still.

"Why do I feel like I'm always in the dark?" he asked. "What's in the file?"

Holly shoved it under her coat, fearful it would get wet in the rain. "Sorry. Again. I forgot to mention it. I sent Derek undercover. He's been doing some research."

"So what are you keeping from me this time?" Callum asked.

"I'm hoping it will be a missing cabinet."

Chapter Thirty-Seven

The journey to the manor was short and silent, save for Holly's voice as she read the contents of the file to Callum. When she finished, she slapped the file shut and they stared at the road. It was the same route they always took, but Holly fancied new dangers were lurking ahead, and she didn't know what to do about them.

Parking by the front door of the manor, the roar of machinery brought Holly and Callum to the rear garden. They found Mrs Masterly in the grounds dressed in a frilly blouse and pencil skirt. She also wore a safety mask and leather gloves. Her feet were swallowed in a pile of leaves and in her hands was a chainsaw.

Mrs Masterly raised it above her head and swung it at the ivy climbing the side of the manor.

Callum surged forward, wrestling it from her grip.

"You could take off your arm," he said, cutting the engine and casting the chainsaw aside. "What do you think you're doing?"

Mrs Masterly flipped up the plastic visor protecting her face. "I'm taking care of a problem."

"By re-enacting the *Texas Chainsaw Massacre*?" Holly asked. "Callum's right. You could have hurt yourself."

The ivy she'd demolished gathered around her feet and Mrs Masterly kicked it, sending a flurry of torn leaves into the air. "I rely on your

CHAPTER THIRTY-SEVEN

kindness too much. Despite my appearances, I am not a doll to be mollycoddled."

Holly and Callum looked at each other. The mention of dolls made them both uneasy, but Holly had to admit Mrs Masterly had a point. She was a grown woman capable of making her own decisions.

Mrs Masterly continued. "And if I choose to use a chainsaw, an instrument I have never used before, to do a job I have never attempted before, then I'll do just that. How hard could it be?"

Judging by the expression on Callum's face, his unease had doubled and he stared warily at the chainsaw.

"Please let me do this for you," he said.

"You have more important things to do. We have to find Greyston's cabinet before it's too late." Mrs Masterly removed her safety helmet, revealing a kink in her otherwise perfect hair. "Now, I have a fear that Mr Xavier is just around the corner. It won't be long before he makes an unexpected visit. He calls me constantly. I don't answer, of course. I just stand there, listening to the phone."

Callum inspected the chainsaw's blade. "This guy is really starting to annoy me now."

"But he's gone now," Holly said.

Thunder rippled through the clouds, followed by a white streak of lightning.

"Am I?" Mr Xavier appeared from around the manor. He hobbled toward them but stopped when the ground became too wet. He leaned on his walking cane, his camel-hair coat flapping in the wind behind him. "I'm here for the cabinet."

Dropping the chainsaw, Callum jumped forward, his hands reaching for Mr Xavier.

For once, Holly was quicker. She grabbed Callum's wax jacket, bringing him to a stop.

"What do you want?" Holly asked Mr Xavier, reigning Callum in like an angry toddler.

He paced the ground, limping with each step. "I've been thinking about our problem."

Holly frowned. "Our problem?"

"In order to receive your grant, I need to see the cabinet. I know you need the money so that's the problem we have, don't you think?"

As the rain dribbled down Holly's neck, she waited, knowing Mr Xavier was hoping for a chance to explain himself, and she didn't have long to wait.

"The problem is," he explained, "your lack of money and my wish to see the cabinet should be mutually beneficial. Mrs Masterly won't let me see the cabinet, which leads me to assume there is a problem with it."

"Maybe she just thinks you're an idiot," Callum said.

Mrs Masterly tutted loudly. "We don't insult our guests, Callum. No matter how odious their behaviour."

Mr Xavier nodded with a smile. "You don't like me so you're willing to lose thousands and thousands of pounds? To lose your home? All I want is for you to agree to my proposal. That's not wrong, is it?"

"You have a creepy way of going about it," Holly said.

"I'm overzealous," Mr Xavier said, "and I apologise. That's my problem, not yours."

"And you lied to us," Callum said. "The cabinet belongs to an occultist. It's decorated in devils and demons."

Mr Xavier raised his hands in defence. "I did it to protect you. People are uncomfortable around such things and I didn't want you to get into a fluster. You might have sold the cabinet elsewhere and I'd be back to square one.

"You're right. Alistair Greyston was accused of practising the dark arts. It was claimed he went missing to spend time with witches and imps and such like. The truth was, he was a radical. He saw myths and

CHAPTER THIRTY-SEVEN

legends as being as integral to our collective identity as any regimented religion."

"Is that why he was placed on trial?" Holly asked, wishing she wasn't intrigued.

"And why he was hanged," Mr Xavier said.

Holly shuddered and sneaked a glance at Mrs Masterly's wan face. "Tragedy does follow this cabinet around."

"If you believe in such things," Mr Xavier said with a knowing look.

"With the cabinet at the manor," Holly said, "you could blackmail Mrs Masterly into allowing you access."

"Forced her to stick to our agreement," Mr Xavier corrected, "but you're basically correct. I've waited a long time to see this cabinet in the flesh. I may never have this kind of leverage again."

Mr Xavier trailed his walking cane through the leaves on the ground. His eyes followed the ivy snaking up the manor walls. They hopped from branch to branch like a bird in search of an abandoned nest, only stopping when he saw the crumbling hole where a robin sat and sang a high-pitched song.

"Which brings us back to our problem," Mr Xavier said. "The only reason you wouldn't let me see the cabinet is that you don't have it."

Mrs Masterly's laugh was shrill and unconvincing. "Of course we have it."

"You did have it," Mr Xavier said. "I called Mr Charleston. It was definitely delivered here. The question is... do you still have it? Judging by that hole in the wall, I'd say you've had some unwelcome visitors."

The accusation was heavy in the air. Holly wanted to speak but didn't know what to say.

"The cabinet is upstairs," Callum said. "Locked away."

"Before I found you here, I thought you might be indoors. I knocked and when I didn't get an answer, I tried the door and walked straight in. No locks, no alarms. Anyone that blasé about personal security could easily fall victim to a theft."

He searched their faces. Holly felt his eyes on her, scouring her, making her feel unclean. When he turned his attention to Mrs Masterly, she withered. But when he glanced at Callum, it was Mr Xavier who looked away first.

"It's very disappointing," Mr Xavier said. "If I can't study the cabinet, then its goodbye to the grant and no investment for Little Belton's future. Still, it can't be helped. As you find my company so repugnant, I'll leave you to your gardening."

He smiled, but it was so narrow, it barely made it past his thick beard. Mr Xavier hobbled on his cane, his injured leg dragging through the tall grass until he disappeared around the corner of the manor.

"He knows," Mrs Masterly said, her voice trembling. "He knows the cabinet is missing."

Very disappointing. The words circled around Holly's head like cartoon birds after a fall. Very disappointing.

Callum started the chainsaw, plunging the rotating blade into the trunk of the ivy. Sawdust sprayed in clouds, coating him in powdery chippings. The groan of the saw changed pitch and Callum turned it off.

"I've cut through the trunk. That will kill the ivy," he said, dusting himself clean. "Give it a few weeks and it will be weak enough for me to take down."

"Aren't you listening to me?" Mrs Masterly asked. "Mr Xavier knows the cabinet was stolen."

"Of course, he knows. Didn't you hear him?" Holly asked, blood thumping in her ears. "*Very disappointing.* This man has chased Greyston all his life. He was within spitting distance of the cabinet for the first time and when it's snatched from under his nose, *very disappointing* is all he can say? He walked out of here without a care in the world."

CHAPTER THIRTY-SEVEN

"What are you saying?" Callum asked.

Holly jammed her hands on her hips, taking on the pose of a superhero saviour. "He knows it was stolen because he was the one who stole it."

Chapter Thirty-Eight

Now all we need to do is prove it, Holly thought to herself.

Added to that was the further complication of Hector's involvement. Her gut told her he was involved and there was a lot of evidence stacked against him. Hector knew about the cabinet. He had money problems. He'd been missing for days and they still had no idea where he was.

Mr Xavier had denied knowing him, but that was proof of nothing. They could still be working together. Or was Mr Xavier exploiting Hector's empty bank account for his own needs?

If Mr Xavier was the thief, he was being incredibly bold by staying in the area, but it also meant something else. The cabinet was close by. A man as preoccupied with Greyston as Mr Xavier would not stray far from his precious prize. The best solution seemed to be to follow him and hope Mr Xavier led them to the cabinet.

There was a lot of ground to cover and Holly and Callum had decided to split up. Callum had opted to prowl the estate. It was his natural habitat and he stood a better chance of tracking Mr Xavier among the moors.

Holly had said nothing. It was a silly idea. The estate was much too large in which to find a single man, but Callum had been adamant. They had bickered and Holly grew suspicious of Callum's true motivations.

Meanwhile, Holly had taken the easier option of hanging outside of

CHAPTER THIRTY-EIGHT

The Travelling Star, waiting for Mr Xavier to emerge.

And she had been proven right.

Who was the tracker now, she wondered?

By the time Mr Xavier had finally left the pub, water had pooled in her shoes. Folded into a nearby doorway, she watched Mr Xavier stumble along the high street. He adjusted the yellow and black rucksack over his shoulder and walked into the Winnows' convenience store.

Holly waited and Mr Xavier returned to the high street, plunging through the soggy village green, taking a right down Stationer's Lane. Holly followed, veiled by the grey drizzle of the rain.

Mr Xavier soon passed the outskirts of the village. He studied the contours of the land before clambering over a wooden stile into a field. The ground was saturated and difficult to navigate. His walking cane sank frequently, leaving him staggering for purchase.

Righting himself, he marched onward to Black Rock Manor.

Holly kept close, ignoring the rasping sounds of her lungs as she gasped for breath. Spending time outdoors didn't make her outdoorsy. Her fitness levels had declined with her increase in weight, and although she'd sworn off her damaging biscuit habit, it was taking time for her body to catch up.

Mr Xavier stopped at the Witches' Hall to inspect the charred poplar tree. He kicked over what remained of the bonfire, running a hand through his glossy beard.

Holly had examined the site many times. She was certain there was nothing left to find.

Mr Xavier lingered. Sheltering under the tree, he retrieved a notepad and pen from his rucksack and looked in the manor's direction. As he made an entry, his hand froze and his eyes scoured the building.

What was he seeing, Holly wondered? The same hallucination she had seen? Mr Xavier didn't believe in the bathing of the Green Man, but he was well-educated in the ways of the occult. Perhaps some ghoul had risen from its grave? Or was he reciting a spell from his notebook?

As the fanciful notions swam about her head, Holly realised how little she knew about Mr Xavier. She had the file Derek had prepared for her. It was filled with information gleaned from censuses and polls, and from the thousand other ways the internet kept track of people these days. It didn't speak of the man, however. Or how unhinged he may prove to be.

Either way, Holly wasn't prepared to allow Mr Xavier near Mrs Masterly again. She crept closer, ready to stop him trying.

Mr Xavier zipped his notes into his rucksack and when Holly thought he was about to march on the manor, he proceeded in another direction.

Holly rubbed her knees.

"Where are you going?" she asked herself.

They continued through the estate, one hopping over sedge grass, the other shadowing him closely. The only other entity present was Long Robert, making himself known by turning the drizzle into horizontal lashings of rain.

The effect was disorientating. The grey sky melted into a grey landscape. Traversing the nondescript field shielded by a curtain of rain, Holly discovered she was lost. There was one guiding light, that of Mr Xavier's stripy yellow rucksack wheeling ahead of her. She kept her eyes fixed on it. With no Callum to save her, she was in danger of finding herself adrift.

The incline steepened and Holly's already aching knees ached further. Her breath shortened. She pulled on handfuls of grass to drag her ailing body up the gradient. The ground grew rocky and there was drumming inside of her head.

The rain melted into a fine mist before stopping altogether.

Mr Xavier washed his face in the pool beneath Juniper Falls, casting furtive glances at Simone's bothy. Smoke curled from its chimney and a light glowed in its windows.

CHAPTER THIRTY-EIGHT

Mr Xavier ducked behind a rock, stashing his rucksack out of sight. Holly ducked too, rolling behind a juniper bush for cover. She waited, unsure what she was waiting for. Steeling her nerves, she peeked through the thorny branches to see Callum staring at her as he approached the bothy.

Chapter Thirty-Nine

Callum beckoned her closer and Holly fell through the bushes, the thorns tearing strips from her clothing. Staggering to her feet, she examined her coat and trousers to see they had been reduced to confetti. Holly tidied herself up as best she could. Rather than running to Callum's side, she rushed to the rock where Mr Xavier was hiding.

"Got you," she shouted.

But Mr Xavier wasn't there. He'd disappeared, leaving behind a single footprint. Holly examined it and guessed it to be a size ten; the same size of boot belonging to Simone's stalker.

"What are you doing?" Callum hissed from Simone's front door.

Holly walked around the rock, scratching her head. There was no doubt Mr Xavier was gone, but Holly couldn't figure out where he'd gone to, unless he'd crawled back under the rock, of course.

Perplexed, Holly joined Callum at the bothy.

"Can you stop being weird for just a second?" he asked, picking stray ribbons of coat from her shoulders. "This is serious."

"What are you doing here?" Holly asked. "You were supposed to searching for Mr Xavier."

"I did," Callum said. "For a while."

"Well, you did a fantastic job," Holly said. "He was ten feet away from you and you saw nothing."

CHAPTER THIRTY-NINE

There was a sharpness to her tone she didn't like, but Holly felt hurt. They were trying to help Mrs Masterly, who was in turn trying to rescue a floundering village. They were a team, working together for the common good. How dare Callum betray that.

And then she remembered Callum's broken heart and how she was partially to blame.

"Would you like me to go?" Holly asked. "So you and Simone can talk things through?"

Callum knocked on the bothy door. "I'm not here for that. I'm here to get my hands on Hector."

Simone greeted Callum with a smile. She wore a cheesecloth dress, the hem fluttering around her thighs like butterflies. She carried a raffia trug in the crook of her arm filled with wild strawberries. Her smile stiffened as she studied Callum's earnest face.

"You looked pained," Simone said. "Can I help you with something?"

"Just being neighbourly," Holly said.

Simone's eyes travelled up and down Holly's tattered attire.

"Did you know it was the ancient Egyptians who invented scarecrows?" Simone asked.

Holly picked out a twig from her hair.

"How fascinating," she said through a clenched jaw.

The rain had paused and the sky was threatening to turn blue. Birds emerged from their hiding places and went in search of food.

"Could we come inside?" Callum asked.

"I'm making tinctures," Simone said. "Come with me to the garden."

They followed her to where the old ruins had been transformed into a walled garden. Stepping through the herbs, Holly listened to the buzz of insects flitting from flower to flower.

"What's this herb?" Callum asked. "I've seen nothing like it before." He pointed at a plant with a crown of blade-like leaves.

"That's savoury. I use it to flavour pork pies and turkey stuffing,"

Simone said.

Holly was suddenly hungry.

"And if I mix it with rose oil," Simone continued. "I can ease singing noises of the ear."

"What's that when it's at home?" Holly asked.

Simone plucked a cornflower from the garden and brought it to her nose to smell. "Tinnitus, I expect. Most of my learning is from medieval texts and they aren't too specific."

Callum hurriedly moved on. "What about this one? I haven't seen it before."

"Mugwort. It's a herb of Venus, the goddess of love. It's used to take the heat out of a woman's blood, if you know what I mean?"

Holly had never heard of a person having hot blood, unnaturally hot, that is. Blood was supposed to be warm, wasn't it? Judging by the way Simone was looking at Callum, with her soft gaze and playful smile, Holly guessed he'd be the one needing mugwort.

"You seem to know a lot about this stuff," Holly said.

"My medicine might be old-fashioned, but it doesn't make it wrong," Simone said.

"Doesn't make it better either," Holly said. "You were quite happy to be treated at the hospital."

"After Callum treated me with charcoal. Just like my ancestors might have done."

"Holly is right on this one," Callum said.

Without the clouds, the garden was bathed in sunlight. The heat had been absent for so long, Holly was shocked to feel it on her skin.

"These herbs don't work," Callum said.

Simone's mouth dropped open.

So did Holly's. Her friend was being uncharacteristically harsh.

"You can put them in teas or make salads with them," Callum continued, flexing and unflexing his fists, "but don't expect them to cure cancer."

Simone rubbed a hand down her face. "I've studied this for years. Researched it. Lived my life by it. I know what I'm talking about."

"No one knows what you're talking about," Callum said.

Holly came forward. "Don't be so snipey. We're guests, remember?"

The lines around Simone's eyes deepened as she focused on Callum. "Is that why you're here? To tell me I'm a fool?"

"Oh, there's only one fool around here and that's me," Callum said.

Holly sidled in between Callum and Simone, sensing the sparks flying off them might start a fire. "That's not why we're here at all. In fact, when I arrived here, I discovered something you need to know."

"My dad taught me about the old ways, using the land to treat yourself," Callum continued, "but he was clear on one thing. Hospitals outrank salad every time." He grabbed a plant, yanking it from the ground and presented it to Simone. "This will kill you, if you're not careful. Just like those mushrooms you ate."

"Stop it," Holly said, jabbing a finger into Callum's chest. "Why are you being like this?"

The question hung in the air, next to the bees flying from flower to flower.

Callum returned his attention to Simone and, to his credit, tried to compose himself. "If you're all knowledgeable, you would have known those mushrooms were panther caps. You would have known they could kill you."

"But you were there to save me," Simone said, setting her trug on the ground. She opened her arms, beckoning Callum toward her.

"That's what everyone wants, isn't it?" he asked. "They want Callum to save them, protect them. Do the heavy lifting, but what about what I want? When do I get something from you?"

"I'm here now," Simone whispered.

"But where were you yesterday?" Callum asked.

Holly's heart beat faster. Callum's behaviour made sense. The pain of his rejection had taken over his sense of duty; an occurrence Holly thought she'd never witness.

Simone's lips trembled. She searched the garden, as if her answer to Callum's accusations lay among her dangerous herbs.

"Why did you say the straw dolls were love tokens?" Callum asked. "Was it for the same reason you think these herbs are magical? Or that there really is a celebration called the Bathing of the Green Man?"

"Why are you being so mean?" Simone asked.

"We saw you on the estate," Callum said. "You were with Hector. You were… hugging."

Simone's chin trembled. "Have you been following me?"

"We'd came here to ask you about a tincture Hector had with him," Callum said. "You would have known all about it because I realise now you made it for him. Anything to soothe his weary body, eh?"

Simone took a step backwards. "I met him while I was working with Mr Charleston. Hector is a friend. The same as you and Holly are friends. Of course I wanted to help him."

"You and Hector are not like us," Callum said. "Hector hasn't been seen in days. He's on the run."

"What are you saying?" Simone asked.

"Hector is involved with the cabinet. He has gambling debts. He needs the money."

Simone laughed. "He's the sweetest man. There's no way he would commit a crime."

"Unless he was desperate," Callum said.

Simone's cheer didn't last long. Holly saw the doubt in her eyes. Simone was asking questions of Hector in the same way Callum was.

She pressed her hands to her cheeks. "He stole the cabinet?"

"And there's something else," Holly added. "You said someone was stalking you, coming to the bothy when you were on your own. You

CHAPTER THIRTY-NINE

were right. It's Mr Xavier."

"What?" Simone and Callum asked in unison.

"I followed him here and I'd be willing to bet it's not the first time he's paid you a visit."

Simone sat on a wall of the ruined building, gathering the hem of her dress tightly around her knees. "But why?"

Derek's file was tucked into the back of Holly's trousers, safe from the rain, but it felt to Holly as if it wanted to be outside.

"We were hoping you might tell us," she said.

Simone's face was blank, her body still. Even the wind had dropped.

"I do not know why Mr Xavier would be here," Simone said. "He's the grant assessor. That's all I know about him."

Holly glanced at Callum's baffled face.

"You don't know him at all?" she asked Simone.

"No, and I don't want to, especially if he's coming to my home. This is where I centre myself. No one comes to my domicile without me being here. I don't feel safe, otherwise."

The parallel between Simone and Mrs Masterly couldn't have been clearer. Both women, both unsure in their own homes. It left an acrid taste in Holly's mouth, but that wasn't what was troubling her at that moment. It was the file and the pages in between.

She saw Callum about to broach the subject and Holly elbowed him in the ribs, quickly shaking her head.

"Perhaps it's nothing," Holly said. "I'll speak to Mr Xavier as soon as I see him. I'll clear it up."

"Am I secure out here on my own?" Simone asked. "And what about Hector? Do I need to worry about him?"

"There's a link between Hector and Mr Xavier," Callum said. "I just can't see it yet."

Simone chewed on a fingertip. "Hector is always talking about money. Always devising ways of coming up with more and it's not about clearing his gambling debts. He said, he'd like to be the kind of person who owns a manor like Mrs Masterly. Even if it was just a small piece of it."

"A small piece like a cabinet?" Holly asked.

The clouds rolled over the sun, casting them in shadow and Holly noticed the buzz of the insects dying to a hush.

"Maybe," Simone said, her eyes glistening.

Holly took out the file and drummed her fingers upon it. There were too many secrets surrounding the cabinet, as if it was forcing those in its orbit to lie. Simone was lying. Mr Xavier was definitely lying. Even Holly had lied to protect Callum from the truth regarding the straw dolls. The situation stank worse than her walking boots after a day of marching through the damp estate.

It had to stop. She had to draw the liars together and expose them for what they were. It was time to discover the truth.

"Tell us where Hector is," Holly said to Simone, her jaw setting like stone.

Simone blinked and clasped her hands. "Why?"

"Because if he's not careful, the men he owes money to will be the least of his problems," Holly said.

Chapter Forty

Callum insisted on remaining with Simone. The mention of Mr Xavier and the potential danger Simone was in had stoked his ire. He'd clearly forgotten about discovering her with another man.

He'd stationed himself outside of her front door, perhaps hoping for some sort of reconciliation.

Simone had also seemed to have forgotten about their spat. She had readily agreed to Callum guarding her. Perhaps her fear had overruled her indignation and Holly couldn't blame her for that, but what they had both appeared to have forgotten was that Holly now had to walk home alone.

She tramped through the fields. The sun was swallowed by clouds as it journeyed toward the horizon. What little light there was started to fade and Holly wondered if she'd ever be able to figure out what had happened to the cabinet.

But with Mr Xavier roaming the estate, she currently had bigger concerns. It wasn't safe to be alone on the moors right now and she quickened her pace toward home.

The shadows began to lengthen, their dark hands grappling for Holly's ankles as she staggered over the rough terrain. The ground was soft, sucking at her boots.

Forcing herself to keep moving, she passed the track leading to the cold shores of Knock Lake. She paused, toying with the shredded remains of her coat.

Mr Xavier was standing with the lake lapping at his shoes. He was watching her, alternating his gaze from Holly and her home.

Holly's exhaustion disappeared. She didn't want Mr Xavier anywhere near her cottage. She didn't even like to think of him knowing where it was. Her eyes narrowed as he marched toward it with confidence, his strides lengthening the closer he came.

"Where are you going?" Holly shouted.

Mr Xavier came to a halt, but didn't turn around. "I was wondering when you were going to make your presence known."

Holly jogged to his side, regretting it when she developed a stitch.

"I wasn't following you," she said between splutters.

"Of course you weren't," Mr Xavier said, shaking the rain from his beard, "but you followed me to that waterfall, didn't you? I used to be a tracker, like Callum's father. I could have returned the favour, but I thought I'd simply wait for you to make your way home."

"Do you want to speak to me?" Holly asked, wishing Callum was by her side.

Mr Xavier's coat billowed in the breeze. He tapped his walking cane against his leg. The clicking sound echoed around the valley. "No, I'm simply a citizen out for a stroll."

"So am I," Holly said, hoping he didn't hear the tremor in her voice.

Mr Xavier pointed toward the lake. "Did you know Knock Lake was once known by a different name?"

Holly nodded. "It was called Murder Lake. They used to drown witches there."

"You're right," Mr Xavier said with a grin. "Thankfully, that practice has long since been outlawed, but I wonder how many unidentified skeletons lie on its bed? Personally, I wouldn't like to guess or to live anywhere near it, would you?"

CHAPTER FORTY

The question felt like a threat and Holly's heart beat faster.

"I inherited the cottage from my parents," she said, needing to explain herself.

As the words escaped, her childhood nightmares arrived in a flurry. She'd always assumed her fear of the lake was spawned from her fear of deep water, but what if it wasn't? What if the dead had been calling her? Women from a bygone age had been murdered metres from where she had slept as a child. Holly didn't believe in the supernatural, but as Callum would say, belief had nothing to do with the truth.

"I knew your parents," Mr Xavier said. "They were good people. How do you think they would feel if they knew their daughter was stalking an innocent man?"

"Are you innocent?" Holly asked. "Why were you at Juniper Falls?"

"I was doing nothing wrong, if that's what you're implying?" Mr Xavier said with a broad smile. "I'd say that was the definition of innocence, wouldn't you?"

Holly tried not to look at the lake or imagine what was in there. "Instead of asking you questions, perhaps I can tell you what I already know."

Reaching into her sodden coat, Holly retrieved Derek's file from her trousers, ignoring the fact it was warm and moist. She pointed it at Mr Xavier. "This is information about you. It says you've worked with Historic England for almost twenty-three years. Why is that?"

Mr Xavier clasped his hands together and said nothing.

"You have a mortgage on a property in Bridlington," Holly said. "That's only fifty miles away."

Holly saw the rolling of Mr Xavier's eyes and continued.

"You moved out of Little Belton."

"I told you that," Mr Xavier said.

"But you didn't move far, despite having to travel the country for your job."

"What else?" Mr Xavier said.

"You have a lifelong interest in Greyston."

"Again, something I told you," Mr Xavier said. "Is there anything of use in that little file of yours?"

"I'd say, you didn't want to move too far from Little Belton," Holly said, "in case a certain someone returned. Someone you'd lost contact with."

Holly watched the manilla file darken as the rain seeped into its surface. She folded it into her pocket and searched for the nearest loose rock.

"According to my file," Holly said. "Simone is your daughter."

Mr Xavier didn't move. As far as she could tell, he wasn't even breathing. He wasn't blinking. He became as solid as stone. Oddly reminiscent of Simone when Holly had questioned her about Mr Xavier.

"I mentioned you to your daughter," Holly continued. "She lied. She pretended like she didn't know you."

Holly avoided his hard stare and looked to her feet. By her left shoe was a hand-sized rock. If Mr Xavier reacted to her revelation with violence, she was prepared to use it in defence.

"I misjudged you. You've done your homework," he said, leaning on his cane, "but my family has nothing to do with you. There is no need to discuss it."

"Simone shares your interest in antiques," Holly said.

"No, she doesn't. My daughter has had lots of jobs. The fact she worked for Mr Charleston is a coincidence. He let slip he had employed a new salesperson to shift the cabinet."

"Which you found out because you harassed him daily."

Mr Xavier took a step forward and Holly looked to the rock by her feet.

"Or she could have told me over dinner," Mr Xavier said.

"I don't imagine you see her that often."

CHAPTER FORTY

Annoyance flashed over Mr Xavier's face. "What is it you want, Mrs Fleet?"

"The truth," Holly said. "You're father and daughter. You're in Little Belton together and yet you've made no time to see her, except to hang around her bothy and spy on her through the window."

"How do you know? Yes, you're following me now, but have you been following me every hour of every day? What about Simone? Have you been following her too? We could easily have slipped away with no one knowing."

"Why were you at Simone's bothy?" Holly asked. "Were you expecting to go in? Maybe chat about what to do with the cabinet you stole?"

"Ah, so it was stolen?"

"As if you don't already know," Holly said.

Mr Xavier pressed a hand to his chest. "I've just paid a visit to what I assume is a witches' hall. You'll know this, given you've been trailing me. I knew the cabinet wasn't there and when I saw the remains of a bonfire, I'd thought you fools had burned it, afraid of its hidden power. I'm pleased to know it still exists."

Stumbling forward, Mr Xavier was upon her, his tall frame bearing down.

Holly ducked, swiping the rock from the ground and raising it above her head.

There was no humour in Mr Xavier's smile. His white teeth glittered through his dark beard, appearing sharp and pointed. "And what are you going to do with that?"

For the first time, Holly wished her roof was still leaking. It would mean there'd be a chance Derek would be up there, that he would see her and run to her rescue. Holly thought of screaming, but her husband was indoors. She saw the light shining through the new window Mr Winnow had installed. The bull looked at her, its horns glowing in the darkening sky.

Murder Lake seemed even more sinister now Holly might be found at the bottom of it.

Mr Xavier slowly reached into his coat.

"I'm not afraid of you," Holly said. "I'll use this rock. I mean it."

He retrieved his hand, opening it in front of her. Sitting in his palm was a straw doll.

"I'm searching for these," he said.

"The Winnow's treasure hunt?" Holly asked, the rock dropping from her grasp.

"I popped into the convenience store for a map and Mr Winnow persuaded me to purchase a hunt. Actually, his tactic was to strong-arm me, but the result was the same."

"I don't believe you," Holly said, despite having fallen for the same tactic.

"That's what I was doing at the bothy," Mr Xavier said. "I was looking for clues."

The light was bruised with purple and the first of the night's stars shivered into existence. Holly pulled her tattered coat close to her chest, her eyes on the straw doll.

"Can I go now?" Mr Xavier asked again.

But it was Holly who moved first, eager to get away. Scrambling up the valley wall, she dug her feet into the slippery slope, using handfuls of shrubbery to drag herself upwards.

Mr Xavier was soon lost in the darkness and Holly was glad. His mocking eyes reminded her of the fool she'd made of herself.

Mr Xavier's relationship with his daughter didn't mean a thing to either of them.

Chapter Forty-One

The bonfire crackled, spitting out red embers like the mouth of a medieval demon. The flames fought bravely against the drizzle, but the logs sizzled with the damp. Holly had known sleep wouldn't come that night so once she assured herself Mr Xavier was gone, she'd marched to Callum's cottage, glad she had done so.

Because they were expecting visitors, apparently.

The door to the cottage clicked shut and Callum appeared by the fire, a fur rug in his hands. He placed it over Holly's shoulders and dropped into the weathered deckchair beside her.

"Why aren't we waiting for them inside?" she asked. "Are you afraid of being attacked in your home?"

"I don't know anything about this Hector guy," Callum said, "and I don't like surprises. I'd prefer to see him coming."

"What was going on back at Simone's bothy?" Holly asked. "You only calmed down when you thought she might be in jeopardy. You were very high-minded with her."

Midges, confused by the light of the fire, hung in a twisting blanket above it. Callum studied their ever-changing shape before replying.

"It was nothing," he said with a shrug.

"I've never seen you like that before."

"I'm not proud of it," Callum said, gazing at his father's gravestone just out of sight, "and I doubt my dad would have been, either."

The fur rug kept Holly warm and dry, but it weighed heavily on her shoulders. "You said, he'd never spoken to you about relationships, but did he ever try?"

The deckchair groaned as Callum shifted his weight. "No, and I beg you not to start now."

"The thing about liking girls is – "

Callum held up his hand to silence her.

Holly giggled. She was embarrassing him and it was fun. Callum might have benefited from her perspective, but when he pointed to his ear, she knew she'd been silenced for another reason.

Holly froze, detecting movement in the darkness beyond. She heard footsteps, and Callum stood from his chair.

"Thanks for coming," he said.

Stepping into the light of the fire, Simone's face was grave. There was no smile, no twinkle in her eye. She was wary, like an animal sensing a trap.

"You didn't give her much choice," Hector said, appearing by her side. "You implied I was in danger."

Hector had lost something of his former self in the last few days. He was still handsome, but he looked tired. There were grey bags under his eyes and his face was heavy, as if he'd have trouble animating it.

"That depends on your answers," Callum said.

"We're trying to help," Holly added.

"Maybe," Hector said, "but not us. You're helping yourself."

The midges were blown away by a gust of wind and were scattered to the four corners of the estate.

"You've been hiding from us," Holly said.

"No, I've been busy." Hector ran a shaking hand through his hair. "That's what happens when you have a proper job."

Callum picked dirt from his fingernails. "Do you consider stealing a

CHAPTER FORTY-ONE

job?"

"Are you talking about Mrs Masterly's missing furniture?" Hector said. "I had nothing to do with that."

"You had the opportunity and you had the motive," Holly said. "You were working at Mr Charleston's and you knew the cabinet was on its way to Black Rock Manor. You came too, waiting for the chance to steal it."

Stepping away from the fire, Simone clutched at her neck. "I brought Hector here to clear his name. We spoke about this before we came. I told him everything you said. I don't want to hear any wild accusations thrown at him."

"Not that I have to justify myself to a third-rate journalist and a gamekeeper," Hector said.

The fire's heat singed Holly's legs. An ember nestled into the hem of her trousers. She should have removed it, but she was distracted by its glow. It flared like a warning beacon, threatening to blossom into a flame. She shook her leg, but the ember held fast, blazing in a sudden burst of light before dying into ash.

"Where have you been since then?" Callum asked Hector through gritted teeth.

"Working."

"One last job to clear your gambling debts?"

Hector bristled. "How did you...?"

But he didn't finish his sentence. Instead, the brief indignant flame in his eyes died, like the ember had in Holly's clothes.

The decorator heaved a sigh. "Everybody knows, don't they? I guess that's what happens in a village. Nothing to do, but gossip. Yes, I was an idiot. I'm in debt."

"Enough debt to commit a crime?" Holly asked.

"Yes, but I didn't. I've been doing work where I could get it."

"We heard how you get your jobs," Holly said. "Call up a stately home and offer your services in the hope there might be something juicy to steal."

Hector snarled.

Callum snarled back.

"As one job finishes, I call around looking for more work," Hector said, his teeth bared. "I'm not ashamed of that and it's common practice in my trade. As you know, my job at Black Rock Manor ended abruptly, but I found work over in Crockfoot. I've been staying there until it was done. I knew about the cabinet, but I didn't know there'd been a theft."

"I've been to Crockfoot," Callum said. "It's rubbish, isn't it, Simone?"

But Simone didn't answer, content to stare into the darkness instead.

"We know you were working in Crockfoot," Holly said, studying her fingernails. "We went to find you. The problem is, you're never where you're supposed to be. The man you were working with said you'd been called away for an emergency. Care to explain?"

"No," Hector said, "but it had nothing to do with the cabinet, if that's what you're implying."

Holly adjusted her clothing. "You were also supposed to be at The Travelling Star with your brothers. Why didn't you take them with you? Many hands make light work, you know?"

"They shouldn't have to pay for my mistakes," Hector said.

Callum tapped a finger against his chin. "Plus, you'd have to share your money with them."

Even in the dark, Holly saw Hector glower. It was a cheap shot and Callum's growing frustration was reaching a peak. She didn't know what would happen after that.

"Where is your van?" Callum asked.

"In Crockfoot."

Holly cocked her head to one side. "Why leave it there?"

CHAPTER FORTY-ONE

"Because the roads are dangerous in Little Belton," Hector said. "Apparently, Little Belton doesn't spend as much money on their infrastructure as Crockfoot does."

"How did you get here?" Holly asked.

Simone coughed into her wrist. "He took a taxi to the outskirts of the village. He came to my bothy and we walked from there."

"So you know where Simone lives?" Callum asked. "You've been there?"

"Several times."

Holly placed a restraining arm on Callum's shoulder. His muscles were bunched, feeling like frozen rope in her grasp.

"Do you have any more questions for me?" Hector asked. "This is an interrogation I don't deserve and it's late. I'm staying with Simone tonight. I want to go to bed."

Callum flinched under Holly's touch. It was impossible to knead the tightness from his shoulders. He was so tense, she was likely to break a nail.

"You bought a ratchet hoist from Roland's. Why?" Holly asked.

"Why do you think?" Hector answered in a bark. "The old one broke. We used it to move heavy equipment around, but the boys were horsing around, swinging from it like baboons, and it snapped. I'm surprised you haven't accused me of stealing that, as well."

"What about the brass fittings you bought?" Callum asked. "Where did they go?"

"They didn't arrive or they were stolen before I got a chance to fit them on Mrs Masterly's wardrobes. What more do you want from me?"

With Hector's raised voice came further violent vibrations in Callum. Holly stepped in front of him, unsure who she was protecting.

"Thank you for your time," she said to Hector, afraid of where their conversation was heading.

"And if you see Mrs Masterly before I do, tell her I'll wait for my money," Hector said.

Callum pushed his hands into his pockets. "She doesn't have to pay you?"

"No, I'd like her to pay me, but I know what it's like to be stretched financially," Hector said. "I've paid off my debts. She can wait to pay off hers."

Placing an arm around Simone's waist, Hector kissed her cheek. "I'll wait further down the lane. Call if you need me," he said to her, leaving without looking back.

Holly listened to his footsteps fade. When they stopped, she searched the night and found Hector's form lurking in the distance. It appeared she had misjudged him from the start and she wondered who else she'd been unfair to.

Chapter Forty-Two

"Are you happy now?" Simone asked.

She folded her arms over her chest. The sleeves of her dress fell to her elbows and Holly noticed Simone's bare wrists.

Where was her weird bracelet?

"Thank you for letting us speak to him," Holly said. "Hector doesn't appear to be connected to the missing cabinet. Not directly, but we've wasted a lot of time tracking him down. That was time that could have been used elsewhere if you'd both been more honest with us."

Simone shot Holly a piercing look. "Who was posing as a danger to Hector anyway?"

"Well, your father, of course," Holly answered.

The drizzle petered out. The grey night sky dissolved into black and starlight appeared, enhancing the contours of Simone's body. Holly looked away, noticing that Callum did not.

"We know Mr Xavier is your dad," Holly continued. "Why would you keep it a secret?"

Simone rubbed goose pimples from her arms. Was she finally feeling the cold?

Or was it fear?

"How did you find out?" Simone asked.

Callum glanced at Holly and she read his mind. She did not know how

Derek had come across the information in the file. Holly didn't want to lie anymore, but neither did she want Simone to know about Derek's involvement. Holly wasn't sure about the legality of what had been done, though she was certain the morality was questionable.

"Because it's not like we look like each other," Simone added.

"Why is that?" Holly asked, trying to move the conversation on.

"Not that it's any of your business, but my mother was Nigerian. My father is of Persian descent. I take after her more than him. Thankfully."

Simone's eyes locked onto Holly's.

"It was you, wasn't it?" she asked. "You ran some sort of background check on me."

"Holly had nothing to do with this," Callum said.

"Why do you always defend her?" Simone asked. "What has she done for you?"

Callum rolled his head around his neck, listening to the bones crack.

Failing to get the response she wanted from Callum, Simone rounded on Holly. "You don't want him to be with anyone else? How selfish are you?"

Quite a lot, Holly thought if she was being honest with herself, but no more than anyone else. She was tired of explaining herself to outsiders. What they thought didn't matter. Holly disregarded the question and concentrated on Simone's words.

"Thankfully?" Holly asked. "Why would you be thankful for taking after your mother and not your father?"

Simone flexed her forearms. Muscles and ligaments rippled under her skin. "I haven't seen him in years. We don't get on. His obsession with Greyston rules his life. There wasn't any room left for me."

Although Holly had left her mam and dad behind, they had remained a staple part of her life. There had been weekly phone calls and her parents had visited London to see her. Holly had left Little Belton. Her parents had never left her.

"I'm sorry you feel that way," Holly said.

Simone looked to the darkened sky. "It's not your fault. It was his. I left home as soon as I could, working all over the country, trying to find myself."

"And you found yourself back in Little Belton with your father not far behind," Callum said.

"This is my village," Simone said. "I was always destined to return."

Did Mr Xavier know that, Holly wondered? Was that why he had remained close to Little Belton?

"If you hate your father," Holly said, "why don't you just keep moving?"

"I don't hate him."

Holly slapped her forehead as a realisation occurred. "It seemed odd. An estranged father and daughter in the same place at the same time."

Callum tugged on his sleeves. "Did it?"

"It makes perfect sense now," Holly said. "The cabinet wasn't a coincidence, was it?"

Simone shook her head. "I didn't go looking for it. I'd heard so much about Greyston while I was growing up, I never wanted to see a piece of his furniture in my life. So imagine my shock when I started working for Mr Charleston and saw the cabinet at the back of his shop."

"Perhaps its dark forces drew you to it," Callum said.

Holly bit her tongue. Why did he always bring it back to mumbo-jumbo?

But Simone appeared to agree.

"I thought the same thing," she said with a sigh. "If anyone could control its power, then my father could. I knew he would have loved a chance to study it up close. I guess I was feeling lonely or homesick. I asked Mr Charleston if he would allow my father to see it. That's when I found out about the repeated phone calls, the demands my father was making. Mr Charleston said no."

"So you came up with another plan," Holly said.

"I sold it to Mrs Masterly knowing my father would track it to her door."

"Did you also know he would have leverage over her as her grant assessor?"

Simone shielded her face with her hands, her sobs escaping through her fingers. "It was a terrible thing to do, but I was wretched. I didn't have a home or a family. At the time, I didn't think it was so wrong."

Callum crept forward, tentatively placing his arms around Simone. She rested her head on his chest.

"You were desperate," Callum said. "You shouldn't blame yourself."

"It doesn't make it right," Simone whispered.

Moving from the fire, Holly felt its warmth desert her. "If you arranged all of this for your father, why haven't you seen him yet? You had a chance to see him when he first arrived at The Travelling Star. You distracted him with the Bathing of the Green Man ceremony, but decided not to be there yourself."

Simone pulled back from Callum's hold, retreating further into the night. "I didn't know how to speak to him. It had been so long."

"Your father has been visiting your home, perhaps hoping for a chance to speak to you," Holly said, shrinking into her scarecrow clothes. "He claimed it was part of Mr Winnow's treasure hunt, but you reported footprints there long before you father bought the game."

"It's a conversation I don't know how to have with him," Simone said, taking another step backward.

Callum followed her into the night. Like Simone, he couldn't express his feelings. He was too awkward or too slow.

This time, he moved fast, closing in on her, drawing her to his body. He lowered his lips to hers.

"No," Simone said, twisting out of his grasp.

CHAPTER FORTY-TWO

Callum jumped back immediately, stumbling over the rocky ground, bringing him in danger of falling into the fire.

"I apologise," he said, levelling his shoulders.

Hector rushed into the ring of light, placing a comforting hand on Simone's arm. "Are you all right?"

Simone stared at Callum, her eyes flashing. "You can be so kind and considerate, but also so cruel. I don't understand you. I don't know what you want."

Callum stared at Hector.

"I suppose you know what Hector wants," he said. "To be honest, it seems pretty clear to everyone."

"Hector is my friend," Simone countered. "He practises traditional medicine and doesn't mock it. He believes in all the creatures we can sense, but not hear. He's not like you."

"I believe in them too," Callum said. "Well, some of them."

"And that's your problem. You're walking a tightrope, afraid of committing to one side or another."

Holly stood by Callum's side, feeling him quake beneath his clothes.

Hector linked his arm through Simone's and led her from the fire.

"I really did like you," she shouted over her shoulder to Callum. "It's a shame you weren't more like Hector, but maybe you'll grow up one day. Until then, leave me alone."

Chapter Forty-Three

When the dawn broke, Holly was already returning to Callum's cottage.

She cradled a casserole dish in her arm and knocked on his front door. It was her fifth attempt and her expectations of it being answered were low. His Defender was parked in the driveway, but there was no smoke in the chimney and no light in the windows. Wherever Callum was, he wasn't at home.

"I wasn't expecting to see you here."

Holly jumped, dislodging the lid from the glass dish. It fell to the ground, spinning like a coin while the contents sloshed over her coat.

Callum lifted the casserole from her grasp, bringing it to his nose for a sniff.

"What's this?" he asked. "It looks like rabbit stew."

"That's because it is," Holly said.

"But you hate rabbit stew."

"My mam and dad used to eat it all the time," Holly said. "I always knew it was going to be a long evening when I came home from school and smelled it bubbling on the stove. They'd try to get me to eat it by saying it was good for the soul. So I thought, maybe it could mend a broken heart, too."

Callum stiffened, water dripping from his long hair. "I went out. For a walk. It didn't help. Come inside. I'll light the fire."

CHAPTER FORTY-THREE

Five minutes later, Holly was resting in an armchair, a fur rug draped over her lap. She felt better, but her skin was icy and her temperature was rising.

Callum continued stacking wood in the fireplace. He paused and patted his pockets.

"What's the matter?" Holly asked.

"I need kindling." Callum looked to the mantlepiece to where his remaining straw doll watched over him. The other two were missing in action. One had been stolen by a raven. The other was lost at Knock Lake, where Holly had discovered the last of the notes.

Callum took the doll and shoved it between the logs while striking a match.

Holly sat forward. "Wait. What are you doing?"

"It was silly to think they were love tokens," Callum said. "At least, they're good for something."

The flame flickered, casting dancing shadows around the cottage.

Holly dropped to her knees beside him and blew out the match.

"But they were a love token," she said. "Those dolls were from me. Clearly, they backfired spectacularly, but they came from the heart."

Callum hung his head. "I appreciate it and sorry for acting like a child. Before and after the dolls. You were doing what you thought was right. Same as always."

"Yeah, but I so often get it wrong," Holly said. "And it looks like you've screwed it up with Simone too, so we're both idiots."

"Is that why you cooked rabbit stew?" Callum asked. "Because we're screw-ups?"

Holly smiled. "I didn't know you were going to get hurt. I should have taken your feelings more seriously."

"Don't worry about it," Callum said. "I don't think I'm cut out for relationships anyway."

Holly had made the stew while Derek slept upstairs. While the sauce thickened, her thoughts had turned to the note in the last doll, the one she'd kept hidden from Callum. She'd tussled with a question all night, sacrificing rest for tortured inner monologues. By morning, she'd decided not to show it to Callum and simply present him with a home-cooked meal.

So it was a surprise when she pulled the note from her pocket and showed it to him while they kneeled by an unlit fireplace.

Callum's mouth fell open as he read its three short words.

Holly Loves Callum.

"What's this?" he asked.

"It's the note from the last doll." Holly fought down her embarrassment as she spoke. "I wasn't going to show it to you in case... well, you know..."

"I got unhonourable ideas?" Callum asked, shrinking into his clothes with embarrassment. "Why show it to me now?"

"You'd said you felt like you were being kept in the dark."

Callum poked a tongue into his cheek. "Technically, Mr Winnow wrote this note."

"Our relationship is one of the most important things in my life," Holly said. "It's hard to define, but it shouldn't make us miserable. We should be happy we found each other."

Callum looked at her through the curtains of his hair. "Did you really cook me a rabbit stew?"

"Actually, it's chicken. I couldn't bring myself to chop up a rabbit, but I honestly don't think you'll notice the difference."

Callum shook his head with a grin. "I should have known."

"What self-respecting person eats *Bugs Bunny*?" Holly asked.

Rummaging through the stack of logs, Callum winked at Holly.

"My love token to you," he said, presenting her with the straw doll, "and there's a big difference between rabbit and chicken. I could smell that a mile off. I'm like a bloodhound."

CHAPTER FORTY-THREE

Although the fire wasn't lit, a warmth spread through Holly's body. Finally, she'd got it right.

"If the stew is chicken," Callum asked, "do I have to share it with you?"

"Absolutely and I'm pretty hungry, now you mention it."

Callum went to the stove, carefully stirring the stew with the same wooden spoon he used for every meal.

Holly returned to the armchair, holding the doll to her chest. "You may not want to hear this, but I feel sorry for Simone."

Callum clattered the casserole dish with his spoon, but nodded at Holly to continue.

"With the theft of the cabinet," she said, "she may never reconnect with her father. It was the one thing that bonded them together."

"It's a shame Mr Xavier stole it then."

Holly stared into the fire. "I'm having my doubts about that. The last time I saw him, he was acting pretty cool. Mr Xavier was on the estate. Hunting straw dolls."

Callum stopped stirring. "He's doing the treasure hunt?"

"Enjoying himself, too," Holly said, remembering the way Mr Xavier had taken pleasure in intimidating her. "He'd figured out we didn't have the cabinet, but he hadn't known it was stolen."

"Was he roaming the estate on his own?" Callum asked.

"We knew he was," Holly said, "but we thought it was because he was up to no good. Turns out he was doing the same treasure hunt you were supposed to be doing."

Callum turned off the stove and listened to it cool.

"What's wrong?" Holly asked.

"Do you fancy going for a walk?"

Holly buried her face into her hands.

"I'm too tired," she said. "Can't we just stay here for a bit?"

"Mr Xavier hurt his leg. Badly," Callum said, pacing the floor.

"There's nothing wrong with you – "

"I'm tired. Like, really tired," Holly said, interjecting.

"And I can't get you out of that chair. A few days ago, Mr Xavier was using a shopping trolley to get around. He wouldn't be on the estate without a good reason."

"Maybe he was using the treasure hunt as a cover to visit Simone," Holly said.

Callum grimaced. "He might have been, but does he strike you as a man with family reconciliation on his mind?"

Every interaction Holly had had with Mr Xavier, she'd been left with the same conclusion. He was a determined man focused on one thing and it wasn't his estranged daughter.

"The last time I spoke to him," Holly said, "he was quite dismissive of Simone. I don't think she's his top priority."

"Which leads me to believe he was on the estate for another reason. It will be hard to track him in all this mud, but I can try," Callum said.

Holly held up the straw doll in her hand. "Mr Xavier was carrying one of these."

Callum rustled his jacket. "Further evidence that they aren't love tokens. Who would send him one of those?"

"What if the treasure hunt was a ruse, but he was using it as an excuse to look for something else?"

"Like a place to stash the cabinet until the coast was clear," Callum said.

Holly got from her seat and marched to the front door. "We don't need to track him. We already know where he's been. Mr Winnow has cameras all over the estate, remember?"

Chapter Forty-Four

"What do you mean, they're fake?"

Mr Winnow stood behind the counter in his shop. He was wearing a coffee-stained cardigan, which he held to his body. He shrugged, his bald pate reddening.

"I thought they were supposed to be part of the treasure hunt?" Holly asked.

"They are," Mr Winnow said. "They're insurance so people don't cheat. You can't trust people these days."

"But they don't work." Holly's eyes strayed toward a display of macaroons. She licked her lips, listening to the growl in her stomach. "What kind of insurance is that?"

"It's the estate," Callum said, studying a shelf of books on the supernatural. "There's no internet. No mobile coverage."

"The cameras would only work if I run cables everywhere. I'm not made of money," Mr Winnow said. "I tell people about the cameras to scare them into being honest."

The treasure hunt may have finally brought Holly and Callum together, but it had done little to capture a thief.

"Well, that's another good idea down the drain," Holly said.

"What do you mean?" Callum asked.

"If Mr Xavier was using the treasure hunt as a cover to snoop around,"

Holly said, "we might have caught him on the cameras. We could have plotted out his movements."

Mr Winnow sidled up to Holly and Callum, cupping a hand over his mouth. "I don't like him. Mr Xavier, that is. He's fine when he's drunk, but there's something about him, don't you think?"

"You don't need to whisper," Callum said.

Checking around his shop as if expecting to see Mr Xavier lurking there, Mr Winnow reluctantly dropped his hand.

"Have you noticed his beard?" he asked. "He kind of looks like the devil, if you ask me."

Holly hadn't noticed, but now that Mr Winnow had mentioned it, the comparison was hard to shake.

"There's no way of knowing where he's been," she said.

"We know he's been here," Callum said. "He bought a treasure hunt. Maybe if we wander around the estate, we might bump into him."

"Maybe," Holly said without conviction.

"Mr Xavier also bought a map," Mr Winnow said. "To help with the treasure hunt. Felt like cheating to me, but I wasn't going to argue with a man like him."

A frown rippled across Callum's brow. "What map?"

Mr Winnow lifted one from a shelf and unravelled it, waving it like a paper flag. "This one."

"That's a road map," Callum said. "It's no good for exploring the estate. There are more marshes than roads. Why would he need it?"

"Especially as he wasn't driving," Holly added.

Callum snatched a packet of biscuits, funnelling them into his mouth, leaving a trail of crumbs on his shirt. "The roads are submerged under rainwater. Maybe that's what he's looking for."

"Where do the roads lead to on the estate?" Holly asked.

"They don't lead anywhere," Callum said. "They pass through on their way to someplace else so why would Mr Xavier need a map of

CHAPTER FORTY-FOUR

them?"

There was only one reason Holly could think of. Mr Xavier was attempting to leave Little Belton.

Chapter Forty-Five

The village green was now flooded under water. A flock of white ducks paddled in circles around the picnic table. The ravens, who saw the village green as their own, looked on enviously from the rooftops.

Water spilled from gutters. Pavements were awash with babbling streams, forcing Holly and Callum to walk in the road. No one else was foolish enough to brave the torrents and they had Little Belton village to themselves.

"How are we going to find Mr Xavier now?" Holly asked.

They hurried through The Travelling Star's welcoming doors.

Big Gregg sat in the corner, his feet propped up on a stool. He looked up from a book he was balancing on his stomach. "Something to warm you up?"

"No, thanks," Holly said. "We want to see Mr Xavier."

Snapping the book shut, Big Gregg stood and adjusted the straps on his false leg. "He's the only person I know who drinks less than you two. You just missed him. He said, he had some business to attend to."

"He's out in this weather?" Callum asked.

"He's a weird one, that's for sure," Big Gregg said. "I mean, have you seen that beard?"

Holly drummed her fingers on the bar. "Did he say where he was going?"

CHAPTER FORTY-FIVE

"Out on the estate," Big Gregg said, waving his book at them. "Long Robert doesn't seem to bother him."

"Why should it?" Holly asked, dropping onto a stool. "Long Robert doesn't exist."

"Of course, he does," Big Gregg said. "I saw him once."

Holly rolled her eyes. "No, you didn't."

"Well, I heard him."

"No, you didn't," Holly said between gritted teeth. "It was probably just some animal. When are you lot going to give up all this nonsense? It's just make-believe. It's raining because of the weather. That's it."

Footsteps thundered down the stairs from the second floor, and Paul and Saul appeared in the pub. Their faces were red and they threw packed bags to the floor.

"Is everything all right?" Holly asked.

Saul dropped to his knees and pretended to search through his luggage.

"Actually, we're in a spot of bother," Paul said, approaching the bar.

"Can we help?" Callum asked.

"Not unless you know how to catch a thief," Paul said.

Holly and Callum looked at each other and waited for him to continue.

Paul rubbed his eyes. "Hector came back at last. Told us he'd been working in Crockfoot all this time. Mending a spire or something."

It was the first time Holly had seen Hector's brothers angry with him. Saul was emptying his bag of dirty clothes while simultaneously thrusting them back inside.

Paul's eyes brimmed with tears, but his jaw was set with concrete. "I don't know why he would keep that from us."

"Perhaps he was trying to protect you," Callum said.

"But we're family," Paul said.

"We don't always make the right choices for the people we care about," Holly said, watching Callum shift uneasily on his feet. "He was doing his best."

"No, he was lying," Paul said. "He told us he'd been using the van for work and that would have been fine, except he wasn't."

"What was he doing with it?" Callum asked.

"Nothing. It was stolen," Paul said. "That's why he couldn't get back from Crockfoot to take us home. He's been using taxis."

"Where is Hector now?" Holly asked.

"Gone looking for the van, hasn't he?" Paul said. "Made us wait here again."

Callum pulled Holly to one side, whispering into her ear. "It's too much of a coincidence."

And Holly agreed. A stolen van was the perfect way to transport a stolen cabinet. Suspicion would fall on the owners while the thief made their getaway, but the roads had been flooded, forcing the thief to create a distraction by burning another piece of furniture. It would buy them time to hide the van and get the cabinet out of Little Belton.

That's why Mr Xavier needed the map.

But Holly needed proof.

"Did Hector say when the van was stolen?" Holly asked.

The doors to the pub blew open, showering the carpet in rain. Hector stood there, his face wet and twisted against the weather. He slammed the door shut and leaned against it, collecting his breath.

"It was stolen on the same day the cabinet was taken," he said.

Chapter Forty-Six

Hector staggered to the bar. "Whisky, please."

Big Gregg cast his gaze to Holly and Callum, folding his arms over a barrel chest.

"Not until you explain yourself to your kin," he said.

Hanging his dripping coat over a chair, Hector faced his brothers, his hands clasped in front of him. "I messed up. I'm sorry."

Paul and Saul looked at him from under their brows.

"It's okay," they said.

"It's not okay," Hector said, rushing to their side. "You two have been carrying me for the past few months. I haven't paid your wages. I've kept you in the dark. It's not fair. All because I'm a terrible gambler."

Holly ran a hand down her crinkled shirt. "I think it's time you told us everything."

Hector rounded on her and she was reminded of how quick he'd been to anger on the first day they'd met.

"This is a family matter," Hector said with a growl. "Back off."

Callum stepped forward. "And she's my family, so watch your tone."

The two men circled one another, days of mutual distrust and frustration in their hearts. They were rival alpha males who'd avoided scrapping for too long, and now that day had come. Holly didn't know who would win, but she inched toward a footstool, prepared to use it in

Callum's defence if it was needed.

"Mrs Fleet is right," Paul said, placing a calming hand on Hector's shoulder. "You don't have to say anything to us. We're your brothers. We'd do anything for you, but you owe the village an explanation and you can start with Holly and Callum."

The pub fell quiet, except for the rain pattering against the window. Hector stared at Callum, unwilling to let go of the fight within him.

"If you're not honest with them," Saul said, "how can you be honest with us?"

While Hector reached a decision, Holly marvelled at the sudden maturity of the two Spectre brothers. Perhaps they had benefited from time away from Hector.

"My van was stolen," Hector said, giving in to his brothers. "What more is there to say?"

"You could say and I also stole the cabinet," Callum said. "It would save a lot of time."

Hector cracked his knuckles. "I told you, I knew nothing about the bloody cabinet until I came back to meet up with you."

"To be fair," Holly said. "We've seen no evidence you were in Crockfoot for more than a day."

Reaching into his back pocket, Hector produced handfuls of crumpled paper. He threw them on a table and straightened them out. "Receipts, so I can claim back on expenses. This one is for a spinach smoothie from that awful milkshake place. This is for an overpriced pickled egg and caper waffle from a Belgium fusion café. That was also awful."

Callum glanced at Holly. "It sounds like Crockfoot, all right."

"Every receipt is dated. They show I was there when I said I was there," Hector said, a note of triumph in his voice.

Holly clicked her tongue while she considered the evidence. "Okay, then. How do we know your van was stolen?"

Hector pointed at another piece of paper. "Crime number and

insurance claim. That's what I was doing when I was called away for the emergency. The police had some CCTV footage they wanted me to review, but it turned out to be nothing. They gave me my paperwork and sent me on my way."

"Straight into Simone's arms," Callum said, staring daggers at Hector. "We saw you with her later that day."

"It was then that I realised I wasn't going to get my van back. That I'd have to find money I don't have to buy another. Is it so bad that I wanted to share my bad news with a friend?"

"You could have stolen your own van as a way of covering your tracks," Holly said.

"Oh, for God's sake," Hector shouted. "I didn't know anything about the cabinet until the night I met you."

The certainty in Hector's voice forced Holly to consider he was telling the truth. That, and the mountain of evidence he had produced.

"Why didn't you tell us about your van?" she asked.

"Simone begged me not to," Hector said. "She thought if you knew the van had gone missing on the same day as the cabinet, you would suspect me of stealing it. Which is exactly what happened anyway."

Callum tugged on a lock of his hair. "Simone knew about your van and she decided not to say anything, either?"

Hector rubbed the tired lines around his face. "She was helping me out. Honestly, that girl is a saint. We barely even know each other. We're not that close and she's been nothing but supportive."

"Well, I think that answers that," Callum said, slapping his hands together. "How about that whisky? Drinks all round."

The smile on Callum's face prompted a relieved Big Gregg into action. He spun in a delicate twirl to the optics and began dispensing drinks.

"What are you doing?" Holly asked Callum from the side of her mouth.

"You heard what Hector said," he whispered back. "They're not as close as we thought."

"That's what you took from that?" Holly asked Callum.

She forced down a further sarcastic response before turning to Hector. "It still doesn't tell us who took your van."

"And all our climbing equipment," Paul said, joining Callum at the bar. "It was in the back of the van when it was stolen."

Holly held up her hands, trying to process the additional information. "When we found you in Bimpton's Quarry, you didn't have any ropes. You said, you were just having a laugh."

"Sorry, Mrs Fleet," Paul said. "We didn't mean to lie."

Saul twisted the straps of his rucksack. "We thought Hector was keeping it from us, to stop us doing something stupid while he was away."

"So you did something even more stupid instead? Like scaling a cliff face with no safety equipment?" Hector asked.

"We meant nothing by it," Paul said.

"Why did you lie to Mrs Fleet?" Hector asked.

"Because we didn't want her to think of us the way other people do," Paul said. "Like you do. As idiots."

Poor things, thought Holly. While Hector was away, they'd matured. Now he was back, they'd returned to being infants. It wasn't their fault. In some ways, it was the same relationship Holly had with Mrs Masterly, but with one difference. Holly could think her way out of a paper bag. Paul and Saul could not.

Hector gathered his two brothers in his arms. "You're better than I'll ever be. You'd never be so stupid as to gamble."

"Except with your lives," Holly muttered.

"I'll replace all your equipment," Hector said, "but you have to promise not to go climbing without it again. Okay?"

"You'll never afford it," Paul said. "They took everything. All the ropes, harnesses, the chalk bags. It will cost too much."

CHAPTER FORTY-SIX

"Chalk bags?" Holly asked. "What's a chalk bag?"

Paul looked at her as if she was the stupid one. "They're what they sound like. They are bags full of chalk. We dust our hands so they aren't slippery when we climb. It's a safety thing."

Holly was distracted by the chatter at the bar and saw Callum sipping whisky with Hector.

"So how was the job at Crockfoot?" Callum asked.

Hector finished his drink in a single gulp and wiped his mouth with the back of his hand. "Same stuff, different town. It was interesting, though. The spire, that is."

Callum shook his head in despair. "There was nothing wrong with the old one."

"You're telling me. Apparently, the town hall was built in eighteen ninety-seven, but the spires cladding was from nineteen ninety-seven. It had been replaced after a mite infestation. Anyway, they wanted all the original fittings. No expense spared."

"Bloody Crockfoot," Callum said, offering Hector another drink. "More money than sense, that lot."

"Except it wasn't their money," Hector said, his cheeks rosy with alcohol. "It was from Historic England. It was another grant."

"Did that grant have to be assessed?" Holly asked, a spark of excitement flaming inside her.

Hector shrugged. "I haven't got a clue, but there was a guy there from Historic England. Right piece of work he was. I was just a grunt so I never met him, but I heard he was there to sign off the work or they wouldn't get their money."

Callum pushed away from the bar. "What was he called?"

"I can't remember," Hector answered, "but he had the craziest beard I've ever seen."

"You were right," Callum said to Holly. "Mr Xavier had been in the area before the cabinet arrived. He was in Crockfoot."

"The same place where Hector had his van stolen." Holly fished in her pocket to produce a twenty-pound note, slapping it on the bar. "Get these boys a drink. They deserve it. I think we've just found our proof."

Chapter Forty-Seven

"Slow down," Holly shouted.

They left the waterlogged road, skidding right onto a track. Hitting a pothole, brackish water coated the windscreen brown. The wipers beat fiercely to clear it, but the remaining view was greasy and amorphous, as if they were seeing the estate through a soiled gauze.

But Callum refused to listen.

"You're going to get us killed," Holly said, grasping at her seatbelt. They bumped along, Holly's bones jostling as much as her rounded stomach. She had never been a fan of rollercoasters, especially when they were real.

The persistent rain had been joined by a wind. The trees cowered under the blows of invisible hands. Branches snapped and splashed to the ground, sinking into murky floodwater. It was the middle of the day, but the sky was black with anger.

Holly fancied she could see a face in the clouds and wondered who it might belong to. Her face was as pale as her knuckles as she held on for dear life.

"We're almost there," Callum said. "Are you going to tell me what's going on? We can link Mr Xavier to Crockfoot, which means we can link him to Hector's stolen van, but that doesn't explain why you're forcing me to break the speed limit here."

"I'm not forcing you and you're forgetting about the map," Holly said, wincing as they narrowly avoided a stranded herd of sheep. "And do you remember what Paul said about the chalk bags?"

Startled by the grumbling Defender, a sheep strayed into their path.

Callum slammed on the brakes, sending them into a spin. Thick mud covered the windows causing the wipers to smoke and desist. The tyres screeched and choked.

Holly was pinned to her seat by the centrifugal force. Her arms and legs were petrified into immobility. Only her eyes moved and Holly clenched them shut.

Callum fought with the steering wheel with one arm. His other was a protective band around Holly's body. His face was white, but there was no fear. He was the calm in the storm and whatever happened next, Holly thought she'd be okay.

"Brace yourself," Callum said.

The Defender slammed into a tree, bringing them to an abrupt halt. Holly's head bounced against the window. Her teeth jarred together and the breath was driven from her chest. The world was a blur, but she heard a creaking noise and felt Callum's wandering hands on her body.

"It's falling," he shouted.

What was? How could anything be falling? The questions in Holly's head were distant, like echoes of something she'd said days ago. Her head was heavy and she struggled to keep it from rolling around her shoulders.

"We have to get out," Callum said.

He grappled about her waist, snapping the seatbelt free. Holly grew weightless. She was being carried. She heard Callum's grunts, felt his insistent hands on her as he tugged her to safety. The air was chilly and wet.

And Holly wasn't weightless anymore. She was sitting in a pool of

CHAPTER FORTY-SEVEN

mud, its icy touch reviving her. The rain washed her face and she blinked the droplets from her eyes.

"What's going on?" she asked, pressing a hand to her aching head.

Callum lifted Holly to her feet.

"We hit a tree," he said, "and now it's going to hit us."

They took a few stumbling steps toward the sheep who caused the accident. Its jaw moved from left to right as it chewed lazily on a gorse bush, unheeding of their presence.

Over the howl of the wind came the creak of splintering wood. Holly turned in time to see a tree collapse on top of Callum's Defender, burying it under a mass of branches. Glass popped as a window was crushed, peppering the ground in shards.

"I hope you've got insurance," Holly said.

"Are you okay?" Callum asked, inspecting the bruise on her head. "I should have been more careful."

Holly wiped a streak of mud from Callum's face. "You saved me."

Her head was throbbing. It felt as if her ribs were attempting to leap from her body, but it could have been worse. Much worse.

"Where are we?" she asked.

"On the ring road surrounding the manor."

Peering through the dark skies, Holly saw the manor's outline standing proud of the horizon. There was a dim light in one of the windows and Holly imagined Mrs Masterly cleaning by candlelight.

"Let's go to the manor and discuss this," Callum said. "You can tell me why you brought me out here."

He made to move, but Holly placed a gentle hand on his arm. "There was a reason Mr Xavier bought a road map to the estate."

"He won't be out in this weather," Callum said. "Surely, he'll have turned back?"

"Obsession doesn't quit and neither do I." Holly slithered through the branches of the fallen tree and onto the dented roof of the Defender.

"If this has taught us anything, it's that walking is safer than driving. Mr Xavier knew that. He was a tracker. Like your father. He knew how dangerous these roads could get, and that's why Mr Xavier has been out here day and night. There's no other way to get around."

Holly held out her hand to Callum, but he hesitated.

"You could get hurt if we stay out here," he said. "There's already been one crash."

"Actually, there's been two," Holly said, leaping to the other side of the road, "but we missed the first one. Come on."

Chapter Forty-Eight

Holly and Callum trudged onward, their feet sinking in the quagmire where the road used to be. For once, Holly was leading the way. She waved away the driving rain and ignored the seeping dampness in her clothes.

They'd been there days earlier, but the conditions had worsened since then. The crash had rattled Holly's nerves and she struggled to stay upright. If Callum could run aground, then anyone could.

The sky lightened, losing the steely touch of imminent thunder. Holly recognised the landmarks surrounding her. She wasn't a tracker like Mr Xavier or Callum, but she had travelled this road enough to know they were on the right path.

"Just around the corner," Holly said, yanking her leg out of a section of marsh. "I wouldn't want to get stopped out here. It's just an endless stream of filth. We'll probably catch Lyme disease wading through this."

Callum batted at a low-hanging branch, covering himself in a cold shower. "You get Lyme disease from ticks in the grasslands. Out here, you're more likely to get Weil's disease from the rat urine in the water."

Holly's mouth dropped open, but she clamped it shut quickly, unsure of how the disease might enter her body.

"We're back to where we started. What are you expecting to find that we didn't see the last time we were here?" Callum asked.

Holly climbed up a small mound that stood proud of the water. Shaking her boots, she found what she was looking for. The tree they had discovered on their first visit remained prostrate on the road. The ghostly handprints were long gone. Everything had been washed away, except for the tree lying forlornly on its side.

"The road is still blocked," Callum said. "How are we going to get past?"

"We're not," Holly said, sliding down the grassy mound. She waded toward the tree, placing her hands where the giant ghost had once placed his. "This is why we're here."

"It's going to take me ages to clear this tree," Callum said. "No one will be using this road for a while. I could move it with a ratchet hoist, I suppose."

Holly gave the tree an experimental push. She didn't expect it to move and she wasn't surprised when it didn't. "I thought that had been the point. To block the road, to stop people pursuing the stolen van, but I was wrong."

"What's it for then?" Callum asked.

"You said, trees this big don't fall over. You also said, it was too big to be pushed, but what if it was pulled?" Holly climbed onto the trunk. Where Callum was confident enough to balance along it, Holly was not and she crawled to the top of the tree on her hands and knees. She pointed to the parallel gouge marks. "This is where they attached the ratchet hoist. They used it to pull the tree over to the perfect position."

Callum nodded as if he agreed, but Holly watched as the nod slowly changed into a shake of the head. "The perfect position for what?"

"Don't you get it yet?" Holly asked, failing to hide her exasperation. "Mr Xavier's map is the key to this whole thing."

As Holly was about to explain, she was stopped by the sound of slow clapping. It came from the heaped branches hanging over the ditch.

CHAPTER FORTY-EIGHT

There was a sarcastic tinge to it that set Holly's teeth on edge.

"Finally figured it out, have we?" said a voice and Holly knew who it belonged to.

So did Callum, apparently. He launched himself along the trunk, diving into the tree. There was a commotion, followed by swear words. Callum finally emerged, dragging a distressed Mr Xavier with him.

He was thrown to the ground where he fell into the dirty water. His camel-hair coat was streaked in mud. Soggy leaves clung to his beard. He attempted to clean himself with a handkerchief taken from his breast pocket.

"You certainly get around," Holly said to him.

Mr Xavier was an arresting sight. Yes, they were tracking him and given Callum's talent in that area, it would only have been a matter of time before they'd found him. It was his matted beard and his soiled clothes that left Holly aghast.

For all his claims of originating from Little Belton, Mr Xavier simply didn't belong there anymore.

"I was out for a walk," Mr Xavier said, as if reading her mind.

"In this weather?"

"No better time for it," he said.

Callum wiped his hands on his trousers and looked to the branches swaying in the wind. "I found more than a devil worshipper back there. You better have a look for yourself."

The grave expression on Callum's face made Holly's heart race. The tree had fallen on purpose. She was sure of it and there could only be one reason. To hide something; something big.

Holly scrambled along the trunk, squeezing through the branches, thankful she had dropped a few pounds. The branches had done a good job. They'd covered Hector's van in a mask of leaves and dirt. It was on its side in a ditch. The panelling was dented, a concave metal bruise forming the shape of a grinning face. The bumper was loose, buried under a mound of chains and next to those were an abandoned ratchet hoist where the van had been used as an anchor to bring down the tree.

Holly called to Mr Xavier from the ditch. "Must have been hard work. Doing all that on your own."

Mr Xavier folded his handkerchief into a square, placing it neatly into his pocket and saying nothing.

The ditch water reached Holly's knees as she splashed her way to the rear doors and found them unlocked.

Taking the handles in a firm grip, she swung them open and saw something she didn't expect to find.

Chapter Forty-Nine

Holly plunged through the mud, sometimes sinking to her knees, but ploughing on regardless, all thoughts of pain or discomfort forgotten. Caked in dirt, Holly burst through the door to the manor, falling into the interior.

Mrs Masterly was waiting in an armchair in the centre of the reception room, her broom resting across her lap.

Holly floundered like an upturned crab. "What are you doing?"

"If I can't keep this door shut," Mrs Masterly said, wringing the broom in her hands, "I'd thought I'd wait for whoever came through next."

"And then what?" Holly asked.

The grimace on Mrs Masterly's face told Holly all she needed to know. Free of the sleeping pills hidden in her vitamin vial, Mrs Masterly had regained her resolve. Thieves didn't just steal material possessions. They took away a person's sense of security, but it appeared to Holly that Mrs Masterly was taking it back.

After a few false starts, Holly told Mrs Masterly of their discovery. As the words tumbled from Holly's mouth, Mrs Masterly's face went from joy to horror.

"You can't be serious," Mrs Masterly said.

Holly clutched at her chest. "I'm as serious as a bout of Weil's disease."

She rolled onto her stomach and dragged herself to her feet, staggering toward the kitchen and the telephone. She made her phone call and returned to the reception room.

"Wait here," she said to Mrs Masterly, "and get Simone. It'll be hard for her, but she'll want to hear this."

Holly launched into the rain, but the journey to Callum's crushed Defender and the stolen van took longer on the way back. Holly's adrenaline had deserted her to be replaced by the weight of what she had to do next. She reached Callum, who had been guarding Mr Xavier in her absence, in time to see the headlights of Mr Winnow's delivery truck hove into view.

Together, they pulled Hector's stolen van from the ditch. Miraculously, the engine started on the first go, and they trundled to the manor to find Mrs Masterly and Simone waiting by the door.

Mr Winnow rolled down the window of his truck. Holly could tell by his face he was about to broach the subject of compensation. Something in her face told him not to bother.

"Why did you do it?" Holly asked. "Why did you put that note in the treasure hunt?"

Mr Winnow rubbed his bald spot, as if he was searching for good luck.

"*Holly Loves Callum*," Holly whispered. "What would have happened if Callum had read that note when I wasn't around to explain it?"

Swivelling in his seat, Mr Winnow fixed Holly with a stare. "I dunno. What would have happened? Callum would have realised how much you cared for him, that he wasn't as alone as he thought he was. Is that such a bad thing?"

Over by the manor, Callum manhandled Mr Xavier through the door. He turned to Holly and grinned.

"But why put it in a treasure hunt of all things?" Holly asked.

"Because that was the last one," Mr Winnow said, slipping his flatbed

CHAPTER FORTY-NINE

truck into gear. "That was his prize."

Holly stepped back as Mr Winnow pulled away. With a toot of his horn, he disappeared into the grey of the estate, leaving Holly to consider his words.

The cabinet had been carried into the reception room amid an audience of marble statues. Mrs Masterly and Simone inspected it for damage.

The cabinet was tall, narrow at the base with a wider top, giving the impression it was defying gravity. It was made from cherry wood, a tree traditionally eschewed in furniture making as it was associated with witches, correctly in this instance, thought Holly. The surface was carved with intricate symbols and stained with coal, lending it a black sheen.

"Is it okay?" Holly asked.

"There are a few dints and scratches," Simone said, "which have devalued it a bit. There's water damage, but considering it's still in one piece, I'd say, we've been very lucky."

Mrs Masterly, awash with relief, dropped into her armchair, wafting cool air about her face. Holly joined her, hovering over one shoulder. Abandoning the cabinet, Simone stood at the other. The three women faced Mr Xavier, who stood as the condemned man next to Callum.

"Have you got anything to say for yourself?" Mrs Masterly asked Mr Xavier.

He opened his mouth to speak, but on catching the frown on his daughter's face, he closed it rapidly.

"Then we'll talk on your behalf," Holly said. "You hounded Mr Charleston for information about the cabinet, making sure you knew of its whereabouts at all times. You were in the area long before you checked into The Travelling Star, having stayed in Crockfoot while work was being completed on their spire."

Callum looped his thumbs through his wax jacket's lapels. "And we also knew you were in the area because Holly searched your rucksack and you had far too many clothes for such a brief trip."

"She did what?" Mr Xavier asked, his eyes narrowing.

"Never mind that now," Holly said, clearing her throat and starting again. "You didn't want anyone to know of your whereabouts because you planned to hijack the cabinet and keep it for yourself. While you were in Crockfoot, you stole Hector's van to use in the theft, perhaps hoping to frame him when you eventually got away."

Mrs Masterly shifted in her chair. "We'd known each other through previous business dealings. My husband believes business relationships are best when they are personal, so perhaps I let slip about my night-time routine. Knowing I took vitamins, it wouldn't have been difficult to swap them with sleeping pills."

"Thus ensuring Mrs Masterly was practically comatose while you drilled holes in walls and staged a distraction," Holly said.

Simone made a squeak and held trembling fingers to her mouth.

"He drugged Mrs Masterly?" Simone asked.

"I will not be held to account by the likes of you," Mr Xavier said, his dark beard crackling with fury.

"I'm sorry," Callum said to Simone. "We know how painful this must be for you, but you need to know exactly who your father is."

Simone bit down a sob. "I never suspected he would sink so low."

Holly watched the rain washing down the windows. "It was your daughter who gave us our first break. She ate some poisonous mushrooms, a silly mistake that led me to discover fittings from a replica cabinet, which had been bought from Roland's Hardware."

Simone cradled her weeping face in her hands.

As the rain continued, Mr Xavier turned away from his daughter.

"I haven't been a perfect father," he said, "but I tried my best. When this is done, I want you all to know that."

Holly swallowed, saddened by the angst on Mr Xavier's face. She

CHAPTER FORTY-NINE

gathered her thoughts. If this was going to work, she needed to keep going.

"It was a clever plan," she said, "but you didn't reckon on meeting Long Robert."

Keeping his eyes glued to Mr Xavier, Callum stepped into the limelight. "With all the rain, the driving conditions were treacherous. When the cabinet was loaded into Hector's stolen van, you must have thought you'd committed the perfect crime, but Long Robert was waiting. You lost control, finding yourself and your precious cargo in a ditch, leaving you no option but to remain in Little Belton until you'd rescued your cabinet."

"Which you tried to do using a hoist," Simone said, pointing an accusing finger at her father.

"That's right," Holly said. "You tied it to a tree, hoping it would take the weight of the van."

Simone glared at her father. "But it didn't."

"The tree was standing in saturated ground. When you applied pressure, it was sucked out by its roots, but finally, you had some good fortune." Holly checked her watch and looked through the window to the grounds beyond. "The fallen tree covered the van. It was hidden from sight, buying you time to figure out your next move."

Mrs Masterly stood from her chair, flanked by Holly and Simone. "Meanwhile, you slipped back into your role as a grant assessor. It was the perfect cover, allowing you to ask questions and keep track of who knew what."

Running his fingers through his beard, Mr Xavier removed a stray leaf. He studied it in his fingers, turning it to the light. After a moment, he let it fall, watching it drift to the floor.

"Please. No more," he said.

The muscles under Simone's clothing rippled. "All Mrs Masterly wanted was your help. She put her dreams on the line for you. And for what? So that your greed and obsession could get the better of you."

Mr Xavier flinched under Simone's words.

"I'm your daughter," she continued. "You loved Greyston more than your own flesh and blood. I've lived with that knowledge my entire life, and to make matters worse, you've turned into a criminal."

Simone wiped an angry hand across her teary face. "Well, there is something I can do about that now. I'll call the police and send you to where you belong."

Mr Xavier tapped his cane against his injured leg, glancing at Holly. He faced the window where he was coloured in blue flashing lights.

"There's no need," Holly said. "I've already called them."

The police arrived and Holly explained the situation before they took away Mr Xavier's cane and placed him in handcuffs. Standing either side of him, as Holly and Simone had done to Mrs Masterly, they each took an arm and guided him from the room.

There was no sense of relief. Holly watched the police car leave the grounds; its lights swallowed by the waving trees. She expected it to feel sunnier, but Long Robert was ever present. Not just over Black Rock Manor, but in it.

Holly and Callum approached a weeping Simone.

"Come on," Holly said. "We'll take you home."

Chapter Fifty

Holly and Callum lingered by the door of Simone's bothy.

Callum's face was sombre. He was motionless and Holly wondered how he was feeling. It couldn't be easy for him, she thought, but Holly could always rely on his sense of duty. Meanwhile, she picked stray threads from her clothes, kicked mud from her shoes, and failed miserably at staying still.

"We can't delay this much longer," Holly said.

"Simone said, this was her inner sanctum," Callum said. "That strangers would disturb her chi. Let's just give her some time to compose herself."

Holly smelled incense wafting from inside of the bothy. It was a flowery scent, reminding Holly of Simone's extraordinary garden. She had brought the outside in.

"Well, I'm not waiting out here like some vacuum salesman," she said. "I need to be in there."

Callum peered through the gap in the door. A floorboard creaked and Simone appeared, forcing him backwards.

"I'm sorry," Simone said. "I've made some changes and I just wanted to clear up."

She opened the door wider and Callum was first in, followed by Holly, shaking the rain off her coat. Incense sticks cast a low-hanging smoke curling around cardboard boxes stacked in awkward columns. Simone's rugs had been lifted from the floor and bound into cylinders, while the bed was stripped of its sheets.

The windows had been cleaned and all available surfaces had been scrubbed. Mrs Masterly would be proud, Holly thought.

"What's going on?" Holly asked.

"I'm leaving Little Belton," Simone said, closing the front door behind her. "I made my mind up a couple of days ago."

"But why?" Holly asked.

Simone's eyes drifted over Callum's face and the cardboard boxes containing her life's possessions. "I got a sense I wasn't welcome here. I tried. I really did, but this is a close-knit community."

"Are you sure this isn't because of what your father did?" Holly asked.

"Discovering my dad was a thief only tells me I was right. When I was small, I thought Little Belton was the whole world," Simone said, "but it's a tiny part of it. I must go to a place where my father's reputation won't ruin mine. Who knows where I'll end up? There are still plenty of places to see."

Simone stepped back, folding her arms over her chest. "Will you say goodbye to me? I didn't pack the tea set away. I thought we might have a toast together before I leave. I have some biscuits I baked myself."

She produced an orange Tupperware container and cracked open the lid. There were two biscuits left. They were brown and crumbly, their scent almost drowning out the smell of the incense. Callum took the Tupperware and lifted it to his nose.

"I didn't want it to end like this," Simone said, "but this will be the last time I see you both. Let's say goodbye properly."

"Nothing beats a home-baked biscuit," Holly said, feeling like she deserved a treat.

As she reached over to take a biscuit, Callum slapped her hand away.

CHAPTER FIFTY

"Your hands are filthy," he said. "At least clean them first."

Admonished, Holly searched her pockets for a handkerchief. She wiped away the grime of the estate from her fingers. They wouldn't pass a close inspection, but perhaps they might satisfy a grumpy gamekeeper.

Returning to the Tupperware box, she found it empty with Callum wiping the last of the crumbs from his face.

"You shouldn't have taken your eye off them," he said. "Plus, I was doing you a favour. You'd only feel guilty for eating it."

"Well, at least one of you is hungry," Simone said. "How about that tea?"

"Actually, I wonder if you could help." Callum placed the biscuit box into the pocket of his wax jacket and stroked his stomach. "I'm a bit under the weather. Do you have anything in your garden that might help?"

"Ah, so you believe in my nonsense now?" Simone asked.

"I should never have doubted you."

Simone lifted her chin, considering her best course of action. "I could make something out of thyme. It usually has to be dried first, but I'm sure I can do something for you."

"Brilliant," Callum said, moving to the door. "I'll come with you. It will give me a chance to learn the plant names before you go."

As Simone wrapped a shawl around her broad shoulders, Callum shot Holly a glance before they stepped into the rain outside.

Even though her stomach was rumbling, Holly lost no time in diving through the cardboard boxes. The first few contained neatly folded clothes. The next lot contained copper pans, pestle, mortars, and kitchen scales. Holly assumed they were linked to Simone's potion making and hoped she'd find what they were looking for before she was forced to drink thyme tea.

Holly heard Callum and Simone's voices from the garden. They weren't loud enough to distinguish their words, though Holly thought she detected a tone of panic in Callum's. She imagined him doing his best to keep Simone occupied, stumbling over words and asking questions he already knew the answer to.

Holly ransacked the cupboards, the cold fireplace and pressed her head under the sink. There was nothing on show. Standing in the centre of the bothy, she turned a full circle, looking for help.

The voices from the garden grew louder. Simone and Callum were returning.

Her heart rate thudded until she saw the faded sunflowers. The curtain to the bathroom was closed. She pushed through it, accidentally tearing the curtain down in her hurry. There was a toilet and a small shower.

And there was also a second sink.

The front door opened.

"We're back," Callum shouted unnecessarily.

The sunflower curtain hung from Holly like a cape. She grabbed the sink's contents and spun to face Simone, who held a bouquet of fresh herbs under a suspicious gaze.

"I may be leaving, but that doesn't give you licence to destroy the place," she said.

Holly held up the coil of climbing rope. "Is this yours?"

A shadow fell over Simone as the rain beat heavier against the windows. "I borrowed it from Hector."

"His brothers had said their ropes had been stolen." Holly lowered the rope, but raised her other hand, waving a red cowl like a rag to a bull. "They also said the brass handles they'd ordered went missing. You used some of them to build a replica of Greyston's cabinet, a replica you burned at the Witches' Hall as a distraction. The rest of them you disposed of in Crosskeys Caves. You'd been there as a child and knew they'd be hidden under limestone before they were discovered."

"Please return them," Simone said, her words sounding more like a demand than a request. "They belong to me."

"We knew the tree had been felled on purpose," Holly continued, "but we couldn't figure out why it was covered in white handprints until I discovered that whoever stole the van had access to Paul and Saul's climbing equipment, including the chalk bags. The day we three discovered the tree, you'd arrived first and panicked in case we found the van. So you dusted your hands in chalk for a better grip and, using the strength you're so proud of, made sure the tree was in the correct position. I doubt it moved any, but it made you feel better. Unfortunately for you, the chalk didn't wash off in time, so you employed a different distraction technique."

Holly looked to Callum for reassurance, but he was leaning in the doorway, wiping a sweating brow.

"You claim to be an expert in plants," Holly said. "How could someone like that fail to identify a deadly mushroom? The answer was you didn't. You knew exactly what they were. You took the mushrooms to stop us from looking too closely at the tree. It was a gamble, but after Callum told you he was something of an expert himself, it was one you were willing to take."

Simone sneered. "Wonderful theories, but you have very little evidence, I'm afraid."

"I found your bracelet with the cabinet," Holly said. "I'd noticed it was missing a while back, but thought nothing of it. I certainly didn't expect to find it in Hector's van. It's broken. What happened to it?"

"I don't know how it got there," Simone said. "Perhaps Hector stole it."

"Or perhaps the clasp snapped while you were trying to get the van out of the ditch. The funny thing about this bracelet is it's full of charms. There are silver leaves, silver hearts, and silver bells, but it also has the keys to Hector's van and the key to the manor. Mrs Masterly thought she was going mad. After a burglary, it would be every person's instinct to lock the doors each night, but no matter how hard she tried, they always stayed open. If we get the key checked, I'm sure we'll find it's a cheap clone. That's my evidence."

"That proves nothing," Simone said, waving the wilting herbs at Holly.

"Once we found the bracelet, I knew you were the thief, but I needed to prove it to Mr Xavier, so we staged a mock trial at the manor. When we found him by the van, he was adamant you were innocent. I saw how hurt he was when you tried to frame him for your crime."

"I did no such thing," Simone said.

"In fact, you were so keen to see him go to jail, you made an error," Holly said. "You expertly described how a hoist was used to pull over a tree. How did you know that if you weren't there?"

The words rang in Holly's ear like the peal of a church bell. She basked in their insight and knew she was right.

This time.

Simone's fingers tightened around the herbs in her fist. Green juice spewed down her sinewy forearm. "I shouldn't have left you alone in here. Never trust a journalist, eh? They're always snooping around in other people's business. You used poor Callum to distract me while you raided my home."

"This isn't your home," Holly said. "This is Little Belton."

"Do you think I don't know that?" Dropping the herbs, Simone wiped her hands on her shawl, leaving a smear. "You never liked me. I'm younger than you. I'm more beautiful."

"But you're not as smart," Holly said. "If you were, you would have known the only reason we walked you home was to get inside this bothy. When we first met, and I'd tripped into the waterfall, you were panic-stricken at the thought of me using your bathroom, afraid I might discover where you stored your ropes."

CHAPTER FIFTY

"I am smarter than you," Simone said.

"What you are isn't as important as who you are," Holly said. "That was apparent from the start with you. You aren't as admired as you might think."

Simone smiled, as a cat might to a mouse. "But Callum admired me, didn't he? If it wasn't for his mixed-up feelings for you, I might have made a life for myself here."

Callum's legs buckled and he slid down the doorframe, clutching at his collar.

Holly threw the rope and bracelet to the floor. She ran to Callum's side, pressing her hands to his damp face.

"What's wrong with him?" she asked.

"You don't know everything, do you?" Simone asked, picking up the evidence Holly had so carefully gathered. "And without this lot, all you have is circumstantial evidence. Perhaps I'll stash them under my dad's bed at The Travelling Star. Crimes can't be left to go unpunished, after all."

Callum tried to talk, but couldn't force the words past his pale lips.

Holly jumped to her feet, stirred by an anger she had never felt before. Her spine cracked. Her hands balled into fists.

"What have you done to him?" Holly asked with a growl.

"I was hoping you'd both be silenced," Simone said. "I can't have this story appearing in a newspaper, can I? At least, this will give me time to get to the other side of the world."

"You're going nowhere," Holly shouted.

She launched at Simone, her arms outstretched, her nails like the talons of a terrible predator, but Simone batted her to one side with a commanding arm.

"Don't be a silly girl," Simone said. "If I can carry a cabinet from an upstairs room into a waiting van on my own, then a woman like you is no match for me."

Holly rolled into Callum's limp form, her head ringing from the blow. Simone secreted Holly's evidence under her clothing. "You failed, as I knew you would."

Pushing them both out of her way, Simone paused by the door, sneering at a languishing Callum.

"You didn't honestly believe those dolls were love tokens, did you?" she asked. "I'd heard about you two. I knew Mrs Masterly would come to you for help. I needed to keep you close, that's all. I needed you to love me enough to share what was happening with the investigation. But I have given you a parting gift. A taste of poison. I hope you enjoy it."

With a cruel smile, Simone opened the door and stopped in her tracks.

Mr Xavier was on the doorstep, surrounded by Mrs Masterly, the Spectre brothers, the police, Derek, and Mr and Mrs Winnow. Their faces were as dark as the clouds above them. Thunder rolled around the skies, but it couldn't match the anger in their faces.

Little Belton had come to call.

But Holly's face was painted in wretched agony. She no longer cared about the cabinet or Simone or being proven right.

She looked down at Callum, cradling him in her shaking arms and let out a sob. "Please don't let him die."

Chapter Fifty-One

Wansbeck Hospital was on the fringes of Ashington, an ex-mining town fifteen miles north of Newcastle upon Tyne. It comprised of twelve wards and a variety of specialisms. The nurses and doctors were deep in their work while the patients waited impatiently for their cures.

Holly rushed from the reception desk, having paused to gain as much information on Callum's condition as possible. The rest of Little Belton went on ahead. She took the stairs to the third floor, went to a second reception desk and was pointed to the last door on the left, nodding to Mr and Mrs Winnow, Big Gregg, and the Spectre brothers hovering further down the corridor.

The hospital room was painted in green, the floors lined in a squeaky linoleum. A window looked out onto a busy carpark where trees lost their leaves to the wind and rain.

Callum stirred in his bed, an IV drip attached to his wiry forearm. He blinked, smiled, and fell back asleep.

Mr Xavier stood at the foot of his bed. Mrs Masterly sat in a plastic chair, chewing her lip. Derek was by her side. He came forward as Holly entered, wrapping his arms around her.

She pressed a kiss to his cheek. "Thanks for being here."

"Of course. We're in this together, right?"

A clock ticked on the wall, its hands moving as if they were wading through quicksand.

"Do you mind?" Holly said. "I need to speak to Mr Xavier."

Derek glanced at the man wearing a soiled camel coat and gave Holly a wink, retiring to Mrs Masterly's side.

"Did you know?" Holly asked, forcing a lump from her throat. "That Simone was capable of this?"

Mr Xavier gazed at Callum's pale face. "She burned down her school," he said as way of explanation.

The Little Belton Primary school had been destroyed under mysterious circumstances. Holly had been shocked when she'd first heard, but knowing the perpetrator made it worse.

"She was a wayward child and I was busy," Mr Xavier continued. "It's a terrible combination in a daughter and father."

"Where was her mother?" Holly asked.

"She left me for a younger, better man." Mr Xavier placed his weight on his cane. "Simone complained the school wasn't teaching her the things she wanted to know. She was interested in the natural world or rather, the world beyond this one. She grew frustrated. I like to think she was merely playing with matches when things got out of control. If this current situation proves anything, it's that I was wrong."

Callum's face was ashen, but his lips were moving. He was trying to talk, even amidst the medicine and delirium in his system. Back at the bothy, the paramedics had administered the same life-saving charcoal Callum had used to save Simone's life, but they had arrived late, and Callum's prognosis was worse.

Mr Xavier rubbed his injured leg and sighed. "We moved away. I couldn't stand the idea of people finding out. I remained dedicated to my work. I tried to instil the same discipline in Simone, but it was to no avail. She rebelled and went the other way, finding meaning in fairy tales and folklore."

"Isn't that what you do?" Holly asked.

CHAPTER FIFTY-ONE

"The occultist Alistair Greyston is my passion, but he is not my life. I don't worship the devil or dance with witches on a full moon. If I want to change my circumstances, I change them. I don't sacrifice a goat in the hopes I'll win the lottery."

"If it was that easy to secure funding," Mrs Masterly said, "I would have found myself a goat months ago."

Mr Xavier turned to her, his head bowed. "I'll be approving your grant for the refurbishment of Black Rock Manor."

"That's the least you can do," Derek said.

"You'll be free to carry out your plans and I wish you the best," Mr Xavier said. "Whether or not you keep the cabinet, I'll not be darkening your doors again."

"That's very kind," Mrs Masterly said, "but we'll be seeing an awful lot of each other in the coming future. I will keep the cabinet and I'll need an expert to act as a tour guide. I make my own demands in this world and I've decided that's the least you could do."

Mr Xavier joined Mrs Masterly in a smile, confirming Holly's previous belief.

The woman was strong and beautiful, inside and out.

"Actually, I should thank you for playing the role of the villain in our ruse at the manor," Holly said. "Callum has a friend on the police force, who owed him a favour. We were able to have you mock arrested. Still, it couldn't have been easy for you to see your daughter like that."

"When you found me at the van, I defended my daughter, but I'm sorry to say that I suspected Simone from the start," Mr Xavier said. "Long Robert had visited Little Belton once before. His rains quashed the flames at the school. This time it made the roads impassable for days. For all her schooling in folklore, Simone had forgotten one thing. Long Robert isn't a malevolent spirit."

"Are you saying Long Robert was helping us?" Holly asked.

Mr Xavier watched the rain strike the window in the same way Holly had at the manor. "Simone needed a van to transport the cabinet so she stole Hector's van, hoping to frame him the way she tried to frame me at the manor. If Simone had taken the cabinet, I knew it couldn't have gone far. The treacherous roads would have prevented her escape."

"That's why you bought a road map."

Holly's mouth fell open at the sound of the tired voice. They each turned to the bed where Callum waved wearily, his eyes red but open.

"You're awake," Holly shouted and rushed into his arms.

"I hope so," Callum said through a mouthful of Holly's hair. "Otherwise this is a really weird dream. Were the doctors able to identify the poison in the biscuits?"

"They were panther caps," Holly said. "The same mushrooms Simone ate. You're lucky you're so strong."

Callum nodded. "I thought they might be. I could smell them through her awful baking. That's why I kept yours in my pocket."

"Why eat one in the first place?" Derek asked.

"I didn't want Simone to get suspicious," Callum said. "One of us had to eat a biscuit and I thought it would be better if it was me."

Slapping him on the arm, Holly returned to the head of his bed. "Your luck will run out one day. Stop using it to protect me."

"What else would I need it for?" Callum asked with a shrug.

Mr Xavier tapped his cane against the metal of the hospital bed. "You were talking about the road map."

"Holly tried to tell me, but I was too thick to figure it out at the time," Callum said. "The map was the key. You'd had the same idea as me. Hector's van could only take a handful of roads. Knowing that, you bought a map to go in search of it."

"How did you know where to find me?" Mr Xavier asked. "The estate is thousands of acres wide. I was a needle in a haystack."

Callum pulled his blankets to his chest. "I didn't. That was Holly. She's a better tracker than I'll ever be. She knew everything centred

CHAPTER FIFTY-ONE

around the fallen tree."

His words echoed off the walls as the room fell silent. The only sound was the tick of the clock and the squeak of the nurse's shoes as they hurried about outside.

Mr Xavier shook his head. "I'm sorry. For everything."

"I'm sorry your daughter was willing to see you go to jail for something she did," Holly said.

"I want to believe that wasn't her intention," Mr Xavier said. "I believe her first intention was to lead me to the cabinet and then steal it away from me, so I never got that close again. It was punishment for choosing the cabinet over her."

Derek stirred from a stupor, shaking the bored look from his face. "That's still pretty demonic, mate."

"Perhaps you can visit Simone in jail and discuss it with her then," Mrs Masterly said, dragging Mr Xavier to the door, "but right now, it's time to go home. We're all exhausted and we still have your new role to discuss."

They said their goodbyes with Mrs Masterly promising to throw Callum a big party when he was well enough.

"I'll see you later," Derek said, turning to leave.

"Wait," Callum said. "You can stay, if you want?"

Derek smiled, but shook his head. "Thanks, but there's a leaking tap at home I need to fix."

"You're doing what?" Holly asked.

But Derek had already left the room, leaving Holly worrying over what she might find when she returned home.

"You look tired," Callum said.

"I look tired?" Holly said. "What about you?"

"Well, it has been a long few days."

Holly nodded her agreement. Friends had become enemies. Enemies had become friends, but Little Belton had weathered the storm.

Connections had been made and bonds had been strengthened. Most importantly, Greyston's cabinet was back where it belonged, ensuring a healthy tourist trade for years to come.

"We had our difficulties, but it all came right in the end," Callum said.

Holly looked to the window. "Except it's still raining. We'll be building an ark soon."

"Did you believe what Mr Xavier said?" Callum asked.

"About Simone burning down her school?" Holly straightened her fringe, suppressing an involuntary shudder. "She's a thief, a liar, and a poisoner. Do I think she's also an arsonist? Seems to fit."

"No, I mean, when he said Long Robert was trying to help us," Callum said.

Holly dropped into the chair, kicking up her feet. "Maybe. I don't know. I'm pretty sure Long Robert doesn't exist so probably not."

"There's one thing I can't figure out," Callum said, fighting his drooping eyelids. "Who was it you saw at the Witches' Hall?"

"No one," Holly answered. "I was in a panic. I might even have been hallucinating. There are hikers and walkers all over the estate. It could have been anyone. The next time I see a young guy with blonde hair and elfish ears, I'll ask him."

A nurse appeared in the doorway. "Excuse me, miss. Visiting time is over. You'll have to let him be for now."

Holly and Callum looked at each other and then back at the nurse. He was in his early thirties. Golden hair spilled over his collar while his sharp ears appeared to twitch.

"Do you work here?" Holly asked.

The nurse smiled in confusion. "As flattering as these scrubs are, I don't wear them for fun."

"You look like someone we know, that's all," Callum said with a chuckle.

CHAPTER FIFTY-ONE

"Someone handsome?"

Holly stood aside as the nurse tucked in Callum's blanket.

"Not really," she said quietly, "but the resemblance is uncanny."

"Must have one of those faces," the nurse said.

Holly paced the floor. "Do you ever go walking or climbing around Little Belton?"

The nurse looked up from his task. "Of course. All the time. I really like it there."

"Ha," Holly said, facing Callum. "I told you. That's who I saw. A man out for a walk. Not some – "

But she stopped talking when she saw Callum was asleep. His chest rose and fell with a gentle rhythm as the colour returned to his cheeks.

"He's been through an ordeal," the nurse said. "We have to let him rest."

"You're right. I was just trying to prove a point." Holly's nose itched, and she searched for a handkerchief in her pockets.

The nurse produced a tissue from his pocket.

Holly snatched it from his hand. "Thanks," she said, releasing a succession of violent sneezes in a row. "I think I'm coming down with a cold. It's all this bloody rain."

"Don't worry about that," the nurse said, pointing to the window. "It's going to stop now."

The pattering against the glass ceased. The grey skies rolled over blue and birds tweeting on the wing emerged from their hiding places. Sunshine soaked up the puddles, as if a new season had materialised in the blink of an eye.

"That's impossible," Holly said, turning to the nurse.

But Long Robert had gone, leaving Holly to scratch her head over another mystery.

The End...for now.

I've loved writing Juniper Falls and I hope you enjoyed reading it. If you have a minute, I'd be very grateful if you left a review on Amazon. It helps me as a writer and ensures the continuation of the series.

Can't wait for the next mystery...?

In **Hadaway Farm**, Holly faces her strangest mystery yet. When a fortune teller predicts a woman's death, Holly separates the truth from the lies in order to save a life.

If you would like to know more about Holly and Callum, please join my mailing list by following this link shaunbaines.org By being part of my mailing list, you'll receive lots of exclusive content including updates, discounts, free short stories and much more. Your data will never be shared and you can unsubscribe at any time.

I hope to see you all soon.